ROLLING HILLS AND THE LOST KEY OF PEACHTREE PALACE

ROLLING HILLS AND THE LOST KEY OF PEACHTREE PALACE

MICHAELA HORAN

Michaela Horan

Contents

To all the fictional worlds that I got to call home, I hope this can do the same for you.

Prologue

There was once a far-off land many miles from any large kingdom, in which cherry blossoms and peach trees bloomed from corner to corner, their beautiful colors staining the world until the summer melted into autumn. Animals frolicked in the lovely haven, content for eternity.

Someday, this isolated spot would make its mark on the map.

One morning, as the birds sang sweetly, not a note out of tune, a little girl wandered through a thin canyon cut into a lush plateau carpeted with pale-pink blossoms. She was Charlotte With No Last Name. She was searching for something special: a place to call home.

Charlotte felt nothing but wonder as she soaked in her beautiful surroundings. She breathed in the glorious air, refreshed by the scent of spring.

She laughed, the sound like a sweet bell echoing against the hills that loomed in the distance.

She made her decision. "This place is enchanting," she sighed, "and it will be my job to beautify it, to make it livable so that other people can enjoy it too."

Charlotte walked along the canyon where it merged into the ground, creating a hill that led to the top of the plateau. When she walked among the blossoms and flowers, she envisioned her own perfect kingdom: children playing in village squares, houses carved into the canyon, and best of all, a palace. Just for her.

As she was a young girl, only sixteen, the idea of a palace all to herself was quite an exciting one. She pictured its white exterior and a dirt path lined with cherry blossom trees leading to a set of grand doors. Charlotte imagined walking aimlessly through the kingdom, with no real destination in mind, the leaves like a coat surrounding the kingdom.

As the sun sank into the hills, Charlotte laid down on the largest hill on the highland to enjoy the sunset.

"You seem so lonely, Mr.Hill, against all these blossoms," Charlotte whispered,as if it were alive. "How unfair it is, Mr. Hill, to be you. You mustn't be discouraged just yet, though." She pounded her fist with finality and decided that this hill would be special.

Charlotte With No Last Name did two things that night. First, she decided to turn this blossom-filled plateau and canyon into her kingdom, and second, she would name it Rolling Hills.

Having given the hill a proper name, Charlotte With No Last Name now decided to give herself one.

"Charlotte is so boring," she sighed. She sat on the hill for a while longer until something came to her. "How about Charlie!" she exclaimed.

She wore the name proudly, calling out into the night, "I am Charlie Hills!" For she was young, and the idea of having a nickname was exhilarating.

Two years passed for Charlie Hills, and she created her kingdom to be a sanctuary. But she was alone, and she craved someone to play and talk with, beyond merely the birds and her hill.

One day, when she was hard at work painting with some flowers she'd found in a grove of peach trees, she was approached by a young man who had wandered into her kingdom.

He walked up to her and said, "Hello, Miss."

She was so startled, she dropped the entire palette on which her flowers had rested.

The man turned red, and bent down to help her pick it up. "I'm terribly sorry," he said.

"No matter," the now eighteen-year-old Charlie replied, trying to sound as proper and formal as possible.

The man, named Henry, and Charlie spent the day under the warm sun, getting to know each other, and she introduced him to all the sections of her kingdom.

"But where are the people?" he inquired.

Charlie hung her head with sadness and explained that she was the only resident of Rolling Hills.

Henry vowed to stay with her and grow the kingdom. Eventually they married and raised a family.

Charlie grew into a sweet woman who played all day with her two daughters, Lucia and Denise. She invited people from other lands into her kingdom, welcoming them with open arms.

One day while her husband was away beseeching more people to reside in Rolling Hills, Charlie discovered something extraordinary.

She was deep in the basement of Peachtree Palace, which had grown to be the home of her childhood fantasies.

She found a small key lying on the floor with no hint of where it might have come from. Could this key have some significance to Peachtree Palace? How and why it had been put there was a mystery to Charlie, but as her gentle hand caressed the key, power flooded through her. It frightened her, and it was certainly a right fear to have. The key vowed not only to show her a magical land but also to constantly feed her power.

In a ceremony, she presented the key to her citizens, showing the magic she had learned. They begged for more light shows and magic, and she answered every week with a performance.

But one day, at a show, something happened.

Charlie was twisting her hands in an elaborate movement, smiling at the applause as she levitated the key into the air with a small gust of wind.

The key moved of its own will, shaking in the air. Startled, she dropped the key, and felt a burst of magic surge out as it clattered to the ground, leaking into all of the citizens.

She rushed away, cancelling the display and leaving the people to wonder what had happened.

But Charlie was too confused to think. She wasn't exactly sure, but she was almost certain that this incident had somehow affected not only her own citizens, but everyone in all of Mytheria. She had no idea how this was possible, but she felt a change in the air around her. No matter where she went, she could feel the potential power in everybody.

Nonetheless, Charlie continued to practice magic, even teaching her daughters the charms and spells and instructing them to pass down their wisdom to other members of the Hills family.

As Charlie grew older, she remained ever mindful to cling to the key, afraid to let it go.

Her daughters, however, now young women, began to ask questions about where the key had come from, and what it was. They searched for it all across Mytheria, hoping to possess the highest level of power that their mother had been given.

More and more, Charlie realized that, if in the wrong hands, the temptation of power gained by acquiring the key could tear her kingdom apart.

So she locked the key far away, hidden from the world. She informed her citizens that, try as they might, they would never find the key.

She continued to grow the kingdom into a beautiful place, but the key stayed hidden.

People searched across the world for the key, but none were successful.

Charlie had granted the knowledge of the secret hiding place to no one. Though many tried to earn her trust, she always answered no.

Throughout the rest of her years, Charlie wrote a book on the history of Peachtree Palace.

People were curious why she had written the book, but she simply told them it was necessary, and that one day in the future, they would be glad she had done so.

She reflected on her life happily, enjoying the memories of all the deeds she had done.

Charlie died at the age of eighty-seven.

The world carried on.

The key was never found. People assumed that it had been hidden miles away, as they had been told. And yet it was so close that if you went out on a clear night, just as the sun was setting and the world was aglow, you could almost hear it whispering to you, calling your name.

And so it remains hidden: The Lost Key of Peachtree Palace.

I

Hattie

I was used to being an unordinary princess.

I was used to the stares and the whispers that I got every time I left the palace, and honestly, sometimes I liked them.

They were an opportunity. A chance for me to stand up and promise that I could be successful, no matter how many people didn't agree with me, no matter how many people thought I was too young to be doing this.

I knew they were right, of course. No ordinary sixteen-year-old should ever have to rule an entire kingdom. But then again, I wasn't ordinary at all, and Rolling Hills wasn't an ordinary kingdom. I was used to the skepticism I'd get no matter what I did.

What I wasn't used to was just how much of those stares and whispers I would get for the simple task of trying to meet some of my citizens.

I strode briskly down the narrow canyon. My loose brown curls blew in the wind, and I took advantage of it, using them to hide my face when I passed another family casting me an odd look.

The weather was beautiful as it always seemed to be, sunbeams shining from every corner of the sky.

Rolling Hills wasn't as fancy as our neighboring kingdoms, as my council constantly liked to remind me, but it was lovely. It had a specific aura that lured one to walk down into the canyon, feeling not a care in the world, but always aware of the beautiful landscapes and the feel of cherry blossoms and leaves swirling softly in the breeze.

The surrounding kingdoms often scoffed at our houses, whose doors were carved into the canyon like someone had used a giant cookie cutter. But nothing anyone said would break the fairy-tale lens through which I looked. To me, to everyone who lived here, Rolling Hills was paradise.

Today's air was touched by a warm breeze. Cherry blossom trees bent down into the canyon, creating a pink blanket in the sky. The leaves flew in the wind, littering the ground with exquisite rosy specks.

I mentally tried to run through my schedule. I'd been away from Peachtree Palace to take a walk around the kingdom for about an hour now, but it might have been a little longer.

Not that anyone would notice I was gone beside Illis.

I flinched as I realized how mad she'd be for not telling her where I was going again. Another family cast me a weird look, and I found myself wondering why it was such a big deal for me to be walking around like any normal person.

"Good morning to you, Your Majesty," said a little girl on the street, startling me out of my thoughts.

She pushed her blonde hair out of her eyes and glanced up at me with a little curtsy, her dark skin glowing in the sunlight.

I rolled my eyes, trying to seem as casual as possible. "You can just call me Hattie."

"Okay, *Princess* Hattie," she said laughing.

I laughed too, admiring her politeness. From what I could tell she was probably around only six years old.

"What's your name?" I asked, trying to get back on task. I always forgot how big my kingdom was, but I wanted to make my goal to get to know everyone who lived there. So far though, I'd barely made a dent.

"Lily," she grinned.

"Well, Lily, it's nice to meet you." I laughed again and turned to her mother who I had just noticed standing beside me. "Your daughter is fabulous. In fact, I believe I owe her a walk. If you don't mind, of course," I said, as I winked at Lily, who nodded her head vigorously.

"I'd rather not take her to the market anyway," Lily's mother said as she brushed a piece of hair out of her eyes.

"Would you like that Lily?" I asked.

"I'd love to," she giggled but then paused saying, "But don't you have a Royal Council meeting today?"

My hand flew to my mouth, and I nearly dropped the petal in my hand. I was supposed to be at one of our Royal Council meetings, held regularly to make policies for the kingdom. I wanted Rolling Hills to be run more fairly, where everyone had a say, but it was difficult. The kingdom had been strictly ruled by the king and queen in all years past. The Royal Council meetings were a way of letting the citizens tell me and my council what they wanted to happen with the kingdom.

"I have to go!" I cried as I ran away. "And don't forget that I owe you a walk!"

Lily smiled and waved after me.

I hurried down the canyon, which now seemed to be stretching like a strained rubber band. I peeked in every house to find a clock, but I couldn't get a glimpse.

Eventually I found a house with a clock above the kitchen, and realized with a start that it was the house of my personal cook and best friend, Misty. I had never really fancied eating in big crowded halls of people, so I opted to eat with her every day.

The truth was, I *could* cook myself, but Misty had been one of my closest friends when I took over the kingdom, so I gave her a job.

Misty was just pulling her blonde hair back into a messy ponytail when I entered. She looked surprised at my arrival, hands dropping from behind her head, mouth forming a perfect 'o'.

"What's up Hattie?" she asked, brushing her hands on her yellow apron.

"Time?" I asked panting, "I need to know the time."

"Time. . ." mumbled Misty, glancing at the clock, "Exactly one forty-five."

"One forty-five!" I exclaimed. "Oh god, I'm late!"

I gave her an apologetic wave and bolted out of the house and down the canyon.

I caught a view of Peachtree Palace ahead. The canyon sloped and faded into the ground, and I was now inside the palace grounds. The gorgeous castle glittered in the sunlight, each tower glowing. Cobblestones led up to the front steps. Cherry blossom trees lined the path, each branch dipping. I could glimpse the stylist's house to the left through the trees, the same stones leading to the door.

I took one moment to enjoy the tranquility of my haven before rushing through the grand doors at the front of Peachtree Palace.

The inside was just as beautiful as the outside. Radiant colors glistened from the light pouring through the windows, making everything shine. Two staircases hugged the walls.

Heels clopping like a panicked pony on the floor, I rushed into the room on my left.

The large space had previously been used as a courtroom, but I had tried to shape it into a meeting room where people could share ideas instead of expecting to be sentenced or something like that.

I threw open the doors. Aubry, the twenty-six-year-old leader of my council was peering at me from her stand behind the podium, adjusting the black bun on her head. She clapped loudly.

"Well! I'll be pleased to inform you that Princess Hattie has arrived at last! We've been waiting, you know."

"Sorry," I mumbled, making my way to a chair at the opposite end of the room. I felt everybody's eyes on my back as I slowly sat down. Though many people liked me, I wasn't fit to be a princess, and sooner or later, someone or something was going to prove that. After all, I was only sixteen. Other than being the daughter of the former king and queen, I didn't really have any business handling a crown.

"No, dear, it's fine," laughed Aubry, pushing her spectacles farther up her nose, her crisp accent out of place with the others. "I was joking! All right, our discussion today: Silkbreak is on the verge of cutting industrial ties with us. Their kingdom is far richer and far more advanced than we are, so we don't want to lose their economical support. Any ideas?"

Instantly, hands flew into the air and shouts rang out.

"Send an ambassador there." Someone suggested.

"Send Hattie, send Princess Hattie!"

My head snapped up. "I could go."

"I don't think so," said Aubry, chewing her lip. "Preparations for this year's Cherry Blossom Festival are already too far under way."

"I don't see any reason we can't wait until after the festival," someone called.

I tilted my head and glanced at the schedule in front of me. "One month after the festival, I'm free. I can handle the negotiations with Silkbreak."

"You're far more needed in the kingdom, Princess," Aubry said, raising her eyebrows at me.

Several people raised their hands. "I agree. Besides, Hattie is far too young to do negotiations with a foreign kingdom."

I placed my head in my hands, the usual sinking feeling filling my gut. I had grown so used to it, I sometimes felt like I should just put a cannonball on my stomach.

"How about a vote?" someone called. "Those in favor of Princess Hattie handling negotiations?"

Hands raised around me, and I breathed a sigh of relief. *No more cannonball.*

Aubry counted quickly, frowned and said, "Unfortunately, the princess will be staying in Rolling Hills for the time being." She glanced at me. *Boom,* and there it was again. "Meeting dismissed!"

As the crowd dispersed, Aubry walked over to me. "I'm sorry Hattie," she said.

I just shrugged, too used to it to pretend to care.

"There is something else, however."

"What do you mean?" I asked, adjusting the slipping tiara on my head. It was too heavy for me, but luckily I only had to wear it for important events and council meetings.

"Well, we have another problem. The books in the schoolhouse are quite outdated, and it will cost a lot of money to get new ones."

"So?"

"So," she said, impatience making her words harsh. "You will need to find an influential villager to go with you to the meeting two days from now, one who will propose that we get new books."

I sighed, stating, "But I don't see why we can't raise funds instead for our students to attend Peachtree Academy."

It was Aubry's turn to sigh. It was a short huff, quick, clean, like everything else she did. "Do I have to remind you yet again that Peachtree Academy is the most prestigious boarding school in Mytheria? It takes skill to get into that school, not money. There are only 6,000 students in the world who currently attend the academy, and none from Rolling Hills. Even though your ancestors built it, no one has attended in generations. Hattie, we don't even have registration forms."

"I'm sorry. I forgot again," I admitted.

"Find a villager to help with the proposal tomorrow. Now get some rest, Hattie, you look awful," she informed me as she accepted my paper summarizing the meeting, now covered with notes.

"Thanks," I laughed, not really sure if I should be happy she was trying to help, or amused and offended that she said I looked awful. Probably both.

I bid her good day and went to my bedroom. Spacious and ornate, it was like a perfect princess's dream. There was a basket of peaches by the door, harvested from the kingdom's own grove. I grabbed one and took a bite. It tasted like heaven.

I collapsed onto my bed and pulled out an old book titled, *The History of Peachtree Palace*. It was a storybook, with tales of kingdoms just like ours, including their histories. My favorite was "The Legend of the Lost Key of Peachtree Palace." It told of the first princess of Rolling Hills, Charlie Hills, and magic. Of course, magic wasn't real, but I had always been obsessed with the fairy tales in the book. To be the princesses in the pages had always been my dream as a little girl. Our kingdom wasn't exactly one of the perfect tales in the pages. It was a great kingdom, but it somehow felt . . . lost, as though something was missing from its history. Legends– they were all we had.

My fingers skimmed over the gold filigree on the cover. Reading it now lacked the magical thrill it once had when my mother read it to me. I reached instinctively behind me, grabbing my stuffed bear, Teddy, and hugged him close to my chest.

Teddy's nose was almost gone, and he was worn down, threads fraying and his fur had lost the sheen it once had, but he was mine. My mother had given him to me when I was just a baby.

I gazed again at the book.

Looking at it brought tears to my tired eyes. *The History of Peachtree Palace* was the only thing I had left of my parents besides memories. And Teddy, I supposed. Their faces were imprinted in my mind. I would forever condemn myself for my incapacity to have helped them the night they disappeared. Instead, I cried, a small child, scared of the fighting I heard outside.

"Mariana, protect Hattie!" Father yelled to my mother.

"I can't! I have to help you!" Mother shouted back without hesitation.

I sat afraid on my bed, trembling, only seven years old. "Mama?"

Mother looked desperate, torn. She bent down and leaned her head close to mine. She was crying a little, and it terrified me. I had never seen my mother cry before.

"Hattie, my darling, I need you to listen to me. I love you so much more than you will ever understand. You are the most important thing to me. But I need you to promise me something. This book," she pointed to The History of Peachtree Palace. "You must never lose it. Someday you will rely on it to save the kingdom."

She stroked my face. "You are far too young to understand. You have no idea how much I love you."

She tried to show me with the biggest hug I'd ever felt. I melted into it, accepting the warmth and love.

Father rushed to give me a squeeze too, lamenting, "Goodbye, my little peach."

And as they left me, I realized that I was, for the first time, truly alone.

My parents disappeared that night. All that was left was an emptiness inside me, some inexplicable guilt, and the book.

My mother was wrong about something, though. That night she told me that I didn't understand how much my parents loved me. But I did. Because I loved them the same way.

2

Misty

A Flabbernack called outside my door. It was somewhere between a squawk and a wail, and made everyone who heard it want to curl up into a ball and never get up. The annoying bird had way too much fun waking all the villagers up every morning like a personal alarm clock we never asked for.

I groaned, thinking of Hattie with her spacious bed and fancy room. She probably didn't have an annoying bird waking her up everyday.

But not for me. I was just a normal villager, living a normal life. There was nothing fancy about me.

Not that every sixteen year old lived on their own, I guess that was special.

I pushed these thoughts out of my brain and sighed. Hattie was the kindest princess to rule Rolling Hills. Besides, she had already given me a salary exceeding what most people earned. The villagers weren't poor, but we certainly did not live in the luxuries that Hattie wished we did. Just normal houses, normal everything.

I sat up.

My house was like most others in the kingdom. A little cave entrance carved into the canyon. I had always marveled at how much bigger these houses were on the inside. From the outside, the tiny caves might seem more like a prison, but taking a step through each bamboo door showed a suitable living room with a larger divot carved into the back for the kitchen. In the corner, there was a small set of stairs with two rooms at the top. Taking a sharp left led to my bedroom, which was a frilly, much-too-organized haven so brightly colored that people said it felt like "stepping into sunshine." I did my best to brighten it up, considering that there were only two windows facing the inside of the canyon.

I threw my fluffy yellow sheets aside and shuffled out of bed.

Sunlight streamed into the room, making my bare skin feel like it was glowing. I felt refreshed after my nice sleep.

I stretched my arms one last time before hauling myself to the bathroom. I swung open my closet door and grabbed a short blue dress.

As I was changing, I heard a knock on the door, and my best friend's voice wafted through: "Hello? Misty?"

My cheeks reddened. "Not now, Liam, I'm getting ready."

He fiddled with the door. "Hold on . . . "

"Liam, take the hint maybe?" I asked exasperatedly.

There was a beat of silence.

"Ah," he awkwardly responded. "I'll just go now."

I could almost hear the wince in his tone as he shuffled away.

I sighed and finished getting dressed, taking time to touch up my large brown eyes with eyeliner. I rushed downstairs, opening my door to let the fresh air in.

The sun was already far in the sky. As I headed over to the kitchen, I wondered how many times I'd ignored the Flabbernack.

I pulled the last of the woebly fruit from the fridge and bit into it. The juicy fruit filled my mouth with happiness.

Woeblies were a rarity in Rolling Hills, as they didn't grow there, but I was lucky enough to know someone at the market who could give me a basket of the sweet fruit every week.

I cleared my plate and tossed what remained into a little waste can used for weekly composting.

Walking toward the table, I plucked my shopping list from my apron pocket, sat down, and started adding to the list. Busywork at the most. 'Cooking for Hattie' was my job, but I wasn't stupid. I knew that it wasn't a real job. I wasn't actually needed. Hattie just liked to make me feel that way.

A knock at my door told me that Liam had returned.

"Morning, Misty," he said as he walked in, looking as effortlessly gorgeous as usual. He sidled over to the bench next to me, purposely shaking his dirty blonde hair in my face. "How is my best friend this morning? Is she tired? You know– that is a stupid question because you are *always* tired."

I ignored him, but my face went hot again.

He stood up and headed toward the fridge.

Still writing, I told him, "If you're looking for a woebly, they're all gone."

"Hey," he said, putting an arm around me. "Are you seriously still mad at me for this morning?"

"You tried to pick my lock. It was locked for a reason." I raised my eyebrows at him.

Liam looked down with a frown. "I'm sorry," he said, and I could tell he meant it.

I turned to hug him. "It's all right." But then I hit his arm, as hard as I could– which wasn't very hard– and scowled "Just never do it again."

"Now that is the greeting I am used to," he smirked. "Hey by the way, have I told you about what I did to Scarlet?"

My eyebrows raised again. I was probably going to have permanent wrinkles in my forehead by the time I was done with Liam. "What did you do?"

"Well," he cleared his throat in preparation. "I visited Elise at her shop, and picked up the strongest love potion I could find. Then, I snuck it into Scarlet's juice at our club meeting."

"Wait a minute, club?" I asked.

"Oh yeah." Liam smirked again. "We meet up every Thursday and write poetry after school. I mean, it's not like we've got anything better to do."

I couldn't help but feel a pang as I realized that this was where he wrote all his poetry, and I wasn't part of the group.

He mimed showing off a display. "We call ourselves . . ."

I nodded for him to continue.

"Echoes Creek! Creek, creek, creek," he called out, cupping his hands and repeating the word softer and softer.

It was my turn to smirk. "Please tell me you have that on a pin badge. It could be a members only type thing."

He considered the thought. "You know, that's not a bad idea."

"Consider it yours." I smiled. "As long as you give me one."

"Done. Anyway," Liam said, clearing his throat again and delving back into the story. "As Scarlet looked at me, I slipped the elixir into her juice. She took a sip and fell . . . fell head over heels for me." He winked and I rolled my eyes as hard as I could.

"Of course she fell deeply in love," he continued."saying how she wanted to marry me and–"

"Yeah no I'll stop you there," I interrupted, trying to prevent the grotesque images from entering my mind.

"There was also a fair bit of," he pretended to swoon. "'Liam, you're *so* handsome.' Beauty–" he winked at me. "–it's how I get all my ladies."

My face flamed, and I snorted. "What ladies?"

He countered with a look of actual shock. "Are you blushing?"

"Liam!" a voice called from next door. His mother. I wanted to grovel at her feet for saving me from his question.

"Well, duty calls I guess. Bye, Misty." Liam rose from the bench and gave me a salute before leaving me to my list.

I let out an exasperated breath and tucked a loose lock of hair behind my ear.

I got back to work on my grocery list. It was filled in a minute, and I gathered my bags from the closet and headed for the market.

Walking in the opposite direction of Peachtree Hall toward the end of the canyon, I passed dozens of children and families carrying crates filled with food and crafts for the market.

Several doors in the canyon were still shut, but most were open, displaying busy families getting ready for the day.

I glanced at my shopping list.

"Okay," I thought out loud. "I need to get all this food and then be back in time to prepare Hattie's breakfast by ten so she can start her day. Easy enough."

I walked a little longer until I saw a banner on the horizon. I had reached the edge of town. The market was crowded with villagers from all kingdoms in the surrounding vicinity. Many wore colorful smocks, buying and selling their food and wares. Several people were sewing blankets and shouting generous prices into the air.

I wandered toward a booth with a child making small knitted diamond shapes with letters written on them.

"Welcome," she said, barely glancing up from her work. "Would you like to buy a God's-eye from the best seamstress in the kingdom?" She smiled smugly. "My prices are the cheapest. I can sell you one for only 3 coinches."

I almost laughed, knowing that in other kingdoms the sew might go for only half a coincho, but this little girl was working so hard that it felt like a crime to disappoint her.

"I'll take one, please," I replied.

She almost looked startled that someone was actually going to pay that much for a tiny knit diamond, but she laid out my color options.

"These are the best fabrics in all the kingdom," she boasted. "Green represents harmony, yellow safety, and pink love."

"I'll buy the pink one, please," I answered off the top of my head.

She set right to work sewing and stitching.

I closed my eyes and let the music and shouting fill my ears. I immediately felt guilty for complaining about my life that morning.

The little girl cleared her throat politely.

I looked up. She was holding a finished pink God's-eye with white embroidered letters that read "Love."

"Thank you, it's beautiful," I said and pulled 4 coinches out of my apron. "Keep the change."

The girl grinned widely and thanked me.

Soon my shopping was done, and I was unpacking all my food, including the fresh woeblies. Hattie walked through the door, looking as beautiful as ever.

Her hair was perfectly straight today and her white dress was stunning.

"Hattie," I smiled. I was delighted by her visit.

"Misty." She nodded.

"What are you doing here?" I asked.

"Coming for my breakfast," she replied, eyeing at the unwashed dishes in the sink.

"Oh!" I exclaimed. "Your Majesty, I'm so sorry!"

"Your Majesty?" She raised an eyebrow and giggled, "Seriously? I told people to stop calling me that!"

I rolled my eyes apologetically.

"What have you been doing this morning?"

"I'm sorry, Hattie, but there was a little girl making these sews, and I couldn't resist having one made." I pointed toward the God's-eye now hanging above my sink.

Hattie smiled. "Oh, okay then, it's really pretty."

"Now," I said, pulling a fake menu from the air. "What would you like for breakfast?"

Hattie sat down at the table and bit her nails as she gazed into space. It was hard to tell what she was thinking.

Hattie looked up abruptly.

"You should help me," she said. I could see the wheels turning in her head.

"Um-"

"Oh, and fried woebly, please."

"Ok, help with what?" I asked, taking a frying pan out from the cabinet.

"Well," she replied, standing up. "Aubry told me that we needed new books for the school and that I needed help. And the schoolhouse really does need a new coat of paint. We can kill two birds with one stone at the meeting tomorrow. Bam!"

"Well," I crept. "I think it's a wonderful idea. The books are very outdated and the paint is chipping badly. But you would need to get the support of one other person, and we both know I'm not . . . "

"I'll choose you!" Hattie decided aloud.

"What?"

"I'll bring you to the meeting with me," Hattie replied, chipper.

I stopped dead, the fruit still sizzling in the pan.

"Hattie, that's not a good idea," I told her. "I'm scared of your meetings, and that's that. I know you think this idea is good, and don't get me wrong, I do too, but why don't you ask Fira or Illis?"

"No." Hattie shook her head. "That won't do. The councilors have to be sure the books chosen are ones that a villager would enjoy."

"I don't know, does it really matter all that much what books are put in the school . . . "

"Please," Hattie begged, her eyes growing round like a puppy.

My brain spun, trying to think of *anything* I could get Hattie to agree to, "Hold on. What if you let me get a makeover from Lovedaya?" I asked.

Hattie smiled.

Lovedaya was Hattie's personal stylist, the one who made her look stunning for important events.

Hattie consented, still smiling. "I promise."

I nodded painfully. "Okay, okay fine you win. I give up. But I won't forget about the makeover!" I turned on her sternly.

Hattie winked and clapped her hands. "Maybe this will inspire more villagers to speak up about change."

"Sure," I agreed. But my mind was elsewhere, pondering what I'd just shoved myself into. Had I sold my soul for a makeover?

3

Illis

I was antsy with nerves, struggling to keep my features in their signature serious expression.

It wasn't that often that I actually had a good idea worth telling Hattie. And there was a council meeting again today, so the timing was practically perfect.

I sat up and glanced at the clock on the bedside table in my suite—eleven past four. In the morning.

Sometimes being an early bird sucked.

I flopped back onto my bed, knowing that there was no way I was going back to sleep.

I laid on my queen bed for a couple of minutes, thinking about how I would introduce my idea.

Eventually, I got up and switched on my light, admiring the suite I had in the palace.

My bed protruded from the left wall; a desk from the right, next to the bathroom. A balcony in the back gave me a perfect view of the whole kingdom.

I grabbed my trademark green pants and lace black shirt from my walk-in closet and dressed. I gathered up my black hair into a ponytail, leaving a few strands hanging in front.

Now fitted into my comfortable outfit, I strapped on my belt with my dagger.

Honestly, being Hattie's personal guard wasn't as difficult as I had initially thought. I barely had to tail her, but I was always a minute away whenever she needed me. It was more the title than anything.

I quickly brushed my teeth and stepped outside into the hallway.

Since my room was closest to Hattie's in the front of Peachtree Palace, I only had to walk a few yards past Fira's door to get there.

I knocked quietly, and Hattie answered, her hair still in a mess from her sleep. Yet she still managed to look gorgeous in the early hours of the day, her deep brown eyes shining, her face glistening without an ounce of makeup.

"Good morning, Your Majesty," I said, bowing slightly, though the few inches I had on Hattie made it so I was practically at her eye level.

"I swear to god," she muttered, "Are you guys playing some kind of joke on me? *Why* does everyone keep calling me that?"

"Good morning to you too," I said, raising my eyebrows, "Did you get up on the wrong side of the bed or . . ."

Hattie rolled her eyes.

"So?" I asked. "What type of business are you bringing to your meeting today?"

"New books and paint for the school. They're really outdated," she replied.

"Oh," I said, slightly crestfallen but trying not to show it.

"What's wrong?" Hattie asked, narrowing her eyes, seeing right through me. She somehow always did that.

"Well I thought I might propose an idea as well," I answered, fidgeting with the bracelet on my wrist.

It was a simple silver band that slipped softly around my wrist. Hattie had given it to me last November for my birthday and I had worn it every day since.

"What is it?" she asked eagerly, smiling at my silly habit.

"Well, I thought it might be useful to have a town square with a big clock in it. And it could have a bulletin board, so people could post events."

Hattie tilted her head in thought, and said slowly, "There's no reason we can't propose two ideas on the same day. The only problem is you need someone to help you, and since I'm already presenting something, it can't be me."

"Okay," I said, trying to think of who I could ask that would actually agree to help me. It wasn't that I didn't know anyone besides Hattie, they just didn't like me all that much. The more I thought about it, it was probably the unwavering over-protectiveness and the fact that I hardly ever laughed at a joke.

"The meeting starts at one thirty today, so be ready with someone by then," Hattie said.

"Okay," I said again. "Do you think Fira would help me?"

Fira, Hattie's secretary. She did all of Hattie's official papers, *and* worked directly with the council. She seemed like the perfect candidate.

"Great idea!" Hattie exclaimed.

I bowed low again, forgetting what Hattie had just told me, and requested, "Permission to leave, *Your Majesty?*"

"Approved," she giggled.

I headed to Fira's room and knocked.

"Good morning, Illis," Fira said softly as she opened the door, her ginger hair automatically standing out against the pale walls of the palace hallways.

"I have a favor," I stated.

"So I've heard," she said, gesturing to Hattie's room, making me wonder if she'd been eavesdropping.

"So will you help me?" I asked.

"Why not!" she smiled softly, scrunching her small button nose.

"That's great," I sighed in relief. "I was worried that you'd be busy."

No one would ever guess that Fira was the eldest of us. She was soft and small, and her round face was almost like a child's. But there was a sort of wisdom in her eyes that I still couldn't fathom came from a nineteen-year-old.

"You're staring into space again, Illis," She chided as we walked down the marble stairs.

I threw her a scowl but she simply shrugged, "Someone has to remind you," she shook her bangs out of her face as we passed the mirror near the front doors, adjusting a stray piece of hair that had fallen out of it's usually perfect bob cut and winking at me, "Hattie might need you and you'll be stuck in the clouds."

My frown deepened, but I tried to shake it off as we headed out Peachtree Palace's grand doors. Outside, the sun was already gleaming, bouncing off the vibrant pink blossoms surrounding the palace.

I closed my eyes and tried to picture a town square directly at the opposite end of the canyon, close to the market; a fountain spouting crystal blue liquid; a small bulletin board pinned with daily notices; a clock standing tall and emblazoned in the colors of Rolling Hills.

I opened my eyes and suddenly I was back in the entry hall of Peachtree Palace. A seven-year-old Hattie was laughing next to me.

"C'mon, Illis!" she exclaimed, picking up a doll and placing her in the toy house.

"Coming," I replied. I danced my doll over to Hattie, and gave the princess a tight squeeze.

"Hattie, dinnertime," a feminine voice called.

I looked up to see Queen Mariana smiling down at me, her blue dress sparkling as she came in for a hug.

"You begin training to be Hattie's personal guard tomorrow," she declared. "You'd best get some sleep."

"How about the disappearances of all those people?" I said, nodding covertly to the kitchens. "I heard you talking."

"Illis!" the Queen exclaimed. She collected herself, glancing at Hattie, "It's under control."

But I still didn't think so. "Can I help?" I inquired.

"No," the Queen smiled. "Now, get on home."

I ran back to my house, smiling at the wonderful time I had spent at the palace with Hattie.

If only I could have begun training earlier. It was the last time I ever saw Queen Mariana.

This memory faded, and I was sitting in my housing unit, my brother boasting about the money he'd retrieved at the market.

He poured the bad of coinches on the table. "Mom, Dad, look at all the money I made at the market this morning. I'm going to cook and treat you all to a big dinner."

I grinned, happy about having a feast. My brother was an excellent cook. I could practically taste all the delicious foods piling up across the entire surface.

"Why do you never bring us any money, Illis?" my mother asked me, raising her eyebrows expectantly.

My smile dropped, and I tried to look as tough as possible.

"I'm going to be a guard." I grabbed my sword, and started to demonstrate some moves I'd learned in class, finishing with a strike, panting.

I had expected them to clap, or smile, or say good job, like they had to my brother.

But my mother's eyes were down, and my father looked furious.

"Girls don't guard," he spit at me, looking disgusted.

"Stop dreaming, Illis," my brother taunted. "It's never going to happen. You're going to grow up to be useless, just like I always thought you would."

This vision faded, and I was ten, my raven hair swinging in my face, beads of sweat pouring down. *Step again and hit the target.*

I lunged at my instructor, Mr. Montair, my faux sword striking directly in between his ribs.

Mr. Montair straightened up and clapped lightly, but I lunged at him again, knocking him down.

"Never let your guard down," I spit his own words back at him, and a smile creeped onto the edges of his mouth.

I turned to see the audience applauding, except for my parents. They sat in the back row, looking down, ashamed at what I'd become.

I tried to stop it, but I felt small tears mix with the sweat on my face as I watched them stand up and leave without looking at me.

They had never believed that Queen Mariana and King David or any of the Hills's princesses had ruled the kingdom wisely. They believed in the old customs from other kingdoms, in which men were always the strong ones.

I bit my tongue hard enough to draw blood.

I could prove them wrong. I always had, and I always would.

This one faded, and I was standing on a podium facing a crowd, my parents nowhere in sight.

Mr. Montair placed a medal around my neck.

"Fabulous job, Illis. I wish I could say you'll never need this training to protect your princess, but—" he stopped himself, shaking his head. After a second he smiled. "You never heard it from me, but you are the best student I've ever taught."

Mr. Montair then faced the crowd and shouted, "Meet Hattie Hills's official guard, Illis!"

Hattie rushed up from the front row and hugged me, sending tingles all through me. She was crying a little as she wrapped me in her arms, "Good work, Illis, and thank you."

"Thank you," I said, surprised to find I meant it.

I took a step back up toward the podium and cleared my throat, preparing for my speech. I looked out at the eager audience, and began, "People who are different in this world have always been told what to do, been cast out. But I had a dream. As stupid as that sounds. I wanted to be a guard for my best friend, so I became a guard, no matter how many people told me I was too young. You can make a difference. You can make decisions. It doesn't matter what anybody tells you. I believe in you. It is time to throw away any reminiscences of old customs, of who gets to lead. It is time to embrace what the princesses have always wanted this kingdom to be. Brave. Smart. Happy." I smiled at Hattie. "And kind."

4

Fira

No no no, this can't be right, I thought, gazing down at the complicated angles that lay on my desk.

I had barely pondered the matter when I heard a ding, and
glanced up to see a ball released from a small metal shoot. It rolled
down a pipe, passing my mirror and bed on the left side of the
room. The ball proceeded to pass my bathroom and closet and wrap
around the room, falling on a metal cylinder with a chime. Clocks
were too elementary for me. This was much more fun, and my own
invention.

I neatly folded the paper, tucking it in my pocket, and walked
over to the mirror, which I had pinned with messy to-do lists and
with photos of my sister, Anice, and her daughter.

My clock told me it was seven thirty in the morning, which
meant that it was about time for me to get ready for the day.

Although I had been awake for an hour, I was still tired and had
to drag myself out of my pajamas and head to the bathroom.

Placing a straightener on the counter to heat up, checking after a few minutes to see if it was hot, I placed it around strands of hair and pulled. Instantly my hair smoothed out, until it fell in a perfect bob around my face.

I walked back into the suite and gazed into the mirror.

My fiery ginger hair blazed, resting neatly on my shoulders, and large circle glasses slipped down my small nose, earning themselves a push back up into position.

The time now read seven forty-five, so I decided to go to the kitchens to eat breakfast.

The hallway outside my room was bright, the sunlight streaming in. I trudged down one of the marble staircases that hugged the walls. The door on the left of the staircases held the meeting room, and the right, Peachtree Library.

Between was a long hallway, part of which were the dining rooms.

As I reached the bottom of the marble stairs, I straightened my posture, and walked quickly into the kitchens.

Cooks were busy preparing meals for other staff members who would work in areas such as the library, or tutors for the school.

A server handed me a gold plate and gestured for me to help myself to the buffet.

There were pastries holding woeblies and peaches. Cakes overflowing with cream, a soft oatmeal, and potatoes sat waiting to be devoured– the regular breakfast spread.

I helped myself to a peach pastry and a potato from the counter.

"Drink?" the server asked.

"One peach blend, please," I said, and the server handed me a thick shake.

"One coincho."

"Of course." I sat down and began to eat my breakfast, devouring it until every last bite had disappeared from the plate.

* * *

Illis and I sat in my suite reasoning how we should start with Hattie's council.

"We should make a blueprint," I suggested. "To give them an idea of exactly what we're thinking."

"Great," Illis said, as she grabbed a large sheet of parchment and placed it in front of me. "You do the math." Her face was as unreadable as ever, but I saw what I thought had to be a smirk twitching at the corners of her mouth.

I pursed my lips, sighing slightly.

"Hey," Illis held up her hands. "That is what you get for being so smart."

I laughed, "Says the girl who completed the guard training course ten years earlier than the average person."

She blushed, an act that was all too normal for Illis, her sharp features reddening at the praise.

I grabbed a pencil from my desk and plopped down in front of the paper, "Ok, I'm ready."

Illis cleared her throat, her face dropping back into a hardened expression, "So the clock should sit on the side of the plazza. There really only needs to be enough room for some benches and the fountain in the middle."

"Be a dear and grab me the blueprints from my desk," I said, not tearing my gaze away from the paper.

I heard shuffling, and Illis handed me the manilla folder.

I licked my finger and rapidly flipped through the pages until I found the main measurements for the sections of the kingdom.

As Illis continued to verbalize her vision, I converted it to measurements and drew it on paper. I could almost see the clock and bulletin board perfectly.

I'd always been the brains wherever I went, and my friends definitely took advantage of the fact that I actually enjoyed doing the type of work so many people hated.

"Here," I said, handing her the completed paper.

"It's perfect, thank you."

"See you at one thirty," I reminded Illis as she stood up and made for the door, giving me a nod before she walked out.

No sooner had she left than I heard a tapping on my window. I spun to see a spudgewubble tapping its paw repeatedly on the glass.

"Giggles!"

I instantly saw the glint in her fur, and the blight reflected clearly in her diamond eyes.

For several days, Giggles had been on a trip delivering a letter to my friend, and her previously golden fur looked brown. After tickling beneath her wings and diving into my desk drawer for some dried peach fuzz for her to eat, I untied the letter she carried for me.

"Was it a hard journey, Giggles? Such a good girl, huh," I cooed as Giggles munched on her snack. I peeled open the parchment.

Dearest Fira,

I hope they are treating you well at Peachtree Palace. Everything is fine where I am living currently. Of course I can't very well tell you where I am, for that would be "strictly against code." Actually I've already broken more rules than you might imagine sending you this letter. I miss you soooooooooo much, and I hope I get to see you soon. At least it's a beautiful sight every morning. But that isn't why I'm writing. I need to warn you of something, and I pray that you will heed it. Something is coming to Rolling Hills. Protect Hattie at all costs. And please read the legend of "The Lost Key of Peachtree Palace." I dare say you will need it.

Your Cherry Blossom,
Cherry (obviously)

I sighed. This letter bore not a hopeful message of her return. I was beginning to wonder if she would ever come back. Cherry was my childhood best friend. She'd left years ago, the same night Hattie's parents disappeared, and she hadn't come back. I guess the difference here was that Cherry wrote to me regularly. Hattie had no idea how her parents were, but I was always alongside her, promising that we would find them soon.

Just imagining Cherry's dark skin and shining eyes made my heart ache to see her again.

I almost laughed at her warning. Terribly ominous. Still, I couldn't help but wonder about it. I had always had no interest in legends, as they weren't real, but Cherry's warnings always seemed to be accurate, even if they were merely "the kitchen staff will run out of woebly today," not that I'd ever bothered to find out how she knew so much.

I rustled through the books at my desk and found the book of legends. The pages were crisp, as though they'd never been opened, and to be quite honest, they probably hadn't. I began to read. The legend wasn't long, and I finished it in the better part of five minutes.

Upon finishing the legend, I snorted a little. It had to be nonsense. Magic keys were the stuff of fairy tales. Besides, logically, if magic existed we would have found out by now.

"This dawdling is not going to get me to the meeting," I scolded aloud.

It took me twenty minutes to get ready as I reapplied my makeup and changed into a white pleated skirt.

I stared at myself in the mirror, steeling myself for answers, the flaming hair and glasses on my head making me look like a fire princess.

5

Hattie

"Look to the left, dear," said Lovedaya, politely patting my cheek.

It was the morning of the council meeting, and I was sitting in the small stylist house next to the palace, Lovedaya doing my makeup. They did my makeup on all important days like today.

"Yes, dear!" They swiveled my chair back and forth to show me today's look.

Lovedaya walked over to the door to relight the steam machines, sending the smell of sweet morning air wafting around the room.

The interior of the hut was painted pale green and was decorated with crystals and flowers. Jewelry hung from hooks on the wall.

I was sitting in a chair before a vanity, with a small white table nearby, which Lovedaya used to house various makeup brushes, the straightener, and hairbrushes.

From the closet in the back of the hut, Lovedaya selected an outfit and handed it to me, saying, "This will do nicely. It's almost summer! Think of the holidays just around the corner. The Cherry Blossom Festival is only a month away, and then I can finally get some autumnal clothes on you, dear." They smiled, obviously delighted at the idea of the changing color palettes.

I clapped my hands, delighted that summer was approaching. I let the clothes fall onto me, and I admired Lovedaya's handiwork in the mirror on the back of the door.

They had chosen a long sleeve collar shirt with a knit sweater vest over it. My hair was perfectly styled into its loose curls, and my brown eyes popped from the color in the vest.

I smiled and gave a little twirl, smoothing down the fitted white skirt. As much as I loved Lovedaya's makeovers, I was eager to leave and pull my mind away from distractions.

I gave Lovedaya a quick hug.

"Thank you so much. You did a lovely job, as always," I complimented.

"Not at all, dear, thank *you*," they said.

Lovedaya ushered me out of the hut, giving me a slight wave as I walked away down the dirt path. It was a lovely day outside.

I followed the path in front of me, advancing toward the palace and broke through two trees a short way ahead, leading directly to it. The sky filled with squeaks as the morning delivery came. Spudgewubbles flew about, occasionally dropping a letter when they found its intended owner.

I sighed, wondering how I'd ended up with such a beautiful, fairy-tale-like kingdom, and how it could be so gorgeous when my parents weren't there.

I dragged myself away from the thought.

Today at one thirty I was proposing my new schoolbook and paint idea, something long overdue.

Trotting back to the palace, I was greeted by a staff member, "Good morning, Princess Hattie."

"Good morning," I replied. "Any news?"

"Yes," he said. "Fira would like me to inform you that she will be assisting Illis later today in her proposition."

I smiled and said, "Good to hear. Thank you." I turned away, adding, "Have a nice day."

"You, as well, Princess Hattie."

I roamed around in my bedroom with absolutely nothing to do for the moment but stand on my balcony in awe at the soft breeze that tickled my nose. I curled up with *The History of Peachtree Palace*, letting the spring air guide me toward happiness, when I spotted something in the pages of the book. A legend I had never read before. I thought I'd read everything in this book, but the legend was new to me.

I read it to myself, and as I did, a feeling of dread crept over me. Charlie Hills was talking to Alvara, Charlie's second in command, who disappeared the night that Charlie died. I read barely a sentence into the legend before I snapped the book shut, unease gnawing at my gut.

I didn't have time for dreadful legends at this moment, or ever. I was the princess of my kingdom. I needed to keep attentive.

So when one o'clock arrived, four girls walked through the door of Peachtree Palace's meeting room.

Aubry stood ready at the podium, addressing the crowd of staff members and villagers gathered for the meeting, her spectacles perched on the edge of her nose. "Please be seated."

The room sat down with a light thump.

"Today we need to propose ideas to transform Rolling Hills into the vision that our princess imagines it to be," she said, smiling at me. "But also what you, the people, want it to be. Who would like to start?"

"I will," Illis said with a slight waver to her voice, fidgeting with her hands as she stood up and made her way to the little podium, looking uncharacteristically nervous.

A councilor peered at the paper, "Your name is. . . *Illis* Mirai?"

"Illis," she corrected. "Like eye-less, but Illis, and I propose that we should create a town square. I have all the blueprints here." She fiddled in her bag, and all of the papers spilled out onto the ground.

"Sorry" she muttered and bent to pick them up. She stood up quickly, her foot catching the edge of the table.

She tripped.

I flinched.

Illis straightened herself. She cleared her throat and continued, "The square could help people connect and plan activities, ultimately bringing the kingdom closer together."

Aubry looked at the other council members with amusement, and maybe some consideration. "Can we see the blueprints?"

Illis stepped up to the podium and handed the papers to Aubry.

There was silence as Aubry peered at the papers. At last, she cleared her throat, acknowledging, "It's a circle."

"Um, well, I mean 'town circle' didn't have quite the same ring to it." She cringed.

"No, dear, it's fine," Aubry laughed. "I was joking. In all honesty, though, it's a wonderful idea. How do you propose we acquire the funds?"

Illis looked at Fira, who stood up next. "Hello, I'm Fira Pele, and I'm running finances for this project. According to our records, trading goods with Silkbreak for the past couple of years has greatly increased our balance. So, we have a large sum of money not yet set aside for projects such as this one. All we need to do is rewire a little of the money flow into a separate folder for projects. I can handle all that. The point is, the money is there."

"Okay," Aubry blinked. "I'm not a money person," She admitted. "But you are on the treasury board and clearly have this under control. Therefore, any objections?"

No one raised a hand.

"Perfect!" Aubry chirped. "Project *Town Square* underway, effective immediately."

Illis beamed and sat down, wiping her hands on her shorts. She glanced over at me, and I gave her a thumbs-up.

"All right, who's next? Go on," Aubry encouraged.

Several people raised their hands, and Aubry picked a young man who walked up to the podium. "Hello. I'm trying to open a hat shop. That's it. I was just told I needed to come here. There's a spot for sale downtown. May I turn it into a hat shop?"

Aubry looked at another councilor, a middle-aged man. He leaned forward and said, "I don't see why not."

"Really?" The young man asked, wearing a surprised grin as if he couldn't quite believe their generosity.

The councilors nodded assent.

The young man squealed, then clapped a hand over his mouth. "Thank you!"

Aubry sighed, gesturing for him to sit.

Several more people came forward with ideas, until there were only two people left to present, Misty and me.

I raised my eyebrows at Misty. She gulped, but raised her hand.

We walked to the podium, together. Misty was noticeably pale.

"Hey, you're going to do fine," I whispered.

"I know."

I smiled at her, then at the councilors and spoke first. "Hello. I am Princess Hattie."

"And I'm Misty."

"The books in the school are very outdated," I said.

"So we'd like to replace them," Misty said, adding a halting, "Please."

"We also need to repaint the school," I further proposed.

Aubry squinted. "Funds?"

"With Fira's help, we've determined the cost of the books within the price range of the extra money we have," I stated.

"Yeah." Misty bobbed her chin up and down.

"So what do you surmise are the benefits of your project?" Aubry asked.

I shuffled my feet and said, "Well, the books will be up to date, the kids will be better educated, and that'll be good for the next generation and just, you know, everything." I glanced at Misty, struggling to find the eloquence that was expected of me.

"Yeah," Misty repeated.

"That's it," I confirmed.

"All right," Aubry said. "Objections?"

When the sight of no hands reached me, I exhaled in relief and high-fived Misty.

"Okay, Project New Books and Paint underway, effective immediately," declared Aubry.

When everyone walked out of the hall, Fira, Illis, Misty and I gathered around a table.

Illis's expression was serious, but I could tell she was trying hard to keep the grin from her face. "I can't believe it. I mean, I never really thought my project would be accepted."

I beamed. "Truly?"

"Excuse me." Someone interrupted. I spun around, and Aubry and the four other councilors were walking toward us.

I smiled. "Hello."

"I'm sorry to interrupt Princess Hattie, but we should introduce ourselves to everyone if we're going to be working together. I'm Councilor Aubry."

The middle-aged man stepped forward. "Councilor Jax."

A striking woman covered in jewels stepped forward. "Councilor Addilyn."

A young, handsome man bowed. "Councilor Cason."

Lastly, a tiny woman came forward. "Councilor Sheila."

Aubry smiled and said, "We're Hattie's advisory team. We make sure she's confident in her decisions."

"Nice to meet you," Misty spoke.

Illis and Fira just nodded, already knowing them.

"Excited about your new projects?" Councilor Cason asked. His voice was smooth like butter, thick and low, as if you could slice through it with a knife.

"Yes, thank you for approving them," I said warmly.

"My pleasure. Anytime I can be of assistance," he smiled.

Aubry cleared her throat. "Hattie, the projects should be complete in a few weeks, so we can begin prepping for their finish."

"Thank you, Aubry."

"Have a nice day!" Councilor Sheila piped, and the councilors strode out of the room.

Misty took a deep breath. "It is so stressful to be around them."

"More stressful than me?" I cocked an eyebrow. "I'm the princess, you know."

Misty frowned. "Ah, yes," she said, bowing before me, "Your Highest of Highness–es."

The group slowly dispersed until only Illis and I were left, "I think I'm going to go to my room," I said, ignoring the skeptical brow she raised.

"You know it's only early afternoon right?"

"Yeah, I know," I tried to act normal as I said, "There's just something I want to look into."

I got to my room and picked up *the History of Peachtree Palace* like I'd planned, trying to find the legend I'd seen earlier.

Somehow no matter how many times I looked through the pages I couldn't find it.

"Where are you?" I muttered, before a wave of exhaustion hit me.

I shook my head to clear it, but it wouldn't leave.

After trying and failing to get the weariness away, I collapsed onto my bed, my peaceful sleep chasing away the thoughts of the troubling legend.

* * *

Only weeks later the projects had been completed, Illis's vision realized, the town square bustling with villagers checking daily notices and ushering their children over to the schoolhouse.

I took a deep breath, standing atop the steps of the schoolhouse. I raised my chin, announcing, "Today marks the day of a new age for Rolling Hills, with the best book system in the world, and it's all thanks to you." My chest swelled with pride.

I took a sharp knife and cut the ribbon that blocked the doorway.

The crowd's cheers deafened ears for miles as I walked through the schoolhouse door to look around before letting the townspeople in.

Desks formed rows facing a board with chalk. Books were piled on a shelf in every classroom.

I smiled.

The teachers thanked me, and the parents shook my hand. Some children hugged me at my waist.

After all of the people had entered the schoolhouse, I grabbed *The History of Peachtree Palace* and a picnic basket.

I hiked up to Peachtree Grove and sat beneath a tree for lunch.

There was a sweeping breeze in the air and barely a cloud in the sky. I heard the sound of footsteps approaching, and turned over to see Illis coming to join me. "Hello," I said.

"Hi," she said, then sat down and cleared her throat. "Lovely day, isn't it?"

"You're awfully polite today," I replied, laughing, but the look on her face made me stop short. She looked solemn, unlike her usual sharp self. "What's wrong, Illis, are you all right?"

"Hattie, someone's disappeared," Illis's words were torn, her tone indicating a dilemma. She fiddled with her bracelet.

"What?" I said, dropping *The History of Peachtree Palace* with a thump on the grass, my mind reeling to catch up to the meaning of the words. The heavy pull in my chest at the realization was so sharp I nearly gasped. "Wait, someone . . ."

"Disappeared, yes." Illis went on, "Well, several people actually, but we've only just found out, I promise. Just this morning we received a letter from a townswoman who said that she had woken to find her daughter, Lily, missing."

"No, not Lily!" I cried. "I met her on the street. She was a lovely young girl. I remember." I deflated, slumping forward as if the breeze was too strong to stand against. "I promised her a walk."

"You see," Illis paused as if deciding whether to share something. I nodded for her to continue. "I was reading *The History of Peachtree Palace* the other night when you left it in the library, and I read something strange. There was a poem. Something that definitely wasn't there before:

Magic inside, do not hide.
Show your class, through the glass.
Broken, building. World unfolding.
Magic reveal what you feel. Magic is real"

"Is it a prophecy?" I asked. "I mean, usually prophecies rhyme, you know, better than that."

"We don't know," Illis admitted. "But we have a lead."

Illis slid a map under my inquiring eyes and pointed to a spot near the edge of the kingdom.

"*The* Rolling Hill?" I asked. Illis nodded solemnly. "What does the Rolling Hill Have to do with this?"

"We discovered a tunnel in it, unable to be opened. We suspect that she was taken there. Rest assured we will be stationing guards at these points," Illis said, pointing at the map. "In your book there is a page that describes someone evil behind plots similar to this one. An evil girl, named Maurelle, who is supposedly out to bring down Rolling Hills."

A frown touched the sides of my mouth. "I've never read that before."

"Actually, I figured that. The writing looked fairly new, as if someone had recently scribbled it in the book."

Illis picked the book up from out of the grass and flipped to the page in question.

I gasped. My brain moved a million miles a minute. I struggled to focus on what I was seeing. My heart hammered in my chest, as if trying to knock focus into me. "But that's . . ."

"Your mother's handwriting, I know," Illis confirmed. She looked as confused as I felt, but while my features felt like static, hers had turned to a sharp attentiveness. "But why your mother would have written something in this book, I can't say. Hattie, things are appearing in the book, things that aren't by the original author, things that weren't here before. We have to be careful, Hattie, and watch out for anything suspicious."

"I'll keep an eye out," I told Illis with as much confidence as I could muster, but my stomach dropped. The first real evidence was there that my parents could still be alive. It was almost too much to hope for, a little spark that I wanted to keep from blazing into a wildfire, but the fresh writing on the page blared up at me.

"Thank you. If this were to carry on . . ." Something passed between Illis and me, something unsaid, a mutual agreement, a dark shadow. We couldn't bear the thought.

My heart was heavy as I trudged back to Peachtree Palace. I couldn't bring myself to go anywhere but my bedroom. I curled on my bed, tucking my feet beneath me.

Safe in my bed, I hugged Teddy tight to my chest, caressing the book at my side, wondering if it had been a prophecy that Illis had read. If so, what was it foretelling? And why was my mother's handwriting in the book? Why were things suddenly appearing there, and more important, how? The night my parents had disappeared my mother told me to never lose the book, that I would need it someday to save the kingdom. All these years, I had thought those words a silly trick to get me to keep a family heirloom safe.

I thought of the prophecy again. One line rang loudly in my head: *Magic is real.* It tolled in my mind louder than a school bell.

What if my mother's words were true? What if there really was something threatening Rolling Hills? And what if I was the one who would have to save it?

6

Hattie

I woke to a sharp rapping on my door. Illis, by the sound of it. I tossed Teddy on my pillow, silently scolding him for not keeping my nightmares away. But his cute little face made my heart throb, and I scooped him up and gave him one last hug.

Knocks echoed on the door, and I heard Illis call my name. I creaked out of bed and opened the door. She handed me a pile of papers.

"What is this?" I yawned.

Illis's stature slumped slightly. "The number of disappearances in the last week I didn't mention."

The papers seemed heavier than they had a second ago. "Oh," I said, and dropped them on my desk with a thump.

"I'm sorry, Hattie," Illis sympathized.

"It's not your fault," I comforted.

Whether she heard me or not, she didn't acknowledge, she just said, "The hill looks no different than usual. But villagers say they've been awakening to black fog, and then people are gone. We've sent teams out at night, but whoever or whatever this is keeps slipping past us. We really are trying to solve this, Hattie, I promise."

I took a deep breath, "And I can help too."

Illis fiddled with her bracelet. "So what are you going to do?"

I looked back at the papers on my desk. "I'm going to do a lot of reading."

Illis sighed and walked away, shutting the door behind her.

I sat inside and invested the day devouring the details of each disappearance, each one more unlikely than the next. I struggled to find a pattern, as Illis returned with more papers.

These sudden disappearances in Rolling Hill all took place at night, amidst black fog, and with no warning. And the tunnel still couldn't be opened. As for the people who were taken–they were all ages, all sizes, all colors. I didn't see any way they could all be connected.

I reopened *The History of Peachtree Palace*, and flipped to the page on which my mother had written.

It looked as though she hadn't had much time to write the short paragraph. I could barely make out some of the words.

Maurelle . . . magic . . . fighting her is the only . . . Mythics . . . threatening Rolling Hills . . . evil . . . Dark Unicorn is . . . Black, the color of death . . . Hattie . . . Hattie, be careful.

I traced my name, my throat tight. In some cultures, writing a word was as good as saying it, and seeing my mother *say* my name again was. . . my chest hitched.

My head was swimming. If this was my mother's handwriting, why did it look so new? A headache crept into my brain, and I fell asleep on my desk, not even bothering to get into bed.

* * *

I awoke to a gentle wind blowing through my balcony window, my mind still whirring from my conversation with Illis two days ago. My head was sore from leaning against the book all night. When I glanced outside, I saw that it was already sunset, making me jolt awake at the fact that I'd been asleep almost all day.

I was wearing my sweater vest outfit that I'd worn to the council meeting again, but the shirt was considerably more rumpled than it had been that day.

After a few minutes, I decided that sitting and worrying was not going to fix anything, so I dragged myself out of my desk chair and over to the balcony.

The fresh air filled my lungs as I breathed in deeply, enjoying the scent of the spring around me.

A shadow caught my eye– the accumulating pile of disappearance charts on my desk, growing by the hour, climbing higher, along with my anxiety.

I was swiftly reminded just how big a kingdom Rolling Hills was.

These moments on my balcony seemed to be the only time I could find solace, and even here, I was fully aware of the guard stationed outside my door for the last two days.

I worried that we might never discover the answer to all the madness. I bent over to grab the only book I kept in close proximity, *The History of Peachtree Palace*. For the umpteenth time I ran a hand over the gold lettering on the cover. The cover was beige, with small illustrations of peaches in each corner. I gingerly opened the front cover, staring at the date inside. This book was hundreds of years old, and yet I held it today.

I gently flipped through the pages to peer at the poem:

Magic inside, do not hide.
Show your class, through the glass.

Broken, building. World unfolding.
Magic reveals what you feel. Magic is real.

I gazed at the poem–prophecy– whatever it was and began to wonder. What had really happened to my parents? They had also disappeared. Was there more to it?

A memory crashed into my mind with the grace of a careening Flabbernack, as if breaking through water that had been frozen for years. When I was seven, Illis asked my mother about the disappearing people. What had happened to those people when I was little?

An idea began to formulate.

I raced to my desk, yanking open a drawer I never touched. It was filled with old manilla folders. I flipped through blueprints and laws and ledgers, looking for *exactly* what I needed.

My fingers raced through the pages, flipping and scanning, until these bold letters marked one folder: **Disappearance Papers**.

Was it possible that the disappearances were connected?

I started reading and realized that all the people who disappeared when I was seven had similar stories of abduction as the children and adults of now, almost too similar.

The more profiles I flipped to, the more black fog I saw. The more blurry photos of the Rolling Hill.

"What happened? What happened?" I mumbled, plopping onto the floor.

I swiped my finger too quickly and a sharp pain pierced my finger. "OW," I gasped, inspecting the paper cut, stopping abruptly when I saw the photo my finger had been cut on.

It was old and grey and torn, and the date in the corner told me it was from my childhood. My heart missed a beat. It was a picture of the tunnel. The tunnel was open, bringing to mind the image of a monster opening its wide mouth.

The stories told of disappearances in the night amidst black fog. And an old tunnel in the Rolling Hill.

I stared at the papers in my hands for only a second before making up my mind.

"Illis!" I screamed.

The door opened with a bang as Illis rushed in, followed by Fira and Misty.

"What?" Illis demanded, looking around, her eyes wide with fear.

I shot up from the floor and began to pace, *The History of Peachtree Palace* clenched between my fingers. "What happened to my parents?" I demanded.

Illis answered as if it was a trivia question, obvious confusion etched in her voice, "They disappeared as everyone knows . . ."

I interrupted, my feet thumping on the floor as I walked back and forth, "What about those people from when we were little? The ones you asked my mother about, a day before she was gone."

"They disappeared in the same way?" Illis proposed.

"Yes!" I cried, trying to ignore how concerned Illis was looking at me. "Black fog, the tunnel, almost everything."

I ran to her side and showed her the photograph of the tunnel

It took a moment before the realization hit Illis like a smack in the face. "Are you saying you think the disappearances are all connected?" But she already knew the answer to that question. I could see it in her eyes.

"Illis, what do you remember about the night my parents disappeared?" I queried.

Illis gulped. "I—"

Misty cut her off in a small voice, her eyes glued to the floor, "I remember."

"What?" There was a stab of anger in my chest. Misty had never told me about that night.

"I was out in the streets, only seven years old." She stopped to throw me a guilty look. "I. . . I heard screaming, and people were running everywhere. There was– fire, I think. But it didn't look normal at all. It was different colors. Like a flaming rainbow. It should have been impossible."

I looked at Illis, knowing her thoughts mirrored mine.

Misty continued, "The next day, I asked my parents about what they had seen, but they had been inside. I asked everyone, but no one was a witness. No one except me." Her voice was strained. She looked up, and there were tears in her eyes, "I'm sorry I didn't tell you, and I always felt guilty, like I might have been able to help. I was just too scared."

"Misty," I said calmly, even though my heart was in my throat. "I need you to tell me exactly what you saw. Do you remember anything else?"

Misty gulped, dipping her chin agonizingly slow. She took a shuddering breath. "The people in the streets that night weren't just from Rolling Hills, Hattie. They were the same ones who had disappeared."

My brain rushed into a million places, but I settled on, "This situation isn't just bad, history is repeating itself in some way!" I tried to slow my heartbeat, but I was getting excited now, like the puzzle was sliding into place.

The girls' faces were white.

Illis knit her brows in concentration. "What on earth would someone be doing with that many people?"

"Maybe someone is building some sort of army," I reasoned, even though the words tasted disgusting in my mouth. "Something to attack Rolling Hills, like before. They must be special. *Magic is real.*" It was a stretch, but a possibility. "The Maurelle girl in the book. My mother warned me about her."

"So you think someone is trying to build a magical army?" Illis was more serious than I'd ever seen her, and it almost made the words coming out of her mouth comical, but I nodded.

"Hattie." Fira's tone was gentle. She stepped forward. "You can't blame us if we think it's a stretch that some evil girl is trying to– wait, what *do* you think she's trying to do?"

A shiver ran down my spine. "Maurelle is weaving her way through all the people from years ago, through my parents, and through the townspeople now until she gets to . . ." I stopped, my voice dropping to barely a whisper. "That's what she's coming for– me."

What little color was left in the girls' faces drained like water.

"You're jumping to conclusions Hattie," Fira whispered.

I pinched the bridge of my nose. "That has to be it," I said. "*Magic is real.* It must be. Everything has been a setup, a setup to get to me."

An ominous wind blew through my balcony, as though some dark fingers might slither through the door and grab hold of me.

"But *why*?" Illis looked at me and I could tell she didn't believe me either.

"Why don't you believe me?" I yelled.

"There isn't any proof Hattie," Illis said firmly, as if I was a toddler.

I let out a humorless laugh. "Who cares about proof? We know where the tunnel is, let's just go now. We can find Maurelle and stop her."

"I can't let you do that," Illis insisted.

My anger boiled up in my stomach, "Whatever is coming for Rolling Hills is going to keep strengthening if I don't stop it. It's my duty as a princess. And– this is the first lead I've had on my parents in *years*. I can't just abandon it. They could be out there alive. I need– I need to find them," I didn't feel the tears until they blurred my vision and Illis's face cleared with understanding.

I wiped my eyes and tried to stop the sting in them, but the tears kept coming as I took a shaky breath. "This isn't about whatever's trying to attack the kingdom," I said, hating myself for how much it was true. "My parents could be out there, I have to go."

I was immediately confronted with a chorus of *What?* and *No!*.

"I can't let you do that," Illis repeated, a frantic edge to her voice.

I attempted an eye roll, but it had little effect, with the tears still running down my face. "You're my personal guard, not my babysitter. If you want to keep me safe, you have to come with me."

Illis opened her mouth to argue, but Fira interrupted, "I think Hattie is right."

Now it was my turn to say, "What?"

Fira inhaled, and sighed. "Of course I don't want you to go, Hattie, but I just don't see any other way we'll ever be able to stop the threat to our kingdom. And," she put a comforting hand on my shoulder, "I know how much this means to you. Just promise me you'll be careful."

"Okay," I agreed.

I smiled, but Fira didn't return it, saying, "I mean it, Hattie."

"All right, all right," I conceded. "I'll be careful." She awarded me a bittersweet smile. I may have had no family at the palace, but Fira was the closest thing I've ever had to a big sister.

I packed a small bag to take with me, trying to ignore my friends' somber faces following me.

"Listen, Fira," I said, pressing the tome into her hands, "You must keep this safe, understand? Keep *the kingdom* safe."

Fira bowed her head in acceptance, clutching the item to her chest. Illis bolted out the grand doors to look around.

"It's okay, Fira," Misty said, rubbing a fond hand on Fira's arm.

I turned and ran out of Peachtree Hall's doors after Illis.

From my spot just beyond the door, I could see something wet pricking at the corners of Fira's eyes, but she pushed it away and looked down, realization widening her eyes when she processed she held *The History of Peachtree Palace.*

The book wrapped in her arms, Fira sank to the floor.

I was devastated about leaving them behind, the entire scenario felt like a cruel retelling of the night my parents disappeared. I turned away and continued toward the hill with Illis, hoping I didn't look outwardly as distressed as I felt. I was the princess after all. I had to do this. I had to be strong.

"Anything yet, Illis?" I asked, my voice trembling through the void of darkness.

"No."

We stood atop the Rolling Hill. The darkness surrounded us like a blanket: If a blanket was made of itchy fabric, so uncomfortable you wanted to toss it off.

It was another twenty minutes on the moist, green hill before any discovery was made.

"Hattie, here," Illis indicated.

I followed her voice to a point some ten yards away.

In the dark, I could just make out a rock covered with writing that looked like it had to at least be decades old.

"The prophecy," I breathed, running a hand down the rough surface. It pulsed with an old ancient feeling.

"That wasn't here before."

"I think," I paused. "It wants us to find it."

I turned away so that Illis wouldn't see the shudder that ran through me.

I placed my palm flat on its rocky surface and quoted, *"Magic inside, do not hide. Show your class, through the glass. Broken, building. World unfolding. Magic reveal what you feel. Magic is real."*

The hill folded in on itself, crumpling into an open doorway.

I looked at Illis and she nodded toward the door. "Ready?"

"If I wait until I'm ready, I'll be waiting forever."

"Couldn't agree more."

We nodded at each other in solidarity and stepped through the door.

7

Fira

"Listen, Fira," Hattie said somberly, as she pressed something into my hands. "You must keep this safe, understand? Keep *the kingdom* safe." The weight of responsibility on thise two words alone nearly pushed me to my knees.

I nodded. I tried to swallow, but my throat was tight.

"It's okay, Fira," Misty reassured, rubbing my arm.

Hattie bolted out the door.

Something wet pricked the corners of my eyes, but I pushed it away and looked down. I held a book titled *The History of Peachtree Palace*.

The book wrapped in my arms, I sank to the floor, dread pushing down on my shoulders.

With a start, I sat up quickly, my breathing heavy. I looked around. I was still in my bedroom. It was a dream.

I sighed in relief. But then I remembered that Hattie and Illis were gone. It hadn't been a dream after all.

I wanted to cry, but I dragged myself out of my bed, opened a full-length window, and sat cross-legged in front of it.

Having sat there for hours the previous night, I had named it my favorite place to try to forget, but out of the corner of my eye, I saw *The History of Peachtree Palace* and remembered all over again.

Today's motive was to persuade the villagers that everything would be all right. I had to make a speech.

I groaned, wondering how I would convince them if I couldn't even convince myself. I had never been an actress, or an extrovert.

Nevertheless, I pulled myself upward to dress.

My turtleneck was black, my dark plaid pants distressed, more a reflection of my internal mood than the demeanor I was supposed to be conveying. I groaned again, throwing a beret on my head as though it would help make me look more put together.

This whole mess had to be some silly dream.

I whispered aloud to myself, "Wake up, Fira!"

I slapped myself and immediately regretted it, for now I was not only still in the 'dream,' but the better half of my makeup had rubbed off on my clammy hand.

Mumbling, I sauntered into the bathroom to reapply my makeup.

I heard the clock in the square chime two-o'clock, and I smiled wistfully, remembering the time before this dilemma.

It had been ten hours since Hattie and Illis had left, but twelve more disappearances had already been reported overnight. At that rate, the kingdom would be empty in a week.

Misty had mostly been confined to her housing unit, scrounging through books in hopes of finding a trace of the *Maurelle* Hattie had told us about.

Hattie and Misty had grown up together. By the age of six, they were the best of friends. When Hattie became princess, Misty insisted that she be granted some sort of role in Hattie's rule. Hattie let Misty cook her breakfast and lunch. It was no meager paying job.

But today, Misty knocked on my door, looking awake and happy.

"Good morning, Fira," Misty chirped.

"You seem awfully chipper," I replied.

"And you seem gloomy." Misty invited herself into my room and shut the door behind her. She looked me up and down, and said, "I get the message."

I laughed reluctantly.

"Where did that silly girl go?" Misty asked, tapping my head. "I know she's in there somewhere."

"Gone with Hattie. She needs as much help as she can get," I teased.

Now it was Misty's turn to force a laugh.

Then we both sighed, thinking about these perplexing, historical events. I didn't like living through a historical event.

Another knock at my bedroom door pulled us out of our heads and back into reality.

I threw Misty a *'why not?'* sort of look, and she glided over to open the door.

A guard stood outside.

"Hello, Misses." The guard bowed low.

Is this what it feels like to be Hattie? I thought to myself, mildly enjoying it. I raised my chin. "Yes?"

"I'm here to escort you to your speech today, ma'am," he decreed.

"The speech, yes," I said, butterflies taking flight in my stomach. "Okay then, lead the way."

He led us from my bedroom, and out of Peachtree Palace.

We made it to the other side of the canyon in ten minutes, and the kingdom was in a swirling panic with villagers all crowded around town square. Mothers clutched their children; children clutched their mothers. I noticed several women whispering in hushed voices near the edge of the square.

I was perturbed to see them gossiping at a time like this.

"People of Rolling Hills," I calmly projected over the people listening. "Princess Hattie and her bodyguard, Illis, have left the kingdom in search of the disappeared people. They left me in charge. Listen . . ." My voice rose into hysteria as the villagers broke out into nervous chatter. I'm not fit for this job, I thought, I'm just a secretary.

"How about the kingdom, huh?" a villager cried out. The crowd buzzed angrily in agreement. "Who's supposed to keep us safe, our children safe?"

"It's being arranged," I replied, keeping my voice steady. "The Panjuanda are in position to patrol the kingdom around the clock, while a dozen or so men are ready to venture into the Hill itself."

Villagers began to yell in protest. None of them fancied an animal patrolling their housing canyon. Cute as they were, the Panjuanda were vicious. I'd stayed up almost all night arranging that some be brought over from a kingdom near us.

"I don't like it any more than you do, but the Panjuanda are sure to protect everyone from harm. Just lock your doors tight in the evening. Our hope is to have Hattie back in a fortnight, but I fear we may have more difficulty ahead than planned."

I then shouted as loudly as I could before the villagers could start again, "Good night! Go! I'm about to start the Panjuanda!"

Everyone scattered toward the canyon, leaving only Misty and me.

"Hi." I nodded grimly.

"Hi," Misty replied, blowing out a long breath.

"What do you think?" I asked.

"Not good," Misty responded. "Hattie and Illis turning and walking out on us was a bad idea. We're in a worse predicament than we started in."

I groaned. "Look at me! I'm easily one of the brightest in the kingdom. 'Want to help, Fira? No, we won't ask her that, she won't be able to help us at all!' But I could have–"

"Fira," Misty's voice broke into my sentence, scattering it into the watery air, "Did you ever consider that Hattie may have left you because she trusts you? She needs someone like you in charge. Well?"

No response came to me.

"Fira?"

"No." I hung my head.

"All right then. Look," Misty declared. "You really need to sort yourself out. I don't even recognize you at the moment. I have to go."

My head stayed fixed on the ground, but I could hear footsteps patter across the square.

At length, I looked up. The sky was blood red. Then the sun dipped below the horizon, leaving us in impenetrable darkness.

8

Hattie

The tunnel was dark and damp. Every squeak made me jump, every corner made me worried. And the steady drip of the tunnel ceiling would have left anyone with the uneasy feeling that someone was watching them.

Illis stood close by, as if guarding me from some invisible force that was posed to invade my body.

I fiddled with my skirt and glanced up at Illis, who looked much more comfortable in her trademark green cargo pants and top, reminding me once again how quickly I had left without even thinking.

I cleared my throat if not just for the comfort of feeling present.

"Yes?" Illis asked.

"Nothing," I replied. "Just clearing my throat."

Illis stopped short and said, "Listen, you're the brains behind this whole 'operation.' Do you even know what we're looking for?" I wasn't dumb, I knew she was annoyed.

I kicked a stone around the floor and confessed, "To be honest I was just so excited by the idea that I knew an answer to a question I've been asking myself my whole life: What happened to my parents? We think Maurelle is a whack physco, so trust me I don't *want* to go near her, but she's also a person who is kidnapping people, and possibly my parents. I was terrified, curious, and eager to get started. At the moment everything seemed to fit together. Now . . ." I gestured hopelessly with my hands.

Illis didn't respond, simply stared at me.

"It's as though we have everything we need to solve a puzzle but one piece. And we don't know what the piece is that we're looking for,"

Illis ran her hand along the wall, "This tunnel must lead somewhere."

Suddenly we smacked into an invisible wall in front of us. My bag clattered to the ground, and I flew backward.

Illis, who was just a step behind me yanked out her dagger and reached back with her other hand to help me up.

I grabbed my bag and withdrew my considerably smaller dagger, placing my back against Illis's, both of us beginning to move in a circle.

After another minute, when nothing emerged from the shadows, Illis lifted her dagger and began to poke at the invisible barrier.

"That's weird," I said. "No one is coming, but no one wants us to pass either."

Continuing to poke at the barrier, Illis replied, "Maybe there's a password."

I looked at her in shock. "Are you kidding?"

"My training required that I think of every possibility," she added quickly.

"But that's like out of a kids' game. Oh, I know! It might be 'Long live Maurelle!'" I guessed. The barrier didn't budge, but Illis persisted in her poking. "Ooh, how about 'To death with Princess Hattie.' Okay, okay." I frowned, thinking seriously, "*Magic inside, do not hide. Show your class, through the glass. Broken, building. World unfolding. Magic reveals what you feel. Magic is real.*'"

Illis's dagger passed through as if it were moist cake. The barrier was gone.

I stood awkwardly, waiting for her to say something.

Illis dropped her dagger and grabbed me by the shoulders, pushing me into a wall. Her face was inches from mine, her breath hot on my face, "Listen," she said, her stony voice solemn. "We have no idea what lies beyond this barrier. But you heard this password. The same words over again. You cannot trust anything you hear, see, or feel beyond this point. It may lead to your death, or worse, your capture, where you'll be tortured to insanity. Do you understand?"

"Don't get too serious-"

"Do you understand?" she repeated.

Illis left the air still and quiet, full of questions waiting to be answered. But all was silent, bar the noise of our heavy breathing.

"Yeah," I whispered.

"All right then," Illis said, holding me a moment, gazing into my eyes, then seemed to remember herself. She cleared her throat, "I . . ." She stopped talking and proceeded forward as if nothing had happened, and I once again rushed in front, earning myself a yank backward, and wondering what Illis was thinking.

"Oh god," I dragged a hand down my face. "What on earth is my advisory council going to think?"

"They'll think you made a rash decision. Because you did."

I turned my attention back to the tunnel ahead. Whatever was down here could not be good.

The tunnel was beginning to get lighter. I attempted to steel myself for whatever was beyond the corner up ahead, but it wasn't enough.

We rounded the corner into a cavern, and a horrible sight met our eyes. Before us stood hundreds of humans. Little children stood next to towering men. They were all talking. Their faces were sallow and sunken in, as if they hadn't eaten in days, possibly weeks.

One person called out in warning to the others, "She will be arriving soon; it is time to rest."

They all crumpled to the ground, like someone had flipped their off switch, taking only a beat to fall asleep.

Stunned, Illis and I stood at the edge of the cavern for a brief second until I noticed a certain child in the middle of the floor.

"Lily," I breathed, racing toward her.

I felt her forehead to discover that it was ice cold. I started to lightly shake her, "Wake up!"

"That is unacceptable." An imperious voice was heard coming from the tunnel at the other side of the cavern. I looked at Illis.

She gestured to a rock, and we both dived behind it.

A figure walked into the cavern in garments of black. Her hair rose into a braided crown that wrapped around her head in a circle. It had to be Maurelle.

She was followed by a little henchman.

Maurelle snapped around to her minion.

He gulped. "What is unacceptable, ma'am?"

Maurelle laughed, the sound making me shiver involuntarily. "I think you already know the answer to that question, Pompy. You need to feed them something. What will be the point of having an army if they are all dead?"

Her henchman gulped again.

"These *people*," she spat the word out, gesturing uselessly at the bodies around the cavern. "Are weak, like you."

"It's just . . ." he blinked in confusion and lowered his voice. "We can't let you-know-who find out. You'll be sent to–"

"SILENCE!" Maurelle shrieked. "I know the risks, now do it!"

She stamped her foot on the ground, and abruptly, all of the figures around the cavern sat up. Taking one look at Maurelle, they slunk into the shadows, not daring to make a sound. Only one child remained.

Unsuspecting, Lily sat in the middle of the floor, rubbing her eyes as if she had just woken from a nap.

"You!" Maurelle screamed at her.

"Yes, miss?"

"What are you doing talking back to me?" Maurelle yelled.

Lily's eyes grew round and she began to cry.

"Unsavory brat," she snarled and slapped Lily hard in the face. The girl stopped crying.

I burned with rage, and I jumped out from behind the rock.

Good job, Hattie. Very stupid. I found my voice. "Hello, you must be Maurelle."

Maurelle lowered her hand and turned to face me in surprise.

I could almost hear Illis groaning behind me, but she stayed where she was.

"Hello, indeed," Maurelle hissed, raising her hand, and for a second, nothing happened.

Then I froze up. I couldn't move at all. I was stuck. I don't know what I had expected to happen. I suppose I thought I would defeat her there and then. My muscles were stiff as a rock.

Cold terror built inside me, and my stomach twisted into knots. Tears glistened in my eyes. What had I done? Me, the dumb princess had directly disobeyed what Fira and Illis had told me to do.

Maurelle walked toward me, purring, "Princess Hattie, I have been waiting for you for a long time."

Shivers shot through my whole body.

"I think I'll keep this one," Maurelle mocked, merely lifting a finger to elevate me effortlessly into the air to trail behind her.

I could just make out Lily's face where she stood, trembling.

I screwed up my face in concentration, thinking as hard as I could. *I will save you. Don't worry, I'll find a way.*

Lily dropped to the ground and stared at me, her mouth open in shock.

It took me only a second to wonder why before I realized. I would have gasped if not for Maurelle's magic.

She had heard me.

9

Fira

Peachtree Palace is said to house the most extraordinary of secret passageways, and though it may be just boast, they are most definitely secret, for no one has found them in decades, and anyone who did is no longer around to tell about them.

I sat with my legs crossed on the library floor with *The History of Peachtree Palace*, my skirt sprawled out around me.

The book had to have some bigger meaning in the full picture, but I didn't know *what*.

The library was a giant room filled with towering brown bookcases, tables and chairs, an ornate carpet, the smell of old pages crisp and rustic, and of course, books.

Each different book was like one tiny drop of intelligence, until the thousands of books in the room made up the sea of knowledge itself.

But there was one drop missing.

I looked down at the one book that could be found in no library in close proximity to Rolling Hills. That couldn't be a coincidence. For all I knew, it could be the only copy in the world.

I turned to the first page and traced my fingers over the dedication.

Even the impossible can become possible.

Not that it sounded like much of a dedication, but my skin still gave a weird tingle at the words.

I absentmindedly flicked through the pages and halted at a piece of paper sticking from the book.

I pulled it out.

It seemed to be some sort of letter, with a small box attached to it. I stopped only briefly to wonder how Hattie had never noticed this, before peeling away the peach seal with my finger.

Dear Fira,

I stopped abruptly. How did this writer know my name? But still I read on.

I know of your surprised reaction to this letter. I know of the great hardships you will endure in the future. I know your death date, and everything about you, though you and Hattie have not yet met when this is being written. I know that you will befriend her and take care of her, and for that I thank you. I also know that there will come a time when I will no longer be there to take care of Hattie. Please understand that if you finish this letter, your life will never be the same again, and you will be in great danger.

Steeling myself for the worst, I kept reading.

I am dead, if you are reading this. But do not fret or cry, for I have joined a place that some can only dream of. I'm safe in the afterlife. But that isn't what I must tell you. There is a place, a magical place. And though some say magic is only legend, magic is real, as is this place. This place is called the Waters of Peachtree, a magical place, full of secrets that some are never destined to learn, and some are forever burdened to carry. I know the destiny of Rolling Hills, and there are only two options from which to choose: one is dependent on you reading this letter and listening to my advice. Or, you walk away and leave Rolling Hills to fall into darkness forever. For your sake and that of others, I hope you heed my advice. Inside the box there is something, an object that will direct you to the Waters of Peachtree. If this item is not there, then I fear I've written this letter to the wrong person, for this letter will only appear when you are ready, and the item only to someone worthy of possessing its power. Please find a loyal friend and bring them with you. A friend like that is the only one who can complete the task you will be assigned. Hattie is more valuable than you might ever know. So go find her, save her.

–Queen Mariana

I reread the writer's name over and over again. Queen Mariana had written this letter to *me*.

Queen Mariana was dead.

The shock hit me like a wave. I had been here this whole time reassuring Hattie that her mother would return. But here in my hands I held the proof that I'd been lying.

I placed my head in my hands. The information felt too wrong. Too heavy. My eyes watered, and I reached a shaking hand toward the box by the letter.

The box was red velvet with a tiny peach in the center. I slowly lifted open the cover and peeked inside. The box had a white cushion and held one item– a key.

It was gold with little gems on the handle. It sat delicately on the cushion. I gently reached my hand down and picked the key up.

Before I could comprehend what was happening, my senses exploded.

I scrambled and clawed for familiarity, but I could not feel the library around me anymore.

I was stuck in another world. The world of knowledge.

The key seared into my hand, rooting me to the fact that I was still in the library. Despite the burn, I clutched it as tightly as I could manage.

It felt as though someone had collected the drops of water in all the books and poured them through a funnel, straight into the top of my head, pounding a painful drumbeat into my ears.

Music played around me. A symphony of pandemonium.

My eyes burned as knowledge seeped into me.

Chaos abounded.

Images rushed by, a harsh outline against the library.

I screamed loudly, barely even hearing myself, as if I was on the other side of a door.

There were scenes of fire, great fire. Running. Screaming. Queen Mariana ran. Queen Mariana fell, dead.

I dropped the key, and it clattered onto the ground, stopping the images abruptly.

My panicked wheezing was the only sound in the library. As I came to, I realized a guard was standing above me.

"Do you need anything, miss?" he asked the question gently, but I could tell he was terrified, and so was I.

My panting slowed. I felt unstoppable with all my knowledge.

It was too much. I tried to catch my breath, but the world was dimming at the edges.

My brain was racing as fast as my heart, thumping in a rhythm far too fast and so loud I was sure the guard could hear it.

What was happening to me?

My brows knit together in concentration.

"Ma'am?"

"Yes," I replied to the guard, taking a shuddering breath that racked my whole body. "Please retrieve Misty immediately. You may go."

I heard a distant "Yes, ma'am." But my mind was elsewhere, for I knew what I had just held. Everyone thought it a legend. But now I knew it was true. The legend was real. The legend that Cherry had warned me I needed to read. It was true.

The 'legend' of Peachtree Palace was real. And I'd found it. I had found the Lost Key of Peachtree Palace.

10

Misty

I sat on my bed, wondering how in such a time of stress it could be so lovely outside.

A small breeze blew through the door, making me shiver in delight.

I threw myself downward, burrowing into the blankets. From my cozy position I could see my extra coinches of the month stacked on my counter.

I wondered if any shops would still be open, considering the situation of the kingdom. I would never know unless I looked.

I got out of bed and grabbed my stack of extra coinches.

Barely hesitating, I walked out the door and into the sunlight.

The sun's rays washed my pale skin with happiness. Children were running in the canyon, and even the Panjuanda were wrestling playfully with each other.

"Excuse me!" I heard a boy's voice, and dived out of the way just in time as he came hurtling down the canyon on a skateboard.

"Yeah, no problem," I said sarcastically as he skidded to a stop.

"Sorry about that," he said contritely. Looking up at his face I realized it was Liam.

"No problem," I replied again with less sarcasm, and he pulled me into a swift hug.

"How are you today?" he asked.

"Fine," I said, trying to dodge the real question he was asking, whether I was really okay considering the situation at present with Hattie and Illis gone.

"Are you sure?" he pressed.

"Yes," I said, firmly trying to convince myself as well as him. "Where are you going?" I asked suspiciously as more boys shot down the canyon. "You *know* that you attract trouble literally everywhere you go."

"Nowhere," he replied far too quickly.

I looked at him, eyebrows raised, and said, "I see."

"I'm serious, Misty, stop looking at me like that." He was trying and failing to grasp his words, spilling out an introduction. "My name's Liam." His face went furiously red.

He thrust his hand into mine and shook it, attempting to cover up his faltering.

"I'm sixteen, like you. I've been your neighbor for a while, but I don't think you've really noticed."

Internally my body choked on laughter but I tried to keep my face straight at his game. "Ah, yes, I see. And my name is Misty."

Unable to contain ourselves we burst into furious giggles.

I looked carefully at his face. His sandy blond hair looked windswept, and he wore the same kind smile as always. I struggled to detect the lie underneath it.

"Well, nice to meet you, Liam," I tried and failed to not smile.

"Same here. And hey," he said, hugging me again. "don't worry about me." Liam tossed me a sly smile before running down the canyon. I stared after him, hoping against hope that he wasn't going to get in trouble.

"What is he up to?"

I snapped back into reality as his sister, Amber, spoke. She was 25, and had moved out a couple years ago, not wanting to be hindered by a younger brother. I knew in my heart that I was closer to him than she would ever be, but she had an annoying habit of always acting all-knowing around me.

"Your brother?" I asked, scoffing. "Nothing apparently."

"You must not know him," she said coolly. "As he's always doing something."

"You're right," I said, agreeing to her terms, thinking of all the times Liam had told me of their separation.

"Of course I am, I'm his sister," she insisted.

"Of course you are," I replied, knowing only I could hear the sarcasm dripping from my voice.

"Well, best be going." She gestured down the canyon, where I could just see Liam running. Before I could even say goodbye she sprinted down after him.

Wow, I thought to myself. *Wow.*

I decided all this dawdling wasn't going to get me to the market, so I took off at a walk toward it.

No families were preparing for the market on such a beautiful day. They were all outside enjoying the sun. It was unclear whether the market would even be up and running.

I smiled sadly. This errand was my attempt to intentionally ignore the kingdom's problem. But as I neared the marketplace, a strange sight met my eyes.

The market was almost barren on the Rolling Hills side. I spotted very few families from our kingdom participating, and hardly any of them shopping. It was a lonely scene. I recognized a couple of booths from Rolling Hills, but other than that, the rest were from other kingdoms.

I sighed. The wind's bite turned much colder.

I shivered involuntarily.

"How are you?" I asked a family selling food.

They all laughed woefully, and the mother replied, "How is anyone these past days? I just wish we knew more about why Hattie left."

I bobbed my chin in agreement and bit my tongue.

"Here," I said and gave them 20 coinches for a bundle of woeblies, normally it would have cost only 10. "Please, keep the change."

"We need more people like you, Misty Baker. People who are kind."

I mustered the sweetest smile I could manage. How had it only been nearly two days since Hattie had left and the kingdom had been alone? It kind of felt like an eternity.

I bid the family good day and made my way toward the canyon, but rather than head down it, I made a split second decision and veered left and down a street to Rolling Hills's downtown. It was crowded, people of all sorts milling about.

Shops surrounded me in a crazy blur, but I only had eyes for one in particular.

I shoved my way through the crowd until I came upon the door for *Elise's Elixirs*.

The outside of the shop gave the illusion of unkemptness, with its many flowering window boxes and chipping bright purple paint.

The bell gave a soft tinkle as I walked through the door.

"Welcome to Elise's Elixirs," someone mumbled, and I caught sight of Sadie, Elise's mom, behind the counter. She lifted her eyes and smiled. "Hi, Misty, would you like me to get Elise?"

I nodded, and Sadie went into the back room.

I looked around the shop. There was an overabundance of shelves with hundreds of different bottles stacked in rows.

I exhaled slowly.

A tiny girl bounced out of the back room. She had adorable circle glasses, and her curly hair, dyed a rather obnoxious pink, was tied in pigtails. "Hey, Misty!" she greeted.

She caught sight of my expression. "What's the matter?"

"Hi, Elise." I sniffled. "I'm just super stressed because of Hattie and . . ."

"Whenever you get sad, you think of your brother," she finished.

I nodded slowly.

She smiled sadly and took my hand.

My brother was dead.

He had snuck out of the house one night without saying anything to anyone, and he'd never come back.

Everyone consoled me, of course, but I was expected to move on. Yet he lingered in my brain, like a shadow I couldn't get rid of.

Elise was the only one who truly understood. Her brother had left with mine, and when he returned, his sanity was cracked.

He now sat in the same room, day after day, staring at the same photos. The same memories, hoping that he would return to normal. It had been two years.

"Hey," Elise tapped my head. "Anyone home?"

I nodded again.

"I'll admit," Elise said quietly. "This may be our record. It's been three months since you've come with *this* problem." She wrapped her arms around me in a hug.

We sat that way for a minute, not daring to move.

Finally I took a deep breath and pulled back, giving Elise my most courageous smile. "See you around, Elise."

She gave me a small salute. "Anytime."

The bell tinkled again as I left the shop, my head in a better place. Yes, three months, it was time to beat our record.

I wandered among the shops a bit more before making my way back to the canyon.

After the long walk, it was getting dark. Most house lights were on, the doors were all shut.

Halfway back to my unit, Liam joined me. We walked in silence for a while, our hands so close to touching that I could feel the sparks between them.

I tried to strike a conversation, blathering, "Now, you're sure you weren't doing anything to get yourself in trouble?" It felt good to have something normal to talk about, good to forget for one second and pretend I was just scolding Liam as usual.

"I promise, Misty," he said, his voice unusually soft. He paused. "You were at Elise's again, weren't you?"

I sucked in a breath, but bobbed my head.

Liam sighed, "How many times do I have to tell you, you can count on me for you too, believe me." His eyes searched my face, which I was positive was now covered with streaks of mascara. He tucked a piece of hair behind my ear.

"I do count on you, Liam. It's just," I sighed again, "it's different."

"What do I need to do to not be different anymore? I'll do anything, anything," Liam pleaded.

I stored the information in the back of my brain for later, and continued walking.

We stayed quiet again until he suddenly stopped. His eyes locked on mine, "You were there, weren't you?"

"What?" I asked, but I already knew.

"When Hattie ran away."

I grimaced. "She didn't run away, exactly. She is going to save us."

Liam laughed, but I could tell it was fake. "You didn't answer my question."

"Yes, I was."

"What happened?" he asked. "What is she saving us from?"

I didn't think, and all my worries came pouring out of me. "Well, there's this prophecy, and a magic book, and people keep disappearing, and Hattie left to save us from some evil girl who's actually trying to kill her, and she might not be ok and–" I stopped myself. Liam's eyes widened, and I clapped a hand to my mouth and groaned, "I shouldn't have said that."

I mentally kicked myself. This was the worst thing I could have told him.

Now it was Liam's turn to ask, "What?"

When I didn't answer he said, "You cannot get yourself mixed up in this, understand?" Liam sounded angry, but I could tell he wasn't really.

"I have to go."

"Misty, look at me!" He yelled, and I halted. In all the years that we had been friends, he had never yelled at me.

Instantly, I could see the regret on his face. Liam knew that there was no way that I would ever be able to resist getting involved. It was a fault of mine in some way, always helping my friends, never myself.

I began to walk away again, but I noticed something about Liam that made me stop short. Liam was close to crying.

"Misty Baker," he said. "*Please* be careful."

I rushed over to him and hugged him the tightest I ever had.

I buried my face in his shirt and whispered, "I will."

Liam hugged me back.

"Goodnight, Liam," I said, quietly walking away from him. "Goodnight."

When I had finally settled into bed, I could hear Amber and Liam's voices coming from the housing unit next to mine. I knew

Liam was scared, but I trusted him to not tell anyone what I had said.

Poor Liam, I thought. I felt bad for him, always complaining that no one understood him besides me.

It took all of my effort not to do something, but what would I even do?

Go over and tell him to come to my house and have a *sleepover*?

Tell him that I understood the feeling of family not being what it was supposed to?

I pinched the bridge of my nose, forcing their talking out of my head.

Soon, I melted into sleep, unable to keep Liam out of every dream I had.

When the Flabbernack called the next morning, I immediately got up. There was a guard outside, knocking on my door.

I groaned internally, wondering what in the world he would want me for this early.

"Be there in a minute!" I yelled out the door.

He gave a muffled grunt in reply.

I threw on a yellow dress. I looked in the mirror and sighed, wondering what more I could do to help.

I yanked the door open, sun's rays beating down on my face.

The guard stood at ready and announced, "Miss Misty Baker, Fira needs to see you immediately."

11

Illis

I'd never experienced the term *frozen in fear*. It was a kind of stunned horror that left my mind scrambling for a foothold and my muscles uselessly tensed.

I watched in helplessness as Hattie was carried behind Maurelle by some unseen magic. She cackled and strode out of the cavern.

I knew somewhere deep in my heart that if I tried to save Hattie, I would only make our predicament worse. I think Hattie knew that too. So I just watched. And waited.

When I could no longer hear any noise other than the whimpers of the children, I rushed over to the child who Maurelle had hit. Lily, was her name.

I knelt beside her despite the rock digging into my knees. I gently lifted her head.

She wasn't crying. She seemed to be beyond tears.

"Hello, Lily," I whispered. "I'm here to help you. But to do that I need information."

She nodded weakly, and the action made her cough. "I'll do whatever I can to help," she murmured, her voice barely audible.

"How long have you been here?" I asked.

"Two days."

Sympathy pervaded my body. "I'm so sorry" was all the comfort I could offer.

"We haven't had food or water since we got here. But I'm one of the lucky ones. Some people have been here since the first disappearance. None of us know what Maurelle is planning, what she is going to do with us. But I think it has to do with revealing our magic– or something."

"Magic?"

"Yes," Lily smiled. "Magic. It's real. Just like in stories. People with magic in their heads, in their veins, and all over the blood on their hands too."

"Oh my god, don't say that!" It scared me how practically this tiny girl was speaking about magic. But after the ordeal I'd just seen, and all of Hattie's evidence, Lily was right.

It took all of my might not to reach up and put my face in my hands.

Hattie had been right after all, but I'd just been ignoring her. Some bodyguard I was.

"Do you know where your mother is?" I asked her.

Lily's smile fell. "She came here yesterday. She died trying to sneak us all some flowers growing from that hole over there." She raised a trembling finger. Tears streamed down her face in soft droplets.

I looked to where she was pointing.

The flowers were all dead.

I reached into my bag and pulled out most of the food I carried, and placed it on the floor. "Please," I said. "Don't fight over the food, share it. You're all in the same shoes. I'll be back."

"Wait!" came a voice across the cavern.

A girl rushed forward, wearing ripped black jeans and a tight black top. Her hair was tied back into a short tail, but a couple pieces of her caramel hair fell in straight strands around her face.

Her eyes were brown, and thin, but they somehow captured the little light in the room when she looked at me. There was no denying she was gorgeous. My face went extremely warm.

She spoke again. "I want to come with you!"

I blinked. "What?"

She sighed, as if it was obvious, and repeated, "I want to come with you, you know, to defeat Maurelle." She raised an invisible sword and struck the air.

"I don't really think that's a good–"

"Please." She stopped stabbing the air and turned to me, real sincerity in her eyes. "Let me come. I've been waiting my whole life to be swept up into a fairy tale like this one. But I learned a long time ago that the world isn't all magic and color. Not everyone can be as lucky as princesses. Some people have to take a stand, because no one else is going to do it for them."

Her words surprised me. They were so abrupt and perfect. I could tell she'd been rehearsing them for a while.

She reminded me of an old ghost in my past, like a younger self. It staggered me to hear words similar to what I had once said. It made me feel as though I could trust her.

"Fine," I relinquished. "You can come."

She nodded and stuck out a hand. "The name's Elnora, Elnora Dafen. Your neighborhood slightly emo kid who looks for adventure in minuscule things way too often. And thanks for not calling me out, I totally practiced that speech before you got here." She smirked and winked, and I blushed again.

I took her hand. "Illis, personal guard to Princess Hattie of Rolling Hills."

Her eyes widened slightly, and she nervously brushed her hair out of her face. "Well, thank you for letting me come."

I cleared my throat, trying to ignore how tight it had become. "Well, we'd best be going. Don't want to lose her." I gestured toward where Maurelle had exited.

Elnora lowered her chin stiffly.

I gathered my bag in my hands and quietly followed the path Maurelle had taken.

Our feet crunched against the rock as we walked in silence, listening for any sign of Maurelle, my cheeks burning the whole way.

After a mile or so, the ground softened to a light grass.

Elnora spoke again. "How did you find yourself with Princess Hattie?" she asked, and I could tell she was trying to understand how a fellow villager like herself could achieve such high standards.

"Well, I never really had any friends. I was different from everyone else." I paused, watching for her reaction. She nodded in understanding, so I continued. "Hattie noticed me sitting alone one day in the grass by Peachtree Grove. We were six. She asked why I was sitting by myself. I told her that my parents had kicked me out for the night, without dinner, because I hadn't brought home any money. I never knew a six-year-old could be so kind. She invited me to the palace, and Queen Mariana fed me and dressed me. I told her my hopes and dreams, and how my parents disapproved. The queen told me that she would set up a trainer for me and have me start a year later. I finished training a day too late before Queen Mariana disappeared. Since that day, I've made it my goal to never let anyone in the kingdom down, especially Hattie."

"Wow," Elnora uttered. "That's . . ."

"Princesses are often misconstrued," I said, kicking a stone. "They're painted in a light of self-obsession. Hattie contradicts that." I chuckled softly, remembering Hattie's round face asking me what the matter was.

We walked in silence for a while.

"Do you think she's going to make it?" Elnora asked.

"I think," I said, still slightly unable to believe any of this was happening. "That if anyone can, it will be Hattie. I think there's more to her than meets the eye, much more . . ." I trailed off.

Our small green-carpeted tunnel broke way to something horribly marvelous.

A giant white castle loomed in front of us, trimmed with black, and stationed with guards.

The same image appeared on the flag and on the armor of all the guards: a black unicorn.

And walking into the castle was Maurelle herself.

12

Misty

The guard held tight to my arm as we ambled down the canyon.

"Excuse me," I said politely, tugging on my arm. "I'm not going to run away, you know."

"Necessary precautions," he replied, but he let go.

I sighed, and marveled at the canyon.

Its walls rose high enough I couldn't see the crest. The space between the walls was only about a third of that distance. But, still, it always seemed to have at least one sunbeam shining through the cloisters of blossoms above.

I kicked a stone out of boredom, and then began to fiddle with my hair.

At last, I stepped on the long shadow of Peachtree Palace, the structure looming ahead.

The sun behind the castle gave the impression that the whole palace was glowing.

The guard slowly opened the doors and escorted me to the library.

Fira sat, breathless, her hair like a flame against the pale library walls. She looked up at the guard. "That will be all." Her voice was much smoother than her physical demeanor.

"Yes, ma'am." The guard exited with a gulp and a nervous glance in Fira's direction.

"What's going on?" I asked once the guard had closed the door.

She didn't respond for a second, looking down at the ground as if hardly seeing anything at all.

"I need you to tell me the truth," she said finally. "If you had a chance to save Hattie's life and Rolling Hills, would you take it?"

What a stupid question, I thought. "Of course, why–"

"Misty! I need you to be completely honest. Look at me!"

I obeyed. I had never seen Fira act like this.

Her usual shy persona had broken free from whatever prison it had been living in. I wondered what she could have seen.

She continued, holding up a letter. "This letter holds the answer to all our problems. But if you read it, you'll be in grave danger. You may die, do you understand?"

I let out a confused laugh. "Fira–"

Her eyes bored into mine, looking more lost than I'd even seen them.

Fira, the smart, quiet, kind girl. Our older sister. It took all of my will power not to ask if she was okay.

I was lost for words and scared. One thing I had learned while being friends with Fira is that she was most always serious.

"Yes, I understand," I firmly replied.

Fira handed me the letter, her hand shaking as it passed into mine.

I peeled away the seal and read.

I looked up, shock seeping into my bones and guiding my tongue. "Queen Mariana!" I blurted.

Fira held up a delicate-looking key. "This showed me everything.

Every bit of knowledge is locked inside my brain, waiting for me to unlock it."

I was stunned. "Your brain is filled with what?"

"All the knowledge of the universe," she softly replied.

I bit my lip to keep a terrified laugh from breaking free. My mind couldn't, didn't want to wrap around that fact, so I turned to something more graspable, "This place, the Waters of Peachtree, it's real?"

"Yes," she confirmed. "And I need you to help me find it." Fira stared into my soul.

"Of course I'll come with you," I said, trying to muster courage that wasn't there.

Fira's hardened posture melted down to a relieved one, and she hugged me. "Thank you!"

I noticed that her body was getting warmer.

I backed up to see her metamorphosing to a sparkling blue, surrounding her like an aura. "Uh. . . Fira?"

"Yeah?"

"You're glowing."

I looked in awe as the handle of the key in her hand broke off and melted down to a ring.

The ring started to glow and spark until it fit perfectly onto Fira's finger. It was dainty and silver, barely noticeable on her hand.

The band was thin but even from here I could see words encrusted into it.

"What does it say?" I asked.

She peered at the letters engraved in a curly font, almost unreadable, and imparted these words: "Knowledge, the world's greatest blessing," she paused and sucked in a breath. "The world's greatest curse."

Fira looked down at the ring, and without warning, rose off the floor. From my position, I started to cough, the air getting hotter and hotter until it blazed.

Fira spun wildly, her head cocked back, mouth open.

Something was flying into her open mouth. I squinted, and it almost appeared that letters were flying into her mouth.

I clamped a hand over my mouth. "Fira," I called, but she couldn't hear me.

The glowing stopped as soon it had begun, and Fira fell to the floor, taking ragged breaths.

"Fira!" I rushed over to her.

To my surprise, she was smiling. "I've unlocked a piece of knowledge."

"What is it?" I asked, trying to ignore the shiver that ran through me at her words.

"This ring, it's the Adar," she said. "Or *Ring of Fire*. It's been a legend for centuries. One object of fire that gives the user unlimited power. But no power comes without cost. People who used the Adar, hungry for power, yearning for it, using it for evil, disappeared, along with the ring. Decades later it would resurface as a new object, searching for one person who would use its power to help, not hurt—"

"And Queen Mariana thinks that's you," I finished.

She nodded weakly.

"Then there's only one thing we can do," I said before I could lose my confidence completely.

"What's that?"

I tried again to ignore the tension in my gut, the gnawing feeling that something was about to go horribly wrong. "We're taking a trip to the Waters of Peachtree."

13

Hattie

I awoke to a misty fog. I looked around but couldn't identify any objects, no matter how hard I squinted to focus on them.

There was a burning in my wrists, and I glanced down.

Was I sitting on a cloud?

I felt at home, at peace. My hair wasn't done, just some loose waves. I could feel the cleanliness of my skin, I wasn't wearing any makeup.

I stood up and began to walk around. There was a gentle breeze brushing past me.

There was the sound of birds tweeting in the distance, and the smell of fresh-picked peaches hung so potently I felt like I could pluck it from the air. It was cool. Although there was no sun in sight, I sensed the serenity of morning.

I wondered where I was. As I studied the atmosphere, it blended in and out of focus. When I concentrated, the atmosphere got confused.

I made to lift my hands and found with a sharp jolt that they would not move past my waist.

I was chained to the cloud.

Strands of the cloud like material held my wrists firm.

That's when I remembered Maurelle's magic, the floating. I remembered Lily on the cavern floor, her terrified face when she heard me.

"Scared, Princess Hattie?" Maurelle's voice leered through the mist.

It took all my effort not to leap into the air.

I rolled my eyes, hoping she would see my pretense at bravery. "You wish I were."

I was terrified.

Whatever magic she had performed was nothing that I had ever heard or seen before. I'd never seen any magic at all, and I wasn't sure if I should feel slightly excited that my theory had been correct.

I looked around.

I'd been captured. I shouldn't have been excited.

There was a snap, and all the mist vanished.

I was in a cell.

The room was white. A bed, table, and other normal house items lined the walls. I was no longer sitting on a cloud, but my wrists were still chained to what could only be described as a torture table in the center of the room. I gulped.

I looked down to see that I was wearing a comfortable white jumper with a black unicorn stitched onto the chest.

I briefly wondered what it was before I noticed Maurelle leaning against the wall on the other side of the room.

"To be honest, you're quite boring while asleep," she said. "Not your usual . . ." Maurelle paused. "Spunk."

I bit my tongue so my teeth wouldn't chatter. trying to act

as brave as I could. "Spunk? Listen, you don't even know me," I snapped. "This is the first time I've ever met you."

"That," she said. "Is what you think. You see, I've been studying you for a long time. Because you have something I want."

"What?" I spat in disgust, trying not to let myself think about Maurelle studying me from afar.

"Answers," she explained. "And a certain book called *The History of Peachtree Palace*."

"Why would you ever want such an old book like that one?" I laughed. "There's nothing special about it."

"You seem so sure."

I faltered, suddenly losing my confidence, "I . . ."

"Now *you* listen to *me*," her voice lowered dangerously, and she slowly stepped toward me, nearing with every word. "I have a weapon that will destroy your wimpy little kingdom like that." She snapped her fingers I flinched away from her, but she placed two fingers on my cheek and turned my head back toward her. "People, gone. Academy, gone. Palace, gone. Peaches, gone. Gone, gone, gone. All of it. gone!"

Maurelle cackled and then turned deadly serious. "Or, you can give me the book, and I won't do anything. Oh, but I'll have to keep you, of course. You have other things of greater interest to me."

"You really think–"

Maurelle grabbed the chain keys off of the table in the corner of the room, making me stop in surprise. She unlocked my hands before swinging the keys on her fingers playfully. "You have no idea what I think, love."

I rubbed my wrists where the chain had held me, biting the inside of my mouth to prevent myself from asking why she'd unlocked me.

"Here, enjoy your freedom. Try to enlighten yourself about what side you *really* want to be on. And, be a dear. Don't tell anyone about our little chats. You see, nobody else at Dark Unicorn knows that you're here, so let's keep it . . . our little secret. "

Maurelle patted my face and smiled sweetly, turning and exiting the room. I heard multiple deadbolts slide into place, and I groaned.

"Dark Unicorn?" I yelled after her. "What in the world is that?"

I was met with cold, empty silence.

My vision blurred, but I pushed the tears away. I couldn't cry again, not now. Not when I had to be the strong princess everyone expected. That everyone *needed*.

I walked over to the books on the table. There were several about the organization, and I felt the tears start to rush up again, my throat tightening.

This was far bigger than I'd even imagined.

Maurelle wasn't just one person after all. She had a whole organization with her too.

My mind wandered to the people in the cavern, people I hadn't seen disappearance papers for.

I sucked in a breath, trailing my fingers over one of the books. "They were the people from when I was little," I whispered, like saying it out loud could provide any comfort.

I noticed a white bed in the corner of the room. A small note was resting on the pillow with a Dark Unicorn on the front and tiny white lettering that read "Welcome."

I scoffed. "Yeah, right." But I opened the note, settling in the bed and leaning into the pillow.

Dear Princess Hattie,

Welcome to Dark Unicorn. I am Maurelle, recently appointed to Dark Unicorn. And now I could very well say the organization is mine. It had many issues before I came into power, but now it is glorious. I am extending you an offer to join me and help create the perfect new world. Otherwise I will move forward with my original plan, and kill you.

I hope you will consider this opportunity,
Maurelle, Dark Unicorn President

I stared at the letter, and rubbed my temples, wanting to burst out laughing and cry at the same time. It was all too confusing, too blunt, too imperfect.

I crumpled the paper and threw it at the wall. I sighed, wondering what on earth the plan was for me, and what the book had to do with all of it.

I collapsed onto my bed. I had a long stay ahead of me, with no plan of rescue set in place.

14

Fira

I took Misty's extended hand and stood. After her proclamation that we would find the Waters of Peachtree, there was still one problem that remained. I timidly asked her, even though I was sure she had no idea, "How do we get there?"

"That," Misty replied. "Is a really good question that I do not have the answer to." After a brief pause, she began to jump up and down. "We're going on an expedition!" she exclaimed. "What should we pack?"

I rolled my eyes but figured that it might be a good idea to bring *something* before setting out to some place we knew nothing about.

Checking to make sure the Adar was still on my finger, I ushered for Misty to follow me.

When we entered my closet, Misty gasped and said, "Fira, you really are *so* organized." Her eyes grazed my clothes, all color coded into a rainbow.

I attempted a bashful laugh, but even to me it sounded fake.

We paused.

Misty spoke. "What do you think is so special about Hattie? I mean, she's my best friend, and I love her to death, but what could be so important about her that someone like Maurelle would be trying to kill her?"

I looked down. "I don't know," I confessed in a defeated voice.

"Didn't the Adar give you all the knowledge in the universe? Can't you unlock it?" She looked at me with eagerness shining in her doe eyes, even though I could still hear the edge in her voice.

"Like I said, I think the Adar hid the knowledge somewhere in my mind for me to unlock. Plus, even if I had it, I couldn't read Maurelle's mind."

"Right," Misty nodded, though I wasn't really sure what she was agreeing to.

After cramming as much food into my small backpack as we could, we headed back to the library which somehow seemed a lot less inviting in the dim lighting.

I gave Misty time to write the letter she wanted to Liam, waiting for her to go tack it onto his door.

When she was finally back in the library, Misty looked at me expectantly.

"I still don't know where–"

"Fira look!" Misty interrupted, pointing at my hand.

I held up the Adar, which had been inactive up to this point. It now glowed brightly, emitting a soft blue light. It pulsed as I moved around the room. It was trying to tell me where to go. "I think we should follow it," I whispered.

In the center of the library, there was a row of tables, one of which was covered with my papers and work from days before. When I walked toward it, the light pulsed faster, my heartbeat hammering in time with the soft light.

Soon it was flashing steadily.

"Maybe the faster it pulses, the closer we are," Misty guessed from behind me.

She joined me at the table. My ring blinked rapidly when I knelt, looking for anything I could have missed.

I inspected the area but couldn't see anything out of the ordinary.

"Do you think this could be it?" Misty breathed, pointing down to a small hole in the floor.

Upon removing the Adar from my finger, it transformed back into the Lost Key of Peachtree Palace. I glanced up at Misty, who nodded.

The key slid easily into the hole, as if meant to fit there the whole time.

I yanked up on the handle, and a trapdoor appeared on the floor, like it melted out of the carpet. I twisted the key and the door unlocked.

"Okay, woah," Misty said. "That was *not* there before."

"Maybe it always was. You just didn't see it."

"Alright here goes nothing."

Together we bent down and lifted the door to reveal a soft glow from the shadowy depths beneath us.

A gold rope ladder swung up, clinging to the bottom of the door.

Peering down, I couldn't see the bottom, just the ladder disappearing into the pit.

I looked at Misty, her eyes glued to the door. She gulped.

"Let me go first," I offered, trying to channel the comforting energy I usually had.

"No it's okay." She took a deep breath. "I can do it."

I helped her down onto the ladder, and she began her descent.

Once she was more than an arm's reach away, I shifted my weight onto the ladder and began to climb down.

I could hear birds calling and water running. The air beneath the library floor was warm, but not sweltering.

I closed my eyes and clung onto the ladder. The beautiful atmospheric change gave the illusion of a paradise. I looked around. It felt as if I was in the sky, though I knew I was underground.

After several long minutes, I heard Misty's feet hit the floor.

"You can jump," she said quietly, her voice awestruck.

My feet hit the ground with a soft thump. There were cobblestones packed into a path, just like the ones that lead up to Peachtree Palace.

The path continued, and as I dragged my eyes upward, they were met with gorgeous grass, and a beautiful town rose in front of me, about a half mile down the path.

Flowers littered the ground like fine dust, and the stones seemed to connect all of the areas in the town.

"Fira," Misty said, "You might want to look a little higher."

She pointed at something in the distance.

At the back of the city were two crystal clear blue waterfalls against a large white cliff. But my eyes were drawn to something else. Between the two waterfalls was a message painted:

Welcome to the Waters of Peachtree.

15

Illis

"Hattie!" I cried and started forward. Elnora's firm grip held me back, her hand tightened around my wrist. The feel of her fingers around my wrist jolted me with the sharp urge to throw up.

"Not yet," she becalmed.

"But–"

"No. If we jump out now, everyone will see us, and we'll be in no position to rescue her," Elnora warned.

I felt my concentration slipping and whacked myself on the thigh.

I'd dealt with situations like this hundreds of times. It was everything I'd trained for.

"I'm sorry," I confessed.

I sat down, and she followed my move.

"You'd like her," I said. When she looked confused I laughed and said, "Hattie."

"Tell me about her," Elnora suggested, sitting far too close for me to concentrate properly.

I propped my chin up on my knees, "Well, she's kind, for one, and is always helping others, especially me. Hattie is easy to talk to. She dreams of making lives better for all villagers. Even though her life isn't fabulous, either. I mean, her parents have been missing since she was seven. She has a temper," I blew out a laugh. "But I've been around long enough to handle it."

"Sounds like one hell of a princess." Elnora smiled softly at me.

"Hattie is really smart," I smiled. "But she never got to attend Peachtree Academy. Some day, if I'm able, I'll make sure she can go there."

A dreamy look crossed over Elnora's eyes. "I've always wanted to go to Peachtree Academy. The amount of knowledge that is hidden within those walls, and chaos to be caused," she sighed, and I let out a small chuckle. "I keep secretly hoping that they will send me a letter: *Dear Elnora Dafen, we are delighted to inform you that your attendance at Peachtree Academy is absolutely necessary!*" Elnora looked at me. "A princess's dream for a poor villager like me. Poor *definitely* being an understatement for what my parents were."

Her face had fallen. It was almost enough to make me ask what her family was like, but just as I opened my mouth Elnora snatched my arm and began to run.

I gasped at the electricity in her grip, struggling for words.

She dragged me alongside her in a frantic swirl.

We traveled around the side of the palace. Panic in the air, she shoved me against white bricks. My heart was wildly thumping, a rabbit skittering down the hill of my chest.

"What was that for?" I whispered urgently.

Elnora pointed. Maurelle's little henchman was wobbling along the path, headed in the direction of where we had been sitting.

He seemed to be humming to himself, clutching a small bag and sprinkling something on the ground. Immediately, any living grass withered into the ground and sizzled.

I grimaced. "Well, thanks then."

Our hiding place was not very comfortable.

I heard Elnora's heavy breathing next to me.

Our bodies pressed against the cool brick of the castle. The atmosphere was thick with a low fog. Glancing down, I realized my feet were just barely visible.

I heard footsteps.

A troop of guards was heading toward us. I tried to flatten myself against the wall, and I closed my eyes, praying that we wouldn't be seen.

The guards continued marching past us. If they saw us, they chose not to act on it.

Some tension left the air as the guards simultaneously turned the corner and marched onward.

I exhaled in relief.

Elnora tapped my shoulder. "Look."

I turned my eyes away from the guards and spun to face her.

She was pointing at a small opening in the wall just big enough for us to squeeze into.

"Perfect," I whispered.

I tucked into the hole and rolled out the other side. On the other side of the wall was a huge hall-like room. The walls and floors were all marble, and in the center was a statue of a unicorn, maybe thirty feet high. It was all black.

Elnora walked up next to me. She looked at the statue. "Why would they use such a gentle creature as the symbol for some dark organization?"

I shrugged, not having any real idea myself. "This unicorn must be very important to the people of this place. It is plastered all over everything we've seen so far. I want to know why."

Then, Elnora grabbed me again and dove behind the statue. I stifled a shriek, my vision blurring as she dragged me to her side.

Only seconds later, two guards rounded the corner and stood exactly where we had been.

"Thanks," I breathed.

"So, were you invited to the meeting later?" One of the guards said.

I leaned forward and looked through a hole next to the unicorn's two-toed hoof.

"Yes, Maurelle personally invited me," the other guard replied, a certain smugness in his response.

The first guard's jaw dropped. "Seriously? I was just making conversation. I didn't think you were actually invited! How? What is the meeting about? I was only invited to escort."

"Well, I'm not allowed to say," he murmured. "But Tulip thinks that something is up, and she wants to find out what."

"What do you think?"

The guard shuffled his feet. "I don't know."

"Of course, anything will catch Rolling Hills by surprise. They don't even think that magic is real."

My heart caught in my throat, and my instincts took over. I leapt out from behind the statue and punched him in the side of his ribs.

He grunted in pain and staggered. I delivered an uppercut to his face. Without looking at the other guard, I lifted my leg and kicked him hard in the stomach. He crumpled to the ground.

I waved Elnora out, who looked very impressed at my display, and gave me a slow clap. But that didn't help the shock in her voice as she emerged from behind the statue to walk toward me. "I never even considered that everyone else doesn't know about magic."

"Wait, *you* know about magic?"

"That's a story for later," she grimaced.

After a pause I said, "Well, come on then."

The guards were wearing everyday clothes, leaving us nothing to possibly disguise ourselves with.

Elnora glanced with distaste at her reflection in the statue, an image she hadn't seen in days, possibly weeks, and sighed. "Ah, well."

I wanted to tell her that she was absolutely gorgeous, but I bit my tongue, wondering where on earth the words had come from.

"Plan?" I asked, having a vague one in mind.

"Oh yes," Elnora grinned. She removed a small piece of paper from the guard's pocket and opened it. It read *Section B5 Room 15*. She waved the paper in the air. "Lucky for us, this guy had memory problems. We have a meeting to attend."

"And then?"

Elnora let out a breath and raised her eyebrows at me, "We're going to save Hattie."

16

Misty

"Wow," I gasped. "It's beautiful, isn't it?"

Fira nodded, awestruck.

We had walked up the white bricks to the quaint town. It was packed with people. Some were walking, some were chatting with the vendors in the booths that lined the streets, but the one thing they had in common was that they were all happy. Everyone was playing or jumping or smiling.

A little girl in pigtails ran over to me.

She wore a yellow pinafore with a daisy on the front. It looked almost like a crest.

"Hello, Misty! Hey, Fira!" she smiled. "My name is Melody!"

"How do you know my name?" I looked over at Fira, who was also skeptical, but shy as usual.

Melody giggled. "Don't worry, Queen Mariana sent me."

We exchanged looks.

Tears welled in Melody's eyes. "Or at least she sent my mom four years ago. My mom told me. Queen Mariana died on an expedition trying to defeat Maure–" she stopped. "I mean, trying to defeat a bad guy immediately after she wrote Fira that letter."

"Queen Mariana knew about Maurelle?" I blurted.

"*You* know about Maurelle?" Melody raised an eyebrow.

"Yes," Fira took over. "That's what brought us here. We need to talk to the rulers of this place. They have something we need in order to save our friend, Princess Hattie."

"You know Hattie?" She looked faint. "Boy, you know a *lot* more than we thought you did." She leaned in and studied us, her gaze very scrutinous for someone so young. "I think you'd best come with me."

We followed Melody through the perfect town. Perfect being an understatement. My shoes didn't even pick up dust to leave tracks.

A quiet swarm of whispers caught my attention, people pointing and saying hushed things that I didn't like the sound of.

"Where's Hattie?"

This isn't going according to plan," the people muttered.

What plan? I thought, agitated.

Eventually, after enduring a few more stares and whispers, we came upon the tallest building. As we walked in, the loudness of the street disappeared and was replaced with soft music. It looked like a standard office building, but the technology was like nothing I'd ever seen in Rolling Hills. As we passed the people working there, I saw that they were dragging their fingers along a screen projected in the air.

It was the kind of stuff that only existed in very wealthy kingdoms and I had to stop myself from wondering how there had been an entire city under the palace, and focus on putting one foot in front of the other.

Melody skipped ahead to a row of about twenty colorful poles with foot pedals attached to the bottom.

"Hold tight," she said, stepping onto the foot handles.

I clambered onto a pole.

"Repeat after me," she instructed. "Seven!"

"Seven!" Fira and I shouted.

The pole quivered and shot up off the ground.

I heard Fira's scream beside me. We lurched side to side whizzing by more identical offices. We stopped abruptly on a floor labeled "5." A blonde man looked up and smiled, hopping onto the pole next to mine.

"Hi there!" He cheerily tipped his hat. "Fourteen!"

We zoomed upward again and stopped at the floor labeled 7.

"Have a nice day!" the man bubbled when we stepped out.

I turned just in time to see him shoot upward.

I barely had time to catch my breath before someone else was talking.

"Welcome to Floor Seven!" said a teenage girl beaming behind a small counter in the back of the room, which was empty except for some chairs. "My name is Harmony!" She looked much like Melody, but her pinafore was blue.

"I see you've met my sister, Melody."

"Oh, you're sisters!" I said.

"Yes, and *you* are Misty. I'm quite ecstatic to meet you." She rounded the counter and shook my hand. Harmony turned to Fira. "You must be Fira!" she gushed. "This is incredible. Is it true you really have the Adar?"

Fira looked at me uncertainly, but nodded.

Fira held up her finger, displaying the Adar, which glowed softly.

"Wow!" Melody and Harmony breathed in unison.

Fira smiled, enjoying the attention, but I shifted uncomfortably.

"Melody, Harmony," came a stern voice from the back of the room, where a door had appeared.

"Hello, Mother," they mumbled, turning around.

A young woman with a loose ponytail was smiling with her arms crossed.

"Hello, Fira, Misty, my name is Medley."

"She's my mum," Melody stated obviously.

"Follow me through this door," Medley said, gesturing toward the wall.

But the door was gone. "Honestly!" she fretted. The door reappeared.

We walked through the door, Melody skipping through at the front.

"Mother!" she squealed, rushing into the arms of another young woman in a chair.

There was a small meeting room and people were lined along a curved wall. I looked around again. The door had vanished.

"Hello, girls," their mother said. "So you've met my wife and girls, huh? They're quite the bunch. And my name is Lyric."

I leaned over to Fira with pointed sarcasm. "I wonder if they have any pets."

Melody overheard and announced, "We have two spudgewubbles whose names are Note and Key."

I choked on my laugh and saw that Fira was having a similar reaction.

I straightened up and noticed the people lined along the walls. They all had the same kind faces and beautiful complexions. This town was obviously not lacking in beauty resources.

They reminded me of Hattie's advisory, but there were a *lot* more of them.

"Well," Fira composed herself. "It's very nice to meet you. You see, we were sent here by a letter. A letter that your daughter seems to have knowledge of."

"Ah yes," spoke a voice from above us, and a gorgeous girl appeared. Her flawless skin took my breath away, and her almond eyes sparkled. "My name is Rosie." She flipped her blonde hair. "I'm under the impression you are here for your mission."

Fira and I nodded, even though my brain faltered at the word *mission*.

"Well, you're in luck then. These people around you, they are my advisors. Oh, and me. Well . . . that's slightly more complicated. I am Queen Mariana's younger sister."

My jaw dropped. "What? Queen Mariana's—"

"I think you had best come with me. I have a lot of explaining to do." Rosie began to walk, and another door appeared. I walked behind her, matching her stride.

"Bye, bye," Melody waved from her position on her mother's lap.

Fira waved back at her and ran to catch up to me.

We walked straight through the door.

The small room in the shape of a trapezoid was quite obviously the residence of a teenage girl. But this teenage girl was apparently Queen Mariana's sister.

Rosie collapsed on the large canopy bed in the middle, which was covered in a blue duvet to match the walls.

Remembering she had company, she quickly straightened up.

"Take a seat." She gestured to the vanity on the left wall and a desk on the right.

I seated myself at the vanity, noticing the mounds of product that sat in jars. Turning toward her, I waited for answers.

"You must be so confused." She frowned sympathetically. "I'm so sorry."

"We just want answers," Fira said.

"That, I can give you."

"Who are you?" I asked.

"My name is Rose Hills, but you can call me Rosie. I'm from the same family your kingdom was named after. The same family as your best friend, Hattie. I'm her aunt. You see, I was born exactly one year before my sister, Mariana, knew she was pregnant with Hattie. But I've never even met Hattie, or my parents."

I looked at the sadness in her eyes, trying to decide if I should feel sympathy, or even more confused.

"Things used to work a lot differently when I was a kid. People put much more stake in the ruler. I was the first of the Hills's family to be a second child, since Charlie's daughters Lucia and Denise. *They* wanted to shelter me, make sure I wasn't hurt. I was always down here and never up there. I was kept as a backup in case anything happened to Mariana."

"That's awful," Fira exclaimed. "Who's *they?*"

"No one," Rosie rushed. "I loved Mariana, and of course I would never want her hurt. But there were times when I wished I could at least see the kingdom I'd heard so much about. When Hattie was born, I longed to meet her, play with a kid my age rather than being locked down here. But things needed protecting. Me, and our secret."

"What?" I asked.

"An old family heirloom hidden underground. Something even I don't know. Hattie is special, part of a special family."

"What?" I asked again.

"Listen, I wish I didn't have to send you somewhere else, but you need to find something important, otherwise Hattie will die."

17

Hattie

I had no idea how long I'd been trapped in my 'cell'. It felt like a week. Though I was a prisoner, my living space was actually quite comfortable. I had a bathroom with water. My sheets were changed; my rugs were cleaned every day.

Yet there I sat, with nothing to do but think about what Dark Unicorn was.

Several others had come to see me.

A man with slick black hair and glasses. Maurelle, two more times, both to jeer at me and dangle in front of me the idea that she knew exactly who I was. Like a cat, I wanted to chase the string.

I wondered to myself what Maurelle's ultimate goal was. Was this all just some childish game to her?

Every time the cell opened, my heart leapt with possibility and then sunk with the realization.

No one was coming to save me. I dreamt about the impossible: my parents, coming to save me.

For one beautiful moment, I could almost see their smiling faces, drawing me in for a hug. I wiped my eyes, fighting the tears that splattered my uniform.

I needed to figure out what Maurelle wanted with my book. It couldn't be a coincidence. But what on earth could she need with it?

Someone knocked on the door, and a slot popped open, dropping a package.

I walked over to it and gingerly lifted it. It was addressed to *Princess Hattie*, but I had the uncanny feeling that someone was watching me and that the emphasis on *Princess* was not a nice one.

Then I remembered what Maurelle had said to me yesterday, that she 'trusted' me and that there was 'no need for recording.'

She had sat on the bed and laughed at my discomfort. Not knowing what was going on was almost worse than any torture, and she knew that. But I consoled myself. I was still alone, and my friends were safe. I could get through this on my own so long as they were okay.

I yanked my focus away from the memory and onto the box. I peeled off the unicorn seal and flipped up the tabs. On the inside sat two small chains and a note:

HAVE YOU CONSIDERED OUR OFFER?

I crumpled the note up and threw it on the ground, shaking.

If I didn't accept a position in Dark Unicorn, Maurelle would do something horrible to me, something even my nightmares couldn't dream up.

But if I did accept, it would lead to the destruction and demise of my own kingdom.

I wished I didn't feel so weak. I was supposed to be strong, that was my job. I guessed I was failing miserably.

There was another small knock at the door. The same girl who always cleaned my room unlocked the cell, carrying a tray of food.

"Good morning," the girl snapped. Her blue eyes complimented her cream dress perfectly.

"Good morning," I greeted her like a friend, hoping that maybe if I did, someone could finally be nice to me in this place. "What's your name?"

The girl looked startled and hesitated, "Um . . ." Dropping her snappy attitude for a moment, she then looked around and whispered, "Arabella." She continued to place the food onto the small table in the corner.

"What is Dark Unicorn?" I probed.

Arabella looked like she'd been slapped. "What did you say?"

I smiled. "What you heard me say. What is Dark Unicorn? Because from what I'm seeing, it seems like a suppressive, evil organization that squashes all the good out of you until there's nothing left." A couple seconds of silence passed. *So much for greeting her like a friend.*

It seemed like she hadn't even registered what I'd said.

Her eyes were locked on the floor.

"Are you all right?"

She was swaying on the spot, her hands flung up tightly around her head, as though she were trying to block something out.

She glanced up at me and said, "You might not want to watch this."

I couldn't help my jaw drop as she knit her brows and pulled a piece of glass out of thin air.

"What are you doing?"

She gritted her teeth, "I said you might not want to watch."

I realized what was happening a split second too late as she dug the glass into her leg, crumpling to the ground.

I rushed to her. "Arabella!" I shook her by the shoulders. "Oh no!" I panicked.

She had fainted.

My eyes raced around the room.

I could slap her. I shook my head rapidly, trying to clear it.

I saw the small cloth I had been using to wash my face. I picked it up. It was still dripping with the water I hadn't wrung out.

I went to Arabella's side and twisted the washcloth, sending the trapped water cascading onto her forehead.

Sputtering and choking, her eyes flying open, she panted. "It worked! It worked! I have to–" She looked at me, and screamed.

"Hattie," she squeaked. "Oh, Hattie, I want to tell you everything!"

She shook her head to clear it, and she slapped herself in the face. Hard.

"Um . . ." I started, but closed my mouth again, no idea how I wanted to finish that sentence.

She stood up, now composed. In silence, she fixed her hair and withdrew the piece of glass from her leg, only letting out a small whimper.

I turned away, feeling the familiar feeling of nausea creep in when I saw the blood.

She wiped a hand over it and it vanished.

"Please pardon me," she said, stoniness intact.

Arabella turned on her heel to walk out of the room.

"Wait," I called. "Who are you?"

Genuine sympathy lit her features for a moment, and she grimaced. "I'm sorry, I can't tell you."

18

Fira

"What?" Misty's mouth dropped to her feet.

Rosie nodded solemnly. "She will die."

Misty made move to speak, but stayed silent.

"What is the object?" I intervened.

My heart was picking up speed at an abnormally fast rate.

Rosie looked pained. "I can't tell you," she said, "But only because I don't know."

I glanced at Misty, my downcast look reflected on her face.

"I'm sorry," Rosie added. "Things used to be different here. I used to be more helpful. I used to know more. I think it has to do with my sister and Hattie and," she paused. "Maurelle." She let the ominous connotation dangle in the air before clearing her throat and attempting to make up for it. "I figure you'll want to stay the night?"

"I didn't know that was a possibility," I confessed.

Rosie beamed. "Of course. I have rooms already set for guests." A door reappeared at the back of the room, but looking inside, I could tell it led to somewhere quite different from the one before.

I cautiously entered the room, Misty at my heels. I turned back to Rosie.

"I can't help too much," she said softly. "But the thing you're looking for lies within the woods, near the waterfalls."

"Thank you, Rosie."

As she waved, and the door closed, I was enveloped by the same scene as Rosie's room, but with a less personal touch.

Misty rushed past me and collapsed onto one of the two beds, checking to make sure the door had sealed before she spoke. "Another mission huh?" She kept her tone light, but I could hear the weariness weigh it down.

I wanted to groan, but I had to be the big sister now. "Hey," I said gently, crossing over to sit next to her. "It's only been one day. Besides, if you think about it, we just discovered a whole new society we never knew existed. Think about the news we'll have when we get back."

"Actually I was thinking about that," Misty whispered. "Why *didn't* we know it existed? I mean, with Hattie being the youngest princess ever, you'd think she would know something like this."

I sucked in a breath, not wanting to let loose the idea that had entered my head. *What if Hattie's council had been hiding it from her?*

No, I thought, that's impossible.

I let out a little gasp as my head tingled and my vision slid out of focus. It felt like an invisible hand was plucking the thought from my head, until I couldn't remember what it was anymore.

"Are you okay, Fira?" Misty shook me by the shoulders. Everything righted itself again.

I took in a deep gulp of air and tried to smile. "Yeah, I'm fine."

She didn't look convinced, but she smiled and said, "I think I'm going to go to bed."

"I'll be with you in a second."

I strode over to the desk and sat down, reaching into my bag and pulling out *The History of Peachtree Palace*. There could be another legend inside that I would need to know, and I supposed I'd spent too long rejecting them.

Misty fell asleep almost instantly, and I could hear her soft breathing in the background. But I glued myself to the desk chair, reading chapter after chapter, finding no new legends among them.

I finally began to feel my eyelids drooping, and finished off my last page and gingerly shut the book.

With the book neatly stacked, my pajama jumper on, and myself tucked in bed, I remembered that the lights weren't turned off. I began to climb out of bed when they shut themselves off, as if responding to me.

I hid my shudder under the covers as I turned over a lulled into sleep.

* * *

I woke up as dawn was just cracking on the horizon.

Walking to the window and opening it, a breeze of pure, fresh, lovely air danced in. I heard birds calling in the distance.

Though it lacked Rolling Hills's blossom leaves and perfect beautiful sunrise, I acknowledged how lovely a paradise I was standing in.

Every bit of grass in sight was green, and the flowers were all vibrant. I sighed, enjoying the lovely view of the town.

I heard Misty rustle behind me, a yawn escaping her mouth, "Good morning, Fira."

"Good morning, did you sleep well, then?"

"Yep, and you?"

"Yeah."

The nervousness emanated off of her in waves.

There was no way to describe the feeling I had short of *weird*. We knew nothing about where we were going, or what we were doing. And we had been ripped from Rolling Hills so easily it may as well have been a dream. Maybe I'd wake up in my bed at the palace, Hattie and Illis back, some unimportant paperwork to do, the whole nightmare over.

A little bell chimed and a woman's voice spoke: "Good morning. All guests should report to Level Two for breakfast in twenty minutes."

I wished there was a bathroom to get ready in, but no sooner had I thought this had a door appeared where we had come in, leading to a bathroom.

Misty's eyes widened, but she bit back anything she was going to say and gestured for me to go first.

The bathroom was filled with products, but we just washed our faces and dressed, leaving the makeup that could have potentially been someone else's.

I suppressed a shiver at the thought. It was beautiful here, but I had to admit the appearing doors were leaving me slightly on edge.

We proceeded from the bathroom and wished for a pole to ride on. A fancy one arrived, decorated with an ornate design. We placed our feet on the steps, called "Three!" and held on as it whizzed downward.

Floor 3 was a dining hall with a buffet lining every wall. Tables were filled with chattering people enjoying their first meal of the day. The smell of fried potatoes wafted through the air. I heard a woman boasting of the fresh peaches imported from Rolling Hills.

Misty helped herself to pancakes, potatoes and peaches, until her plate was almost spilling off the edges.

I raised an eyebrow.

She shrugged. "Hey, if we could *potentially* die the least we can do is be well fed doing it."

I copied her choices, and we sat, eating in silence.

I noticed Rosie in the far corner and waved her over.

"Good morning, girls." She beamed. "How did you enjoy your night?"

"It was wonderful, thank you," I replied.

"Oh, it was nothing really." She shuffled her feet. "*We* should be thanking *you* for coming to discover how to rescue Hattie."

I rolled my eyes like it was the most obvious thing in the world, proud of myself for being so bold. "She's practically my little sister, I'd do anything for her."

"That's good," Rosie said, looking deep in thought. "Very good . . . Well, I'm off!" She skipped away toward a door that had appeared.

Misty noticed a piece of paper on the table and called out to her, "Hey, you dropped–" But she was gone with the door. "– this."

"Look," I breathed, my finger tracing the parchment. "It has our names on it."

She looked down at our names scrawled on the paper.

I unfolded the paper to reveal a map with a large red X in the forest. In the corner a small note was scribbled: *Sorry, I can't be of more help. –Rosie*

"I guess this is the only thing we have to go on," Misty said gloomily.

"Well," I said, trying to force some form of optimism into the air. "I guess we'll just make do with what we have the best we can. Okay?"

"Alright," Misty reluctantly agreed.

"Alright," I repeated, reassuring myself, even though the feeling of gnawing dread had crept back in. "All right."

19

Illis

The hallway seemed long and winding as our hearts beat in our throats. The clack of shoes on the floor the only sound in the hall.

Elnora walked with the note tucked in her hand, her gaze straight ahead. My eyes stayed locked on the approaching door. Small white letters were painted onto its black body: **B5, 15**.

"This is it," I stated obviously, my hand hovering over the knob.

"Well, let's go," Elnora said.

When I hesitated, she pushed past me and yanked the door open.

It made a loud creak, and the sound of the chatter inside reached our ears.

Elnora gave me a small bow and let me pass, the door booming behind us as she shut it. The high-ceilinged room was crowded with people, and considerably darker than the hallway had been.

"Invitations," spoke the guard, so casually he might have been asking for a ticket to a fun fair.

We handed him the invitation and he passed it under the monitor to scan it.

For one heart-stopping moment the tiny machine didn't make a sound. The guard looked confused, but he passed it through again and it bleeped.

"Enjoy!" he cheered, keeping the invitation and putting it into a pile of others.

I breathed a sigh of relief as we walked into the room. A large stage stood at the front, chairs all around it like a concert hall.

On the stage was none other than Maurelle herself, her voice booming through the hall. "Take a seat, people of the Dark Unicorn!"

Chairs scratched on the ground, and Elnora pulled me down into the chair next to her at the back of the room.

I ignored the small lurch I felt as her hand closed around my wrist, shaking my head to clear it.

Right now wasn't the time to be thinking about the past.

Maurelle's voice filled the air again, "Rolling Hills. Such a small kingdom that somehow forced me," she coughed. "*and you*, to reside under the cover of ground. But now look at us. We have risen to an empire never to fall!"

Elnora shuddered next to me, and I glanced worriedly at her.

When she glanced at me, the irises of her eyes were slightly darker, and she was taking shaky breaths.

"Look around you! You see what we have built, together. We are one team, and I, as your leader, refuse to take orders from them any longer!"

Instead of cheers, there was eerie silence.

A servant walked on stage hoisting a chair with someone sitting on it, hands bound, face covered.

I gasped as a bag was removed from her head.

It was Hattie.

She struggled against her binds but did not move her mouth.

I jumped forward but again Elnora held me back. "Not now," she growled, her voice thick. "We can't blow our cover."

"Ah, Princess Hattie has come to join us," Maurelle purred.

Hattie found her voice. "You know very well that I was forced here," she replied calmly, but only I could tell that her breathing was more shallow than usual, and her hands were fidgeting beneath her binds.

"Forced!" Maurelle's laugh then became deadly. "Who would ever do such a thing?"

Hattie opened her mouth to respond.

"It was a rhetorical question," Maurelle snapped. "Now, Hattie, let's discuss your fate, shall we? Oh, how could I have forgotten?" She cast up her hands and a black cloud flew into the air, soaring over and into everyone.

Elnora grabbed my hand and ducked, right as one passed above our heads.

"There," Maurelle said. "*Now* give me a cheer."

The crowd cheered louder this time than before but abruptly ended in silence.

A small child whispered something in Maurelle's ear.

She patted the child on the back and smiled at her kindly. "This little one wishes to know the story of my exclusion from Rolling Hills. So be it." She sat down on the chair and began. "A long time ago, for I am old,"–Hattie rolled her eyes–"there was a woman, my best friend. Her name was Azami. She thought I was special because of my interest in magic. Dark magic. Others didn't. Being a mythic was a rarity. They pushed and teased Azami for being around someone like me. I couldn't bear to see Azami suffer, so I turned away from her."

Hattie watched Maurelle carefully in thought as if she knew what was coming next, as if she knew the name.

"But Azami was part of the Hills family, rulers of the land."

Hattie's eyes widened.

Maurelle continued, "Her parents disagreed with Azami's views and decided to punish her. They knew that only one thing would truly harm her, teach her a lesson, and that was to hurt *me*. The night was dark, the only light from the stars above. Azami's father dragged her by the arm into my house. I was confused as to why the king was here. Azami knew. She tried to run to me, but her father held her back, saying, 'Not now, Azami.' Tears stained Azami's face. I understood what was about to happen. I lunged for the door, hoping for escape. She cowered in the corner as her father brandished a *whip*."

I sucked in a breath.

"I screamed for help, for forgiveness, promising to stop my magical doings, but he continued. Azami cried with me, and at last she jumped in front of her father's whip and he struck her. I watched his eyes grow wide in shock. 'Run!' I recall her telling me. I knew at that moment that it would never be safe for me there. So I ran, and I never looked back."

Something that could have been sympathy bloomed in my chest, but I squashed it.

"The next year, Azami's parents both died, and Azami became queen, but I knew it would never be safe for me, not with people who thought the same as Azami's father. Azami bore a daughter, who then in turn had Mariana, who offered to let me move back into the kingdom, but it was far from my mind. There's no where in Mytheria I can go where I'll ever be truly accepted. I staged attacks; she fought against me. So now I wait here until the right moment to strike, when I will–and I promise, I will– finally get to watch Rolling Hills burn to the ground in front of me, forever a shadow in my memory. And we will rise to see a new future with me as your ruler."

I was deafened by the screams and cheers of "hope" that echoed through the halls. Hattie shut her eyes again and struggled. Elnora's body rocked with fear. The guards clenched their hands toward the ceiling and fire shot out. Some were weeping, some were calling, some fell at Maurelle's feet. It was terrifying, it was horrible, and for one moment of my life I felt utterly hopeless and scared.

Maurelle stood on the stage and laughed.

20

Misty

The dining hall seemed much smaller, like a spotlight was shining on just Fira and I. We had only one lead, a map. We had no idea where it went or what we were looking for.

Obviously, a perfect situation.

"Let's go," Fira tutted impatiently, and I realized she'd been standing up.

"Right," I said, straightening my shorts and getting up as well. "Time to leave."

A pole appeared in front of us and we hopped on. I didn't even need to shout the number, but it started downward to the first floor.

I tried in desperation to make the ride seem slower.

I heard a small ding again, and we stepped off.

Melody, Harmony, Medly, and Lyric were waiting in front of us.

Melody walked forward and said, "We've come to see you off." She held out two stiff cards. "Rosie said to give these to you. They will allow you into this city at any time. You are always welcome here." She then rushed toward the poles and tackled us in a hug. She whispered, "Goodbye. I'll miss you."

"Goodbye, Melody," Fira replied.

"Goodbye," I echoed. "I'll miss you too, but hey, it'll be another adventure, right?" I laughed at how stupid it sounded. I thought to myself, don't know what it is or where to go.

Melody shuddered, and as we stood up we could see that Melody was crying.

"Why are you crying?" I asked.

"No reason," she replied hastily, wiping her eyes.

"Well, all right then." Fira announced, "We're off."

"Goodbye." The family waved as we walked out the door.

"That was odd," Fira said as we exited the city the opposite way we'd come, and I watched it fade into the distance.

"What? She might just be emotional," I pointed out.

"I don't think so," Fira said cautiously, lowering her voice. "It was something else that wasn't us, I think."

"What do you mean?" I asked, my feet crunching against the rocks.

"She only reacted like that after you said something about the adventure."

I said nothing. Could it possibly be something about the mission we were about to take? Did Melody know something about it?

"Misty," Fira said, quietly, "I think this is going to be dangerous."

"Me too," I admitted, shocked at the lack of hesitation in my voice. "I think I knew it all along, I just didn't want to believe it. Things are happening so fast, and I guess I just keep thinking I'll wake up and be back home. None of this feels real."

To my surprise, Fira hugged me. "Nothing is going to happen to us or Hattie, okay?"

"Okay," I answered, though most of me didn't believe it.

Eventually we reached the end of the city and were faced with a looming forest.

"The trees are beautiful," Fira said.

And so they were. The trees all held white blossoms, looking like gems hanging from a chandelier of winding branches. I looked at a small wooden sign. It read *Crystal Forest.*

"Ready?" she asked, not sounding ready at *all* herself.

I took a deep breath to steady myself, looking forward at the looming trees. "Yeah."

We walked into the forest, which looked like a winter wonderland, except that the temperature reflected the spring day.

As the sun rose in the sky, we found a small clearing.

A pond lay at the center, crystal clear with flowers all around it. Spudgewubbles of all colors were playing a game, chasing each other.

I picked one up, feeling it wriggle slightly and give a little squeak as it gazed up at me.

It reminded me of Liam's love of animals, and longing swept through me. I wondered what he might think of this place.

I could practically hear his voice.

Just think Misty, we could run away there together. Away from responsibility and stupid families. Just us . . . forever.

My heart lurched as I remembered the letter tacked to his door.

Dear Liam,

I'm leaving Rolling Hills, though you probably figured that out already and will likely hate me forever. *And honestly if I make it back, I fully give you permission to. But I can't ignore this. You told me not to get involved, but I have to, Fira asked me, and Hattie needs me. You always called it my greatest flaw. Maybe it is. I already miss your voice. I'm not sure exactly when I'll be back or if I'll be back at all. I wanted to say something in person, but I had to go. But I couldn't leave without saying goodbye, just in case. Since we've been friends, you've always been there for me, and I you, or at least I hope. You're too important to lose, so I promise I'll come home.*

—Misty

The edges of my eyes stung, but the Spudgewubble curled into me and squeaked, and I had to let out a small laugh.

After coaxing the Spudgewubble back to the ground, we left the clearing, but my thoughts stayed on Liam and Rolling Hills.

As the trees surrounded us, my mind wandered to the time that Liam and I met, when I was five years old.

"Hey!" a boy shouted. "What are you doing up there?"

My heart skipped because this was the boy that everyone talked about in my play group. He is pretty cute, I thought.

I sat up quickly and brushed off the leaves from the peach trees that had fallen on my sundress.

"Nothing," I replied.

He ran up the hill to sit next to me.

"I'm Liam," he said and stuck out his hand.

"Misty." I flashed a goofy smile.

"I like your hair."

I giggled, feeling the two half ponytails. "Thank you."

The memory shifted to the day my brother had died, the same spot, very different emotions. I had been so shocked, and felt so lost.

Somehow Liam had understood.

Liam held me tight in a hug and whispered, "Shhh It's okay, Misty. I've got you."

I cried and hugged him back. "He was just gone," I sobbed. "Just gone. He didn't even—"

A bite of wind caught us and he pulled me tighter as I whispered, "He didn't even say goodbye."

"Shhh." He turned to me, so close I could count all of his eyelashes. My breath hitched. "You don't have to talk, Misty, just cry if you want, I won't leave. I promise."

The breeze blew cold as the sun set, but he didn't move, just like he promised. At one point we sunk to the ground together.

For a moment I saw his teasing facade melt down. For a moment he was every bit as caring and smart and kind as a prince from a fairytale.

Finally, when the sky was nearly dark, he stood and helped me get up. He put his arm around me, and we walked to my house together.

"Goodnight, Misty," he whispered, barely audible.

"Goodnight, Liam."

The memory faded away, and I sucked in a breath as the forest came back into focus.

At this very moment all I wanted was to see my best friend again, to feel the same thrill I had the first day I'd talked to him, when all seemed right with the world.

21

Illis

I gestured for Elnora to follow me, and sidled out of the crowded room. The guard threw us a skeptical look, and I muttered, "Bathroom."

The black door shut on the cheering mob, and Elnora slid to the floor, looking uncharacteristically scared. Terrified.

I slid down next to her, our backs pressed against the cool wall.

"She's convincing," I observed, even though I hated myself for the thought. "It seems like she has most of the people on her side, with Dark Unicorn. I wonder if anyone would ever turn against her now."

"No one would have the courage," Elnora said quietly. "They've all seen what she can do. Her terrible display of magic. Most of the people down here are, or were, outcasts. They might be hiding some pity behind their undying loyalty for her and the clan."

"They might just. Her magic, it is incredible, awesome, even beautiful in a way. But horrifying to imagine what she could do with it. Even take down whole kingdoms in one wave of her hand. World domination. She has a bad way of trying to save people."

Elnora laughed, but only half-heartedly. She drew her knees up to her chest and said, "She's awful– Maurelle. All I remember is darkness and cold, no light, despair. 'You're outcasts,' she told us. 'I know what you have inside of you– magic, power. You are different. I can help you, don't worry.'"

My heart skipped a beat when I realized she was talking about her time in the cave.

Elnora was shaking, so I placed an arm around her, despite every nerve in my body that was scared to touch anyone at all.

"None of us wanted to believe her, of course, but when she showed us, it was beautiful, but we could see danger in it. She never told us why we were this way." Elnora furled her hands into fists. "She just showed us."

Elnora's hand opened and a jet of sparkling light danced on it. She waved her other hand and it swirled up into the air, fizzing like a sparkler.

"Elnora means *light*, you know. I never made the connection. But your power, it's all based on who you are. Your personality, your name. Everything that binds you to yourself."

"It's beautiful, Elnora," I uttered in awe. "Absolutely gorgeous."

She closed her hand and the light vanished.

Our hands dangled by our sides, so close they were almost touching. My heart fluttered.

We sat in silence. "Illis," she said. "How are we supposed to survive this, whatever *this* is?"

The wall seemed colder as it dawned upon me that Maurelle had an entire army, we didn't.

"We're doomed," I said gloomily, for a second not even caring that I was ruining the moment.

"Yes, it does seem that way," a voice wafted down the hallway, startling me out of my thoughts.

My heart lurched and I jumped a mile in the air, my hand instantly feeling for my dagger.

Halfway down the hallway a girl with long auburn hair and a Dark Unicorn uniform was leaning against the wall.

I started to panic. Had she overheard us talking? Did she know we were intruders? Was she here to help?

"Hi, hello," she laughed. "Yes, I have been listening to your conversation. Don't mind me." She stared at us awkwardly for a moment before dropping into a serious expression. "All right, well, my name is Arabella, and I've seen your friend. You know. . . Hattie."

It took me a second to realize she was being serious.

"Where?" Elnora demanded, pulling her guard back up, her brows creased.

"On a fluffy cloud in the sky, surrounded by desert," she said in a dry, matter-of-fact tone before noticing we weren't liking her quips. She sighed. "She's in her cell. She's been there for less than a day, but she thinks she's been there for weeks. A slowing charm. It's a simple spell really, but it's unbreakable by anyone but the caster herself, who unfortunately in this case is our girl, Maurelle."

"Can we trust you?" I asked, eyeing her sly smile and jazz hands.

"Not so easily, no. You are right to be suspicious. But am I here to help? Yes. Do I hate Maurelle as much as you? Yes. Have I hacked the cameras and sound so they don't see me here assisting you?" She glanced up at a camera on the wall. "Yes. So, if I were you I would believe that it is safe to trust me, but I'm not you, so you decide."

"What do we have to lose?" I proposed, turning to Elnora.

"In your case, a lot," Arabella responded. "I can think of a long list in my head right now. Would you like me to tell you?"

"Um, no thank you." The uncomfortable quiet that followed was almost hilarious.

"I doubt it will make a difference because you can at least know I agree with your motives," Arabella replied, smiling. "And I expected you to say that. But don't fret, love, with me on your side, you probably won't die."

"Probably," I muttered.

Elnora stood up, and I followed her lead, not missing how her hand was still slightly poised to bring magic, her stance stiff and ready for a fight.

She was better at this than I was, by a lot.

I blew out a furious breath and chastised myself. *Stay attentive.*

"What do we need to do?" I asked.

"I have a plan. It's all quite simple," Arabella said. She paused, waiting for one of us to ask.

I rolled my eyes and took the bait. "What's your plan?"

"Why, I thought you'd never ask." She smirked. "I have the codes to all the doors and access to Princess Hattie's cell. We can sneak her out once I get the clearance pass. It will be slow, but it should work. You two barely have to do anything at all. The plan is for Maurelle to strike in a day's time. If we act quickly, we can stop her before she attacks. Unless, of course, she gets to us first, which she very well might. Sounds good?"

"I suppose that will probably work," Elnora replied hesitantly.

"Probably," I muttered again.

I heard movement, and glanced over my shoulder, realizing it was from people shuffling behind the door to the hall. "Let's move."

We had barely ducked around the corner when a flood of people filed out through the door.

"That was a close one," Elnora whispered, sweeping her forehead with the back of her hand.

"Arabella," I said. "Where should we hide? It wouldn't be a good idea to stay here."

"Don't worry," she responded smugly. "I know a place where you won't be found. Follow me."

We tracked down a hallway and turned right, right, left, right, left. . . I lost count of how many turns we took.

We arrived at a small door with many guards walking by. It was different from the others.

It was glowing with a pulsing light, indescribable, with an odd aura shimmering about it.

"Magic," Arabella explained with a grand gesture. "Invisible to any guard eye, and Maurelle." She moved her fingers, and I heard whatever lock was behind the door click open.

"Now, I must go," she said dramatically.

"You're abandoning us?" I asked, resisting the urge to stamp my heel in indigniance.

"Yep. Good luck, see you later." Arabella waved and began to walk away, but then spun back around. "Of course not, but don't you think it would be suspicious if I suddenly stopped working? If I just disappeared? I couldn't risk falling out of favor with Maurelle, as awful as it sounds that I'm even in favor with her," she shuddered. "But don't worry, she'll keep you safe."

"Who's *she*? Who are we talking about?" I asked, confused.

"The keeper of everything behind this door. Tulip. Tulip Hills, the only sibling of your old Queen Mariana— her younger sister."

2 2

Fira

The map in my hand seemed to quiver with excitement the closer we came to our destination.

The map itself was laid out with all the forests and clearings we had passed. The one thing we hadn't reached was the edge, it looked like the bottom of a cliff, but Rosie had drawn a big red *X* over it, so we'd been walking that way the whole time.

"We're almost there," I said, tracing my finger over the trees on the map.

"I wonder what the thing is that we're looking for," Misty said, again stating her concerns. I rolled my eyes, but she kept talking. "And how it will save Hattie."

I nodded. "And so you've told me."

The walk was starting to stretch on hours, and as a simple secretary I had to say, I was *not* enjoying the exercise.

We plopped down against a tree and took out peaches to snack on. I stretched my aching feet out, groaning.

"Not as fresh as in Rolling Hills," Misty bemoaned as she took a bite, glumly chewing.

I noticed it too as I took a generous nibble. "Not surprising," I said. "You know, when I was little, I used to go every day and pick up the peaches straight off the trees to deliver them to Peachtree Palace. The cooks would always say the same thing, 'Good morning, Fira. How are you? Have you delivered our peaches?' but they knew I always would. I would say yes, and they would take my basket. The head cook's daughter would always sit with me, and we would talk and eat the fruit until our mothers would shoo us away, saying, 'There will be no peaches left for the Hills.' We would go to the library and sit together. Once, when we were about ten, we started to see Hattie in a side room, her face buried in a textbook. Then, we'd just spend the rest of our day daydreaming about being a princess until our parents came and got us. I don't think either of us really understood though– what it must have been like for Hattie when her parents disappeared, I mean, she was only seven."

"God, I miss long and carefree days as a kid," Misty sighed, but it was laced with longing. "Life was easier."

You still are a kid, I wanted to say. A sixteen-year-old shouldn't be forced to burden the responsibility of saving a kingdom.

I knew she was thinking about her brother. She never mentioned him, never talked about him with anyone. If someone didn't know her from a young age, they would never guess she had had a brother at all.

I picked at the grass until Misty started talking again, "I wonder–"

"What the object is, I know!" I sighed in exasperation, but was unable to keep a straight face.

Instantly the tension in the air defused as she laughed with me, and for a moment I forgot about the stupid mission, and just enjoyed seeing her smile again.

The trees steadily thinned as we continued walking, and we reached a clearing not unlike another we had previously come upon. This one, however, seemed overrun, outside the Water of Peachtree's boundaries. A snow-crested mountain rose in front of us, blocking our view with its peak.

"I think this is it," I told Misty. "There, do you see that?"

I pointed to the X on the map, right at the bottom of a cliff, then back up at the mountain in front of us.

A door was carved into the mountain, mimicking the round style of the houses in Rolling Hills.

"What do we do?" Misty asked.

The door looked like a giant boulder, and I was unsure if even both of us could open it together.

Even so, I squared my shoulders and said, "We open it."

My fingers slid into the small openings, and I leaned back, pulling with all my might. A grunt of effort escaped my throat. The door wouldn't budge. *A push-pull sign would be nice.*

"Hey, Misty, can you help with this?"

The door let out a moan of protest as we slid it open, but we persisted. When the door finally flung open, I fell to the ground, landing hard on my arm.

I rubbed the elbow that I landed on.

Misty gasped. "Woah."

On the inside was a dark passageway. Before I could blink, lamps flickered to life until there was a dull glow lighting all the way down. As my foot touched the opening of the passage, the lamps brightened, revealing marble floors and walls. Paintings lined the walls, paintings of princesses. There was something special about them and their regal stances that I couldn't quite place.

"They are the Hills princesses," Misty voiced in awe.

I saw it now.

The first Hills princess, Princess Charlie, sat in the Peachtree

Palace library, her appearance almost identical to Hattie's. I sprinted down the line until I reached the last painting. It was Hattie. She sat in the same spot as the others, among the bookshelves of my favorite room. Her smile was so real.

She didn't look much younger than she was now, but there was something distinctly *off* about her. I wondered when this had been painted.

Did she know it was stuck down here, whatever *here* was, in the very same spot hiding the object that would supposedly save her life? I guessed not. There seemed to be a lot of things we didn't know about the Hills family.

I tried to find excitement in the paintings, but my skin tingled unpleasantly. The entire place was eerie.

Misty tapped my shoulder and pointed. I screamed, startled.

At the end of the passage stood a woman. She looked fairly young and had an odd glow about her, as if standing with her back to the moon.

"Greetings, Fira Pele and Misty Baker. I am delighted to see that you have acquired the correct hints to lead you here."

"Who are you?" Misty demanded.

"Why–" the woman chuckled. "–my name is Odelina."

Misty gaped, a hand flying to cover her open mouth. "I'm sorry?"

"Odelina. Have you heard of me, Misty Baker?"

Misty rolled her eyes. "No, duh," she said sarcastically.

I was surprised. The name rang no bells in my head, and I didn't feel the Adar moving to tell me anything.

Odelina inspected her nails. "Well, who am I then?"

"You're the servant from the fairy tale," she stated, as though it were common knowledge.

"*Servant* is a tad bit harsh. Do you agree, Fira Pele, carrier of Adar?"

I clutched my ringed hand protectively. "Tell us who you are."

"Fira," Misty clucked her tongue. "She's the servant of the great Alvara. The guardian of Rolling Hills. But it's all rubbish. You must be named after her. It's a fairy tale, that's all." She nodded as if trying to convince herself.

Odelina tilted her head, silver hair falling over her shoulder in a sheet of starlight. "Did you maybe not consider that the key's legend wasn't the only one that was true? And honestly Misty Baker, after everything you have seen, does anything seem impossible? "

"Even the impossible can become possible," Misty whispered. It sounded familiar, but I couldn't put my finger on where I'd read it before.

"Exactly."

"I'm sorry," I interrupted. "What is the legend?"

Misty raised her eyebrows, her expression saying: *seriously*? "I thought you'd read it. I mean, you read so much."

"I try not to waste my time with fiction like legends and fairy tales," I said defensively.

"But this particular one, it's *The History of Peachtree Palace*."

I wondered why I'd never seen it. From the way Misty was reacting, it seemed pretty important.

"Please elaborate for her, Misty Baker," Odelina said with a sly smile. "*Then* I can help you."

Misty walked back to the painting of Princess Charlie, and began. "Charlie had a friend named Alvara. As Rolling Hills grew, Charlie obtained the power to rule the world. But she didn't want it, so she locked it away. Alvara was younger but wiser, and knew that she would be no good as the ruler once Charlie was gone. But Alvara discovered the object, obtaining all of its power. She desperately tried to restore the power to the key, which only resulted in magnifying her own powers. Alvara had become one of the most powerful people ever."

Misty traced her finger over the edge of one of the paintings.

"She managed to put some magic back into the key, but never enough. When Charlie died, she wanted Alvara to be princess, which greatly injured her own daughters' feelings. Alvara gave up the job to Charlie's daughter Lucia who became the second princess of Rolling Hills. Alvara lived apart from the kingdom with her servant, Odelina, to whom she told everything. When Charlie died, Alvara, in grief, vanished, leaving her only daughter behind. But legend says that her descendant has resentment toward the line that caused its matriarch to disappear. It is said that unless someone stops them, they will do away with the 100th princess before she has any children of her own, halting the Hills line forever." Misty took a deep breath. "Which is why it can't be real."

"It is," Odelina stated.

Tears filled Misty's eyes.

"Why does that mean it can't be real?" I asked.

"Isn't it obvious?" Odelina asked.

I shook my head hopelessly.

Misty shuddered. "Maurelle is the descendant of Alvara, and Hattie is the 100th princess."

23

Hattie

Maurelle's guards seized my hands in a strong grip, and ordered, "Come on."

"I'm not going to run away, you know," I informed them.

"You're a prisoner. You'll try, eventually."

I was surprised at how civil they seemed. I had always pictured prison guards as big hunks of muscle with only a few words or grunts emerging from their mouths.

The cell approached quickly, and they shoved me inside, promptly locking the door.

"Bye. Thanks for the visit," I said to the wall.

I sighed and collapsed onto my bed. After the traumatizing events of Arabella's visit, not even the meeting with all of the Dark Unicorn clan could shake my unwavering certainty that the time of escape was coming closer. I had a vague idea in my mind that Arabella would have a big role in my plan, but I hesitated to act on it.

I went to check nature's status.

I could see a starry sky through the crack, but my cell and I seemed to be positioned in some sort of cove, which was almost always dark.

I reckoned it was high time for me to get some sleep, so I crawled into the messy bed I hadn't bothered making earlier, not even troubling to change into a different set of clothes.

My eyes slid shut and instantly I began to dream.

I was standing in an empty hall. The lighting was dim but inviting, a rosy glow. I chanced a look down to see my outfit still plastered to my body. It was then that I became aware that someone else was here.

It was a woman, a familiar woman.

"Hello, Hattie Hills," she said.

I searched my memory, trying to figure out where I'd seen her before.

"You know me. I am Odelina. I worked at your palace for a brief time, making sure you were safe."

"You," I said, discovering I could talk. I acknowledged that this dream seemed undeniably authentic. So I did the only sensible thing, I punched myself in the arm, regretting it immediately when the pain felt very real. "Where am I?"

"You are in the empty hall of Peachtree Palace, at the time when Charlie Hills first built it."

I could tell now that it really was the same old architecture in my palace, with the staircases hugging the walls, and the grand doors on the three main walls of the room.

I couldn't help the small smile that graced my lips at the sense of home.

"This is the place where the true spirit of Rolling Hills first began. It is also where it will end, if you do not help save it."

I heard a roar behind me, and when I turned around, the hall was on fire.

I screamed and tried to run away, but Odelina blocked my path, a small orb in her hand.

She raised her hand and a key appeared out of thin air.

My heart pounded, the fire growing hotter around me as Odelina put the key into a small hole at the front of the orb and slowly turned it.

The orb opened, and my head exploded with pain. Magic. Wonder. Darkness. Light.

I dropped to the floor, clutching my head in my hands. "Make it stop!" I screamed.

"I can't, Hattie Hills." Odelina's voice was barely audible over the ever bellow of the fire. "It is your destiny."

I heard a sickening crack, and looked up to a horrifying sight.

The beam of the palace ceiling was cracking open, and in one final crunch it came free, falling right towards me.

I threw myself out of the way, curling up into a ball until I felt a hand on my shoulder. "This is your destiny, Hattie Hills."

When I looked up, Odelina was gone. The palace was burning around me except for one mirror in the center.

I crept toward it, trying to block out the pandemonium around me.

I looked up into a mirror and saw that my eyes were glowing brilliantly to match the glistening gown now donning me.

Without my permission, my hands began to form the shape of a crown, my pinkies and thumbs joining, the rest of my fingers pointing upward.

I lifted the crown to my head. A blinding flash plunged everything into darkness.

I woke with a start, promptly looking down. A scarlet mark the size of my fist branded my arm.

Calling it a dream didn't feel right. It was a concept I knew my brain couldn't create on its own, more like an invasion of my consciousness, as if Odelina were actually there talking to me.

A vision?

At the thought I actually laughed out loud, placing my head in my hands. A vision. I was seriously considering that some magical vision had overtaken my head.

A week ago, I hadn't even believed in magic. And now there were powers and prophecies and for some reason, my kingdom had to be the center of it.

I rubbed my temples. The main thing I couldn't figure out was *why?* Why was Rolling Hills the center of all of this? And why on earth had Odelina been talking to me?

I remembered her, the quiet servant, the only one my mother never questioned, the one who sat in the corner taking notes. But now I could guess what the notes were about. Me.

I splayed a hand across my forehead, finding a thin layer of sweat. The walls spun, and I wondered what revelation my *vision* had been trying to show me.

Before I could think too hard about it, the cell door creaked open, and Arabella walked in with a tray of food. She avoided my gaze and set the tray down on the table. I saw her finger tap the edge of the tray, and she walked out the door.

I cautiously approached the table and picked up the tray, inconspicuously running my hand along the bottom. Sure enough there was a small paper stuck there. It was taped shut, so I peeled it off carefully.

I tried to stop my hands from shaking, but I couldn't help their slight quiver as I opened the note.

Dear Hattie,

My name is Arabella, undercover agent for Dark Unicorn. I can't tell you anything more than that I am on your side. I promise it will make sense someday very soon. In the meantime, though, I hope I didn't frighten you the other day. My body was under the influence of a spell, and I had no control of my actions. But back to the main reason I'm writing this: I was tasked with the job of coming here to this Dark Unicorn fort precisely to help you in a time when you would be stuck within Maurelle's grasp. Your friends Illis and Elnora are here to help rescue you.

I wonder who Elnora is, I thought.

We plan to break you out in less than a day's time, but for you it might feel like a week. A spell is placed on you to make time feel slower. Though you may believe you've been here for a month, it has only been one day since your capture. Maurelle is planning a large attack on Rolling Hills, and we need your help to stop it. There is something we need to find that only your other friends can deliver. Don't worry.

–Arabella

I wanted to jump around in happiness, and scream at the same time. The letter was so unbelievably vague, that I had no idea what was going on other than that I was going to be rescued.

Rescued.

I felt confused and lost, but another feeling persisted. For the first time in what felt like a month, true hope blossomed in me, and I smiled.

I had a chance.

24

Fira

I saw the realization cross over Fira's face.

"She can't be, she just can't," Fira said, pinching the bridge of her nose.

"Exactly," I replied.

"I think the math quite adds up," Odelina said solemnly. "Hattie Hills is the 100 th descendant of Charlie Hills, and she doesn't have much time left."

"That's not true," Fira insisted. "Misty said the legend states that *unless someone stops them they will do away with the descendant.*" We can stop her. I have the Adar and Hattie will have. . . whatever it is we're looking for."

"What *is* it that we're looking for? You know we still have no idea what that is," I pointed out. "And we're running out of time."

"The item lies deep within these caves. You must find it and call my name. If you successfully acquire the object, I will transport you to wherever Hattie will need you the most at the given moment. But first, you need to know what you're looking for. I can't tell you, but if you're nice, I could give you a hint."

"Of course we want a hint," I said, pausing when Odelina blinked in my direction. "Please."

Odelina cleared her throat.

"Though I wouldn't fly if you throw me up
I'd come back to you with aim and luck
And I could be bounced with little weight
But if you put me down, I'd never lie straight."

There was a beat of silence.

Fira burst out laughing. "You're joking right?"

When Odelina didn't respond Fira said, "Well, that's easy. It's a ball."

"Very good." She smiled like she knew that the rhyme was far too simple for anyone to solve, let alone Fira. "Here in this cave there is a room. You will find the ball inside, but be careful. It is more dangerous than it seems. This ball is not ordinary. Good luck, you're going to need it." She smiled sadly, looking as though she wished she could help more.

Odelina snapped her slender fingers. She disappeared in a cloud of fog.

"That was easy," I said. "Anyone could have figured it out in a millisecond."

Fira nodded but mused, "But it's almost *too* easy, and I have a suspicious feeling. 'It is more dangerous than it seems,' what do you think that means?"

"Maybe some sort of challenge?"

"I think so too," Fira agreed.

She started to glow blue. She clutched her head, grabbing at the wall for support.

"Are you okay?" I squeaked in panic.

The glowing stopped as suddenly as it started. "Yeah," Fira replied. "I unlocked something in the Adar again, almost like a game."

"What is it?" I said, trying not to let the overwhelming feeling of fear rise again, like it seemed to do every time Fira mentioned the Adar.

"We must proceed with caution. There is danger in our midst. The Adar can help me, but we have to be careful."

My stomach knotted. I gulped. "Alright."

"Let's go." Fira charged forward in a steady stride down the marble tunnel.

I followed in more uncertainty than her strong steps, stopping for only a moment to admire how much more sure of herself Fira seemed since getting the Adar.

The silence was eerie as we passed countless portrait settings of all the princesses, the only sound our shoes clacking on the marble floors.

Can the legend really be true? I asked myself. Are we really the *only* people that can help Hattie stop Maurelle, by bringing her this ball thingy?

In my heart, I hoped not. I hoped I could run away from any responsibility to Rolling Hills. But in my head I knew that I had to try. It almost made me laugh that *I* had to be the one for this. I wasn't the strongest, or the smartest, or a princess. I was just plain, boring, and ordinary, and I definitely wasn't capable of saving Hattie's life.

But maybe I could prove myself, show Hattie how loyal I was to her, because I suspected that my job wasn't really important and that Hattie just kept me around because I was her friend, as much as I hated to admit it. The thought made me sick of myself.

Hattie was probably being tortured right now, and the only

thing I could think about was that maybe she'd like me a little better if I could save her.

I glanced again at Fira, her newfound confidence radiating off her almost as bright as the Adar's glow.

It seemed adventure was good for some people, but not for me.

"Look at these," Fira whispered, running her hand along a painting. "They are all in the same positions, in the same spots, but through all the exceeding generations."

She was right. The portraits---I saw now---were all identical, yet they were all different people in very different times.

I examined two, side by side. Both contained a princess at a young age, though one had blonde hair and the other brown.

They each looked about three, and each held a peach in her hand. The girls' heads were tilted at exactly the same angle, and they both wore a laugh of pure joy pasted on their smiling faces. They looked happy, not at all scared of anything.

"What is this place?" I asked, a chill running down my back. "Legends never talk of anything like this. A place where all history is painted into the walls of marble. A spot like this is never mentioned."

"I never read legends, remember," Fira said. "I always wanted to separate myself from fiction, focus on my studies. It seems that what I was ignoring might turn out to be true after all."

"No." I firmly placed my hand on her shoulder. "We can stop it. We can still save Hattie."

A tear trickled down Fira's cheek, and she hastily wiped it away, looking at her hands. "Who would have known I had the power to do this inside my body." She fiddled with the Adar on her finger, a dreamy look on her face.

I could've, I wanted to say, but I didn't. I guess I wasn't the only one with some self confidence issues.

"Well, it looks good on you."

"Not the glow though," Fira said with a smirk.

"Don't start," I said with a giggle. "The glow looks *amazing*."

Despite ourselves, we both burst out laughing, and for a second, the sound filled the void of the empty hallway.

We heard a clatter, and our laughing ceased.

Fira cleared her throat, reemphasizing, "We really should be paying attention." She strode forward, not looking back, and I followed, not really having a choice.

The tunnel finally dissolved into a circular room surrounded by doors identical to the one we had entered through, and a door that I did not know was attached to the tunnel slid shut. We heard the distinct sound of a lock.

"Oh no," Fira uttered.

I was about to ask what was wrong when I realized what was about to happen . . .

The room spun so rapidly, I flew against the wall and fell to the ground.

The spinning abruptly stopped.

As the room came back into focus around me, nothing looked different. But the orientation of the room had greatly rotated, so I couldn't identify which of the doors we were about to go into.

I slowly rose and looked around to see Fira mimicking my movement.

"What just happened?" I asked, trying to braid my frayed nerves back together.

Fira cast a dark look at the doors. "The room has spun, so we don't know which door is which."

Panic began to knot my throat. "So how do we know where we came in?"

She fixed me to my spot with a glazed expression. "We don't."

25

Illis

"What?" Elnora's voice rang sharp and clear as a bell in the morning. "Queen Mariana didn't have a sibling."

"See that, is what you think," Arabella corrected. "She lives here, and has her whole life. No one knew that Tulip was a sister of the royal throne, not even Mariana. It was a secret to all."

A million questions flooded my brain, but I picked the easiest one. "Can we meet her?" I asked.

"No." Arabella pulled out a paper and smiled. "Kidding. But I *will* write a letter to Hattie explaining our situation. We must pray that your other friends have found what they're looking for."

"What?"

"Oh nothing. Tulip will explain it to you. Go on, she's waiting."

Arabella walked off at a quick pace, leaving us staring at the door.

"After you, madame." Elnora gestured to the door.

I pulled the door handle toward me, and it slid open to reveal a dimly lit room with rose lights fastened along the walls. Candles burned in the corners, and small machines let off different-colored mists that twirled to the middle, entangling in the air.

"Enchanting isn't it?" came a voice from behind us, and I whipped around, hand on my dagger hilt.

"There will be no need for that." A young woman stood before us, soft brown hair and eyes to match. Like Hattie's. She looked about our age. "Hello, I'm Tulip Hills, but I think you already know that."

"You owe us an explanation," I hissed.

"I know," she said and walked past us to the center of the room, where a table sat, with cushions surrounding it. "Here, I'll make you tea."

Her palm turned upward and a kettle appeared in the air. Tulip poured the water into glasses and placed some herbs inside.

"What are these mists?" Elnora asked curiously, looking at the colors. Yellow, purple, pink and blue mixed in the air above us.

"You don't know?" We shook our heads. "They represent the four classes of mythics: Sunflower, Protea, Marigold, and Aster. A Sunflower is kind, a Protea is courageous. A Marigold is creative, and an Aster is wise. Everyone has some inkling of magic in them, even if it is small. These classes are there to define us and help us learn about our own abilities in magic."

"What are mythics?" I asked.

Tulip smiled softly. "People with the ability to wield magic, my dear."

She paused and closed her eyes. She breathed deeply inward and pointed at the door. "Arabella is a Protea. The princess herself is a Marigold. I can sense that you, Illis, are a Protea. You, on the other hand, Elnora, are a Sunflower. I can see that you already know some magic. Care to demonstrate?"

Elnora gave a sharp nod and twisted her hand, sending light flying across the room. Her sparkles intertwined with the mists, and they began to shimmer and dance.

"Beautiful," Tulip breathed.

"Wait, slow down," I urged, my brain moving too fast to comprehend what I was hearing. "You mean *I* can do magic too?"

"You, Illis, hold out your hand." I did as she said. Her finger traced my palm, but before I could rip away from her touch, I felt a surge of energy course through my veins and up through my arm. "Now try to summon your power."

I was about to tell her that I had absolutely zero idea how to do that, but abruptly I was in a memory from when I was little.

My legs were pulled up to my chest, my vision was blurred.

I glanced down at the small bruise beginning to form on my arm.

I tried to breathe in and out like I'd been taught. Tried to tear my eyes away from the marks on my body.

I heard laughing in the other room and flinched.

This was my punishment.

They did tell me not to take the training course.

My eyes fluttered open. "What was that?" I demanded, starting to hyperventilate.

It was too real, too precise. It was magic.

"Incredible," Tulip whispered. "Your power was locked so deeply inside of you, you have only just discovered it."

"*What was that?*" I said again, my voice cracking as I stared at my hands.

"You can access the memories of time," Tulip said. "You are able to bring memories to life in your mind. But if I'm not mistaken, you may be able to access other people's memories. It is an immensely difficult branch of magic. But with proper training–"

"No," I interrupted.

"Excuse me?" Tulip responded quietly, but she knew what I had said.

"No, I don't want to access other people's memories. I'm not magical, I'm an ordinary, regular girl, trained to kill since I was a kid."

Tulip looked affronted. "You're just scared. You will learn in time."

"No!" I yelled. "I don't want that. I don't want to see my memories. I don't want any of it. Take it back."

"I can't do tha—"

"TAKE IT BACK."

The room went silent, and I could feel Elnora's eyes on me, but I continued anyway, my voice now barely a whisper. "I can't go through it again."

Elnora sucked in a breath, and I flinched. "Illis—"

"Please don't," I whispered, hating myself for wanting so badly to know how she was going to end the sentence.

Before I could lose myself completely, Tulip said, "Come with me."

We stood up, my hands still shaking.

I wanted to smack off the smile that Tulip wore as she led us to a door at the back of the room.

"I'll see you in the morning." She pulled the door open and shoved us inside.

"Hey!" I yelled, but when I turned around the door was gone. "Come back!"

I punched the wall as hard as I could and hissed as pain cracked up my arm. I hadn't even left a dent.

Elnora was staring at me, and I was internally chanting

Don't cry.

Don't cry.

Don't cry.

I closed my eyes and counted in a breath. One. . . two. . . three. . .

Blew out a breath. One. . . two. . . three.

When I opened my eyes again, Elnora was still looking at me, but this time, her gaze made my breath hitch.

Her lips parted slightly like she was about to say something, but the lights went out unexpectedly, throwing us into darkness.

With panic, I turned to notice that the wall in front of me was getting closer. I felt the walls closing in around us.

I backed up and ran into Elnora, her hot breath tickling my neck.

"How tight of a fit is it in here?" she wheezed. "I can't even move."

"Pretty tight," I replied with a small laugh, trying to clear my head to focus on the problem, but my stomach was filling with an unfamiliar rush.

She was far too close to me, but she didn't pull away.

"Hey, Illis," she whispered.

"Hey."

Suddenly the little room quaked and rumbled, and the moment was broken. I was falling, and then we were both on the ground with two heavy thuds. I heard a scream and then we were released.

The floor slowly slid apart, and I grasped helplessly at the ledge, but it disappeared into the wall. We fell through the box, and it took me a moment to realize the change in light. Stars sparkled around us.

I heard a squeal and felt Elnora's hand groping for mine.

I closed my hand around hers and looked up. She looked back at me and laughed. "This is almost like flying."

We took it upon ourselves to spin around in circles, spiraling downward, and giggling uncontrollably. I looked up to see the small box we had stood in, floating in midair.

It suddenly occurred to me that we didn't know where we were going and that we were Hattie's rescue. All at once, my instincts kicked in, and I grabbed Elnora, no longer laughing. I tilted our bodies downward, and we spun faster.

Abruptly we stopped, and a room materialized around us. We fell with a thump onto the cushions we'd been sitting on mere minutes before.

Tulip sipped her tea, smiling slyly at us.

"What was that?" I asked, suddenly feeling very tired of the question.

"My memory," Tulip replied. "I am very strong, and I tapped into your power, making you believe I was bringing you to a closet, then dropping you into the abyss. The thing about magic is that you can find it everywhere, even when you aren't looking."

A million questions popped into my head, most of them starting with why she was ever in a floating box in space, but I settled on, "That was . . . my magic?"

"That was your memory?" Elnora asked, and I turned to look at her. She just shrugged, "I feel like *that's* the bigger question here, just saying."

Tulip ignored her and answered me, "Yes. Now maybe you can accept letting it into your life a little."

Tulip shuffled over to a cabinet drawer in the back of the room. I heard it slide open, and she withdrew two items. Tulip handed one to Elnora and one to me. They were pins. Elnora's was yellow, beautifully carved into a sunburst shape with a diagonal banner across it that read *Sunflower*. Mine was purple, and the word in the center was *Protea*.

"What are these?" Elnora asked, turning the pin over in her hands.

Tulip smiled. "These are your class badges. Congratulations, you're real Mythics now."

26

Fira

"We're trapped," Misty uttered, and I could tell she was working very hard not to let her voice rise into hysteria.

"Yeah, definitely looks that way," I tried to reply calmly, but my senses were still throbbing in fear.

So what do we do now? I asked myself. Think, Fira, think.

The bracelet on my hand vibrated, and I looked down. "What do you want?"

If our predicament hadn't been the way it was, I would've found my talking to a bracelet ludicrous. We were stuck in a circular room, however, with no idea of where to go, so talking to an inanimate object was the least of my problems.

"*Hello.*"

I jumped a mile. The last thing I expected to hear was Illis's voice talking out of my bracelet, let alone that my once stationary bracelet was talking at all for that matter.

"I'm talking through the bracelet that Hattie gave me for my birthday," Illis went on in a rush. "Don't ask me how, I'll explain it when you get here. We need you to come as quickly as you can. We've found Queen Mariana's sister! She's the one who helped us contact you. We're in Maurelle's fortress. Please come quickly. We need you guys now. We have so much to tell you. Bye!" The bracelet shook and died, along with Illis's voice.

"Okay, that was so weird." Misty looked perplexed at the bracelet.

"Yeah." I noticed I was staring at the object around my wrist, and I shook my head, clearing the reminiscence of my thoughts. "I wonder where they found Rosie."

Though I had other ideas on the matter, Misty scrunched up her face in concentration, peering at the doors. "So which door should we go to?"

I closed my eyes in a flash of pain, and felt myself glowing blue again.

Go to the door on your right.

"Go to that door." I pointed and then opened my eyes realizing that I was pointing toward the door behind Misty, her face still in awe at my glowing.

"How do you know?" she whispered.

"The Adar told me," I said, noticing a slight discomfort flicker in Misty's eyes.

Nonetheless, Misty braced herself and walked through the door. I followed, slowly, studying every aspect of the area, hoping to pick up any clue.

It was a small room, lit by tiny lamps on the walls. In the center of the room sat a small orb, glowing a soft pink.

"Hattie, come on, use your power."

"I can't. It's too hard."

"I believe in you."

"Hello, Hattie."

"Who are you?"

"I am Maurelle, and I am afraid I need your power now."

"Why, what do you want with it? This is my power."

"Oh, don't worry, there is no need to fret, you won't remember anyway."
"Did you hear that?" Misty's voice trembled as she looked at me.
"Yes," I replied softly. "I did."
Misty walked a slow circle around the orb. "What is it?"
The pieces slid together. Maurelle was after Hattie. She wanted something from her. Hattie had no recollection of Maurelle in her past. Her parents were always away. One lonely princess.
The words escaped my mouth before I could stop them. "It's Hattie's power."
"What?" said Misty, her eyes widening considerably.
"Don't you see?" I said. "*Hattie's power.* Maurelle is after something Hattie has, but she doesn't know about it. Odelina seemed to have an extensive knowledge of what lies here. The legends that you read, the ones I ignored, they are all true. Magic is real, just like the prophecy said, and this is Hattie's."
A puff of smoke appeared, and Odelina stepped out, clapping. "I've got to say I'm impressed by how quickly you unraveled that little mystery. Usually, people go into the wrong room, but you do have the help of the Adar after all."
"What is in the other rooms?"
"Monsters, curses, the list extends." Odelina lifted an unconcerned shoulder.
I narrowed my eyes, "Who else has come here before?"

"Well, among others, one lovely young woman named Maurelle."

Misty's hand flew to her mouth.

"The puzzle really was pretty simple now, wasn't it?" Odelina wore a sly smile.

I glanced over at Misty, who's hand was still firmly over her mouth. I spoke, "When you consider all the various pieces, they just—"

"—fit together, like one giant puzzle," Misty finished, looking scared rather than relieved. "With only one piece missing. Oh no."

"What?"

"Illis's message." Misty looked horrified. "She said they'd found Queen Mariana's sister. But that's . . ." she paused, struggling for words.

I realized then what she was trying to say. "Impossible," I protested, fear creeping through my stomach. "They went through the hill."

"We went through the library, which, as far as we know, is the only way into the Waters of Peachtree," Misty added.

"Rosie hasn't left the Waters of Peachtree her entire life. She said so herself."

"And yet, suddenly, as soon as we leave, she has a house in Maurelle's fortress."

"So we've been . . ." I trailed off.

" . . . playing into Maurelle's hands . . ." Misty inferred.

" . . . the whole time," we said in unison, staring at each other.

Odelina made no comments, merely stood there, her face unreadable.

"Help!" I cried. "You said that once we found the ball, you would transport us to wherever Hattie needed us the most. You promised."

"So I did," she replied. "And I would never break a promise, especially not to you lovely ladies."

Gently, she picked up the orb and handed it to us. We grabbed on to it. I could feel an odd sort of heat, and my hands began to sweat. The scene started to replay itself, and I glanced over at Misty, almost glowing in the pink light, and her expression revealed that she could hear it too. The scene gradually got louder, pounding in our ears. I resisted the temptation to clutch at them, but my hands stayed firm on the orb.

"Hattie, come on, use your power."

"I am going to transport you on the count of three," Odelina announced.

"I can't. it's too hard."

"Okay, ready?" Odelina prompted.

"I believe in you."

"Yes," we agreed.

"Hello, Hattie."

"Who are you?"

"One. . ."

"I am Maurelle, and I am afraid I need your power now."

"Two. . ."

"Why, what do you want with it? This is my power."

"Three. . ."

"Oh, don't worry, there is no need to fret, you won't remember anyway."

The world twisted around us, and everything went black.

27

Illis

Elnora and I lay beside each other, looking up as she swirled her hands in the air, creating beautiful sparkling light in the room.

Tulip had left on some important duty, and told us to stay where we were, telling us firmly that the guards patrolled heavily on our side of the compound. And Arabella had gone to get a clearance pass so we could break Hattie out of her cell.

We didn't contradict her. Once she had left, we took one look outside the door, saw guards at every corner, and decided to relax instead.

Elnora had been twirling her fingers in the air for almost half an hour, making bright figures dance around the room.

Finally, she dropped her arm and looked at me, "Illis?"

"Yeah?" I hoisted myself onto my side, propping my head on my elbow.

"About what happened earlier." She fidgeted with a piece of her hair and my stomach dropped.

"I–"

"No," Elnora interrupted, then caught herself. "I'm sorry. I just wanted to say it's okay." She took a deep breath, "I wouldn't want to relive my past either."

I grappled for words. I don't know what I was expecting, but it wasn't that.

I opened my mouth to respond when there was a loud crack, and two figures appeared above us. Gravity was not defied, and they fell downward, landing on us in a convoluted tangle of bodies.

Someone kicked me hard in the nose, and I heard Elnora shout, "Sorry!"

I managed to pull myself up and draw my dagger, pointing it at one of the unfamiliar faces and growling, "Who are you?" To my surprise, it was Misty.

"Illis! Woah!" she screamed. "It's me and Fira."

I noticed the other figure poke her head out in hello.

"What are you guys–"

"What is *that*?" Elnora asked loudly. I noticed what she was pointing at. A small glowing orb was rolling around on the floor.

Misty looked uncomfortable and glanced at Fira. "Do you want to?"

"Do *I* want to?"

"Want to what?" I interrupted.

Fira held up her hands. "Can you just do it?"

"I don't want to!"

I took a deep breath, "Can one of you just explain what's going on before I change my mind about using this dagger?"

Fira blinked at me and Misty cleared her throat. "Well um, no need to sugarcoat it I guess. We think that magic is real, and that this–" she gestured to the object. "–is Hattie's power."

The room stayed quiet for a few seconds before Elnora burst out laughing. "This makes a lot less work for us."

Fira looked at me, confused. "What is she talking about?"

"We know that magic is real," I said shortly.

"You do?"

"Yes," Elnora replied. "Tulip told us. Well actually, anyone who can do magic is called a mythic, but there are four classes of mythics: Sunflower (kindness), Protea (bravery), Marigold (creativity), and Aster (wisdom). From what Illis has said, you seem like an Aster to me, Fira."

Fira's eyebrows raised. "Who are you again?"

"I think the better question is who is Tulip?" Misty asked.

"Queen Mariana's sister."

Fira and Misty looked at each other. "We have a lot to tell you." We sat down in a circle, and Fira began to talk, "We didn't stay in the kingdom as we were told. I think that much is obvious."

"Wait a minute *what*?" I said loudly, just realizing the gravity of the situation. "You left?"

"Let me finish," Fira sighed, exasperated. "We found a note in *The History of Peachtree Palace*. The note told us things of the future, what would happen if we didn't save Hattie. Hidden inside was a small box."

Misty sniffed. "The letter was written by Queen Mariana."

"And?" I started.

"Mariana's dead," Fira said. Tears formed at the corner of her eyes. "And I've been here reassuring Hattie that she would come back, that they would be a family again. But she's gone."

The shock hit me like a wave, and I stared fixedly at the wall. My only motherly figure was gone, forever. The only one who'd ever believed in me, loved me, and said that it was all right that I was different. My emotions were reaching a boiling point. Hattie was trapped, Queen Mariana was dead, we were stuck.

"There's no way out of this," I mumbled, not even sure if I'd said the words aloud.

Fira looked at me and stood up, her face a mask. "What did you say?" she sounded dangerously close to her breaking point as well.

"Calm down," Misty said in a low voice. "It's bad enough without us fighting among ourselves too."

Fira glanced at me for a second, then plopped back down to the floor, looking slightly annoyed, though I knew she was just upset.

I wondered how she'd felt, being there alone, and discovering that her queen was dead, all the time she had been convincing Hattie and herself that she wasn't.

"What was inside?" Elnora asked quietly. Her words brought us back to our senses. We all looked at her, confused and she raised her eyebrows. "The box."

Misty cleared her throat and said, "The Lost Key of Peachtree Palace."

I opened my mouth, then closed it again, not really sure what I was going to say.

"Legend says that the holder of the key will gain powers. I thought it was just created solely for the purpose of luring in young readers, catching their attention, and sending them on adventures. The trouble is that it's true. The key gave me powers."

Misty's hands fiddled in her lap. "Fira called me from my house, and we found a small area that the key fit into, unlocking a trapdoor. Then the key transformed into a ring," she said, pointing at Fira's hand. "The Adar."

"We went down and found the Waters of Peachtree, a secret civilization to protect the people in line for the throne. An old practice. We met Queen Mariana's only living relative, her younger sister, Rosie." Fira held up her finger to speak when Elnora started to interrupt. "She's just a year older than Hattie, but has never met her, for she was never allowed to leave. We traveled to a cave filled with paintings, and all the princesses were represented, like in a museum."

Misty jumped in, "We met Odelina."

"The one from the legends?" I asked.

"Yes, she helped us obtain Hattie's power. And here we are."

"What does the Adar do?" I asked.

"It grants the wearer knowledge," Fira said.

Misty corrected her. "Unlimited knowledge. Like, *all the knowledge in the universe* type knowledge. But it has to be unlocked, like a puzzle."

We sat in silence until Elnora brought up the disturbing question we were all thinking, "If Rosie is Queen Mariana's only living sibling, and she's in the Waters of Peachtree, then who's Tulip?"

Just then the door creaked open and Tulip walked inside, looking happy. "Ah, hello. I sensed that there were more than two in this room." She closed her eyes and her finger drifted toward Fira. "We have an Aster and a Sunflower." She glared at us, making my insides squirm with discomfort. I had to resist the urge to glare back. I wondered whether she knew what we had been discussing.

A knock came at the door and Arabella stepped inside. "It's time to go. We need to act now. They're planning to move Hattie tomorrow. I got the clearance badge so theoretically all we need to do is show it to the guards in front of her cell and they should let us pass."

I looked into Arabella's eyes, and I could almost see it reflected that she believed the same things we did.

I knew by the fierce look that she wasn't working for Maurelle.

My eyes wandered to Tulip, wondering who she really was, and what on earth she could want with Hattie.

28

Hattie

It felt like ages since Arabella had delivered the letter to me. I tried to comfort myself knowing that a slowing spell was currently working on me. But even though I knew that it was there, I couldn't help worrying that something had gone drastically wrong.

I knew that I had been left on my own with just my thoughts for company for far too long. My brain seemed to be folding in on itself, consuming me with ideas. It felt like I was going insane. I tried desperately to keep my head straight, but each "day" I felt myself slipping further down.

My door creaked open for what felt like the millionth time. There stood Arabella, wearing the same white dress as the last time I'd seen her. It was the first time I had seen her since the letter.

It felt like a kick to the gut.

It was still the same day.

My brain felt ready to explode. It felt like forever ago since I'd last seen her, at least a week. Yet here she was, the same day.

She walked quickly into the cell and grabbed my arm. "We've

been told to escort you to a new cell. No talking." She kept her grip firm, but I sensed the falseness of it. She led me through the door where three guards stood alert. I wondered how she had bypassed them. They wore helmets and armor, and began to walk behind us. The stature and stride of them looked vaguely familiar, but I could not place my finger on where I had seen them before.

As I was led through the base, I tried to ignore my feelings, but I longed to believe that I was being rescued.

The longer we walked, the more I realized how much I had missed seeing something different than the blank wall. The hallways were bare, but a welcome change to the same view I'd been trapped with.

Arabella was unreadable. Her grip had not strayed, and I struggled to see what she was thinking. She led me into a room, and the guards followed, the door closing and plunging us into darkness. The lights flickered on.

A young girl about my age with soft, upturned brown eyes and caramel hair stood with her finger on the light switch. "Bravo!" She clapped.

Circling me, the three guards pulled off their helmets, and it took me a minute to register that it was Illis, Misty, and Fira. Tears rushed to my eyes before I could stop them.

"You're here!" My voice cracked from lack of use.

They enveloped me in a warm hug, and I melted into it, trying not to let it bother me that Illis had stayed poised with her arms crossed, only giving me a small nod.

I was used to it by now. I knew she would come to me in her own time.

"Yes, we are," Fira said softly into my hair, her voice warm as a hearth.

When I finally pulled away, I remembered the girl at the light switch. "Who are you?"

She cleared her throat. "Elnora, my name is Elnora."

"Oh. Nice to finally meet you Elnora." Aware that Misty and Fira were behind me, I slowly rounded on them. "Wait a minute. Why are *you* here?"

They looked at each other.

"We may or may not have found a note that gave me the Lost Key of Peachtree Palace."

"What?"

Fira bit her lip and continued, "Then we may or may not have followed the note to a magical organization that hides descendants of the royal family, in case someone in Rolling Hills dies. And then we may or may not have found a secret cave, met Odelina from the legend, and found your power."

There was a beat of silence.

"And you were planning to tell me this *when?*" I shouted.

Fira bit her lip again. "Sometime," she crept.

"What about the kingdom?" I wailed.

There was silence, and I let out an exasperated shriek. "You left the kingdom unattended? GUYS!"

I started frantically pacing. "So magic is definitely real, the kingdom is unattended, there are eight million mysteries that need solving, and we're stuck in a secret base with people who want to kill us, and a powerful evil sorceress!"

"Yeah," Elnora sighed. "Yeah, that about sums up our situation."

"Oh my council is going to *kill me.*" I dragged a hand down my face.

"If Maurelle doesn't first," Arabella put in. We all turned to look at her and she shrugged. "What?"

"How did you even get me out?" I asked.

"I got us a clearance pass, then had Illis and Elnora dress up as guards. It was pretty easy. I just worked a little of my–" she flipped her hair and winked. "–charm."

"Who wrote the letter?" I demanded.

They exchanged uncomfortable glances.

"Who was it?" I repeated.

Illis cleared her throat and answered, "It was written by Queen Mariana. Your mother."

Thoughts of magic hadn't surprised me, but the mention of my mother sent my head spinning. I started to go faint, and Fira's hand dove to catch my head. "She's alive?"

"No."

I wasn't exactly sure who said it, but all of them looked scared.

"What? It can't be true," I whispered.

This time I saw Fira's mouth move, grief etched across her face, "She's dead. So is your father. She died on a mission four years ago. Her letter simply knew of the future."

"No, that can't be right," I said stupidly. "They must be alive." A weight settled in my heart. The answer to the question I had been forever asking was revealed. But I wasn't shocked. Not in my heart.

The tears fell and stained my clothes, but I wasn't shocked. Somewhere in me I had felt it. Four years ago.

I sat beside a tree, the beautiful pink blossoms rained around me.

I gazed at the sunrise, dawn cracking beyond the horizon. I stretched my eleven-year-old body, and snuggled into the grass.

My eyes closed and I fell deep into sleep.

I dreamed.

A dark cave.

My parents.

"Quickly, this way," my father cried, and I struggled to catch a glimpse of the oncoming conflict.

Fear weaved into my mother's eyes, and she began to run. But my mother was too slow, a blast of light flew toward her, and the room exploded. I awoke with a start.

My stomach was twisted into knots.
It was a dream, I thought, a dream.
But I felt emptiness in me that wasn't there before.

"Hattie," Misty's gentle voice cut through the pandemonium raging in my head. I felt her soft hand graze my arm and settle on my shoulder. "Oh, Hattie." Misty crouched down and hugged me tight.

I wiped my eyes on the sleeve of my uniform, trying to stop the tears. Fira came and stood beside Misty.

I heard Fira's voice. "I was here the whole time, promising you that they were alive. I'm. . . I'm so sorry."

Unaware of exactly what I was doing, I stood up, gulping for air, and wiped my face again. "So yeah, they're dead. My parents are gone." I took a deep breath. "But I don't think they would have wanted me to just give up. I believe they would have wanted me– wanted us– to go and defeat Maurelle."

My eyes panned the room. Arabella looked at the floor, hard and ready to face any challenge.

Misty sat beside me with a small smile on her face.

Illis stood stationary. I was unable to tell whether she was sad. She gave me a curt nod.

Fira's ginger hair stood out like fire against everything in the room and– I noted with a small wave of pride– she looked uncharacteristically brave.

Elnora was the only girl I didn't know, but she still looked at me with fierce determination. I was her princess, and she would fight for me.

For a moment at least I could forget about the impossible challenge, and let hope in. We were the perfect team.

For a moment at least, I could try to shove away the pain. I was the princess after all, it was my job. My mouth curved into a sly smile, as I spoke the storybook words I'd always wanted to. "Let's go get her."

29

Misty

"Wait!" Illis said sharply as Hattie walked toward the door, grabbing her shoulder.

"What?"

Fira stepped forward and said, "We need to give you something." In all the confusion, we had forgotten about Hattie's power. Elnora picked up the orb, and, softly, the scene started to replay again.

"What is that?" Hattie asked suspiciously.

"It's your power," Fira said softly. "You're a Marigold, the mythic class of creativity. You had your power ripped from you at a young age."

Hattie opened her mouth to speak, but I answered her question, "It was Maurelle. Maurelle stole it from you."

Instead of looking startled, Hattie almost looked relieved, "That's the orb from my dream," she said as she slowly reached out a hand, her eyes itching with temptation, but then halted. "Wait," she remembered, "In the dream there was a key. It fit into that hole." She pointed to a small opening.

Fira pulled the Adar from her hand, and in an instant it transformed into a key. "This, Hattie, is the Lost Key of Peachtree Palace."

Fira unlocked the orb, and the room brightened, light pouring from the slightly opened orb.

Hattie's eyes widened. "Can I hold it?" she asked.

Frowning, Arabella said, "So, the thing is, we aren't exactly sure what will happen if you do. You might die."

"I'm willing to risk it," Hattie snapped. But then she took a deep breath and said contritely, "I'm sorry."

Elnora raised her eyebrows, but Illis nodded and turned to Hattie. "All right, but if you start to act funny, we won't hesitate to rip it out of your hand and smash it on the floor." I almost laughed, but caught sight of Illis's serious expression and stopped.

Slowly extending her hand, Hattie touched the orb. Her other hand wrapped around it, and she held it close.

Instantly, her body started to glow. Her eyes closed, then snapped open, beams of light shooting out.

Wind soared through the room, knocking me over.

I shielded my eyes with my hand, and saw the others doing the same. Hattie began to talk, though I could barely hear her through the wind. "It is okay. I am all right."

"WHAT DO WE DO?" Illis screamed as Hattie rose into the air. She spun in fast circles, reminding me too much of Fira in the library.

I clutched my side and closed my eyes, remembering Illis telling me what Tulip had said. Everyone has some inkling of magic in them, even if it is small."

It didn't make perfect sense, but it was something significant. We needed to join our powers. "USE YOUR POWER! QUICKLY JOIN THEM ALL TOGETHER!" I shouted.

I closed my eyes and concentrated on what was inside me.

At first there was nothing there, but suddenly a pulsing energy came from Hattie's direction, syncing with my heartbeat.

A trickle of water fell from my hand, but the stream quickened, and my hand was now shooting a jet of water.

Half of me wanted to dance in joy and the other half wanted to scream and run away from the fact that there was *magic coming out of me.*

I quickly realized there was no time for either as the water pooled around my feet and leaked inside one of my shoes.

I looked around frantically, having no idea what to do with my hand now gushing water, but the same pulsing energy wrapped around it like invisible fingers and pointed it to the center.

I noticed Elnora aiming her lights in the same direction.

Flames roared, and I saw Fira twisting her hands and conjuring fire.

Arabella's hands shot what looked like small shards of glass that danced around, reflecting Elnora's light.

Illis closed her eyes, and rapid-fire memories shot through my brain of Liam hugging me, meeting Hattie, my parents, home, safe.

All at once the world exploded. The lights were blinding.

And then abruptly everything went still.

* * *

All I saw was white, everywhere. That was the first thing I could notice.

I glanced around and saw the others in a state of wonderment as well.

One woman sat in the center of the whiteness, with no visible walls. Or it would have been the center if there were one. Or she would have been sitting if there were a solid chair. And there very well could have been walls, but we had no way of grasping the sense.

"Hello," she said, looking at each of us in turn. "Arabella Bolour, Elnora Dafen, Illis Mirai, Fira Pele, Misty Baker, and, of course, Princess Hattie Hills."

"Where are we?" Hattie asked, and the panic in her voice sent a wave of sympathy washing through me.

I couldn't imagine what was raging in Hattie's head. She had been rescued only to find out that her parents were dead, been forced to learn about mythics and stupid journeys we technically weren't supposed to be on, been given a powerful orb, and been infused with a power that was unfamiliar yet solely hers.

The woman's voice was smooth as butter. "You are in a place." I rolled my eyes. Of course we were in a place. "It is a bit beyond the reaches of your normal lives. It is not exactly real, but not exactly fake. Meaning to say that you are not dreaming, but you are not awake." She smiled.

"Of course. That makes total sense. I completely understand now," Elnora said, her tone telling me that I wasn't the only one with a couple of questions.

"Well then, I've done my job." The woman stood and began to walk away.

Elnora groaned, "Fine, fine, wait." The woman turned around. "Who are you, and what are we doing here?"

"I bear no name. I am simply the Guardian of the Place That is Not Real or Fake. As for why you are here, well, I assume you want answers."

Hattie nodded her head vigorously.

"Well, ask away then," said the Guardian of the Place That is not Real or Fake.

I started to talk, "You mean we can just–"

"Ask any question you want," she finished kindly.

Hattie was the first to speak, "What are the mythic classes?"

"The mythic classes are the four categories under which all the mythics of Mytheria's magic falls under: Sunflower, Protea, Marigold, or Aster. Everyone has some inkling of magic in them even if it is . . ."

"Very small," I finished.

"Correct. You see, the classes were created long ago by some unknown name. Although only the Legendary Powers have been passed down, they still remain somewhat the same throughout history."

"What are they?" I asked. "The powers, I mean."

The woman clasped her hands. "Two of them are here, I believe. The Adar–" Fira looked at her ring. "–or as it has lately become known, the Lost Key of Peachtree Palace. And the power inside Hattie. Some of it is always alive in every Hills ruler, which is probably how you ended up here. Only a very powerful magic force could have brought you. And the Hills' power works almost as an amplifier of sorts. It can make the people around you stronger."

"So that was the pulsing? That's how we were able to use our powers?" Fira asked, and I was glad I wasn't the only one who'd felt the energy.

"And it brought you here," confirmed the Guardian of the Place That is Not Real or Fake.

"What does Maurelle want?" Arabella asked, staring at the ground.

"Inclusion," the guardian replied. "By no means am I saying that what she is doing is right. And her story of being an outcast isn't what it seems. She could have handled this situation in many different ways, none of them resulting in this. But I cannot help but wonder how things might have been different had some of the Hills's princesses not ignored their mythic abilities and rejected it from their lives, outcasting those with abilities."

"I have one more question," Illis uttered, the first words since we'd arrived in this weird limbo. "Who is Tulip Hills?"

The Guardian of the Place That is Not Real or Fake screwed up her face in concentration, and it looked as though she genuinely had no idea what we were talking about. "I know everything about the Hills family, and to my knowledge, there is no such person as Tulip Hills."

Arabella looked down, and I knew that she had looked up to Tulip, even idolized her. She was an illusion, no more real than swiping a hand through Elnora's light.

All of us exchanged glances, but Arabella's eyes remained down. "Thank you," Illis said.

The world exploded once more. The face of the Guardian of the Place That is Not Real or Rake disappeared, and we flew through the space of white.

We landed with a thump on the floor

I didn't dare look at anyone.

I heard someone get up, and Arabella shuffled away, all of her witty retorts gone.

The information we had obtained was beyond anything I had expected.

Our only ally in this place was an imposter.

30

Fira

My brain was swimming with questions, all of which made no sense. "What do we do now?"

Hattie looked up and answered with costumed conviction. "We'll defeat her, just like we said we would."

I tried, but I couldn't ignore the hint of hurt laced into every word.

"Easier said than done," Arabella muttered.

Illis stood up first. "We need to get our supplies and get out of this place before Tulip gets back."

"Yeah," I said, joining her and getting on my feet. "What do we need?"

"An army that we don't have," Arabella said. "Ooh! Maybe, like, a cannon would be nice."

"Well," Hattie said, looking thoughtful. "I doubt it will take them long to realize I am the princess, but we might as well try to stay undercover for as long as possible. In shorter words, I need something different to wear. Walking around like a prisoner will only draw more attention to me, and therefore to you."

"Good idea," I said. I found a cabinet with a white shirt embroidered with a black unicorn and turned away as Hattie slipped it on. "There. Now you don't look so much like you just escaped from a literal prison cell."

Hattie looked down. "Perfect."

Elnora walked toward the back of the room. She stopped short at a different cabinet. The drawer was unlocked, and she slid it open to reveal a stash of badges. They looked similar to the ones that they already wore– Illis and Arabella's purple, Elnora's yellow– but they were also in pink and blue. She took out three: pink, blue, and yellow.

Elnora cleared her throat and pinned the badges on in a faux announcer voice, "Misty, Sunflower."

She pinned the blue one on me, "Fira, Aster." And lastly she pinned the Marigold one perfectly onto Hattie's new top. I studied my badge, running my finger along the word inscribed onto it, *Aster*. The entire thing felt right somehow.

Only minutes later, we left the safety of the room, though how safe the room was to begin with was debatable.

We moved through the halls silently but confidently, giving the guards no reason to suspect us.

Arabella led, making sure that her lanyard with the image of the Dark Unicorn was displayed prominently on her chest.

We neared the door behind which Maurelle would be. A guard stopped us, his helmet emotionless. "Identification, please."

Arabella held out her lanyard., "Dark Unicorn, three-year member, Section 11, Sector B's Force Captain."

"Arabella Bolour, you may pass. As for the others, identification, please."

"I vouch for them," Arabella interjected.

"You will need more than a vouch. Identification, please," repeated the guard.

Illis cracked her knuckles. "Here's my identification." Her hand met his jaw, and he slouched to the ground.

Hattie had a look of obvious shock. "Where did that come from?"

Illis shrugged and rolled back her shoulder. "Training."

The door was unlocked, and Hattie opened it with ease.

Inside was what could only be described as a room of death: a black bed with a black canopy, black carpets and black walls.

The only natural light came from a window in the back of the room that overlooked a field of withered grass, the yellow blades bent over in subjugation.

Maurelle sat on a small black seat. Her hair was twisted into a braided crown above her head. She wore a midnight dress that only further accentuated her too-pale skin.

"Welcome," she said, extending an inviting hand. "I have been expecting you."

I shuddered involuntarily. The energy Maurelle put off was like a graveyard.

She took our silence as an invitation to continue talking. "You know, Pompy, my sidekick, if you will, informed me a month ago that we would capture the princess and hold her captive, but that someone would try to stop us." She pouted her lips, which were stained charcoal. "I think we found them, don't you?" Her eyes traced the room. "He looked into the pool of dreams, which is no longer the property of Rolling Hills, if I am at all correct. I believe you'll remember it, Hattie. The small tub full of that liquid that can help you predict the future. It was in your parents' bedroom. It used to be a lovely soft rainbow. Now it settles more in the vantablack range."

"Whatever you want from us, we're not going to give it to you," Arabella said bravely from behind me.

"Ah, Arabella, I didn't see you there. Yes, I am afraid that you've, how do they say it? Oh yes. *Gone sour*," Maurelle sneered, her lips curling. "Did you discover that your precious Tulip was not in fact Queen Mariana's sister? She is working for me, you fool!"

Arabella's eyes filled with tears and I could see how angry it made her that they were even there as she swiped at her eyes.

Hattie stood by her, a hand on her shoulder. Illis stood in a ready position.

"Oh, I've got you all in the same place, haven't I? The—"

She clamped a hand over her mouth, trying to detract from whatever she was about to say by flicking her hand up and down to transform her outfit. Her short dress twisted around her and became tight pants and a fitted shirt embellished with the faint outline of a unicorn.

A black cape seemed to grow from her back and she took a slow step forward. "Unfortunately for you, I don't think I can allow you to get away just yet."

She swiped her hand viciously, and a jet of blackness shot out toward Hattie.

The air instantly filled with screams, and Illis unsheathed her dagger.

She struck at Maurelle who dodged the jabs with a bloodcurdling laugh that sent electric currents up my spine.

I tried to find a calm moment in the pandemonium. I stared at my hands intently. "Come on," I muttered.

They flashed red, then died.

I gave an exasperated yell. I was aware that around me everyone else was trying to use their power, but the only ones successfully doing so were Hattie, Elnora, and Arabella.

Arabella's face was streaked with tears as she continuously thrust her hand forward, unleashing the small glass shards.

Hattie was destroying the room with her power.

A glow surrounded her whole body as she walked. Maurelle shot another shadow toward her, but Hattie deflected it with a swipe of her hand.

Hattie's voice was deathly quiet. "You are going to regret that."

Suddenly the pulsing started again, moving faster and faster as Hattie began to glow brighter. One last time, I poured all my energy into my hands, hoping that it would work. I felt hot and I looked down– fire was roaring.

I danced in a circle. "YES!"

The glass window behind Maurelle shattered, and she took the opportunity to step onto the ledge.

I realized what was happening a split second too late and shouted, "No!" She dropped back through it, a smile on her face.

Hattie's features were horrified as we rushed toward the window. Maurelle spun in the air, turned in on herself, and began to fly back upward.

Her twisted smile stared into my soul. "What do we do?" I screamed, but Hattie already had an answer.

She lifted herself onto the sill, and Illis tried, to no avail, to pull her down, but Hattie looked at her and pleaded, "Please let me do this, Illis. I can probably catch myself with my magic."

Illis mumbled, "Probably." I saw she recognized something different in Hattie's eyes, and her hand lowered away from Hattie's arm. "Okay, but all of us have to come."

Hattie looked confused and said, "Alright!" But then yelled into the air. "SOMEONE COME HELP US! WE NEED YOU!"

It was stupid of course. No one was coming to help us, but I still crossed my fingers behind my back and threw out a silent plea of my own. I was terrified. We were no match for Maurelle's powers.

Just when I was about to ask what to do, the floor rumbled.

From the trees at the barrier of the compound, four people were running.

A kaleidoscope of rainbow colors seemed to be flying across the world as they used their powers. In the distance I saw a train of flowers approaching, drawing nearer to the window. On top of the train was a person who couldn't realistically be there, unless . . .

Dirty blonde hair sat in messy curls down her back, and a dark pink dress showed off her flawless shape. Her dark skin gleamed in the sunlight. Her voice rang out like a sweet bell in the morning, as her brown sandals touched the sill next to Hattie. "Hey, Fira, I've missed you."

She was right in front of me. It was the friend who sent me letters, the one who I thought would never come back.

It was Cherry.

31

Illis

Fira's jaw dropped, and she began to cry.

I desperately wanted to remind her that we needed to concentrate and find Maurelle, but as the girl hopped down and hugged her, I realized that my efforts would be pointless.

"Oh my goodness, Cherry, it's you," Fira sobbed. "Where have you been?"

"I've wanted so badly to tell you," Cherry said, but she seemed to get distracted as she turned toward Hattie, pointing at her badge. "A fellow Marigold. I'm a Marigold too. I can manipulate plants actually." She twirled her hands and pink flowers twisted around Hattie's wrists in a bracelet. "Oh, I must introduce myself. I'm Cherry Zara, Fira's best friend, or at least I hope. You must be Princess Hattie. Oh my goodness, I've waited years to meet you. A shame that it had to be under these circumstances."

"Yes, nice to meet you," Hattie leered in uncertainty.

"Oh, I won't bite," Cherry replied sweetly. "I know you're strong enough to defeat Maurelle, you just need to believe in yourself too."

Fira pinched the bridge of her nose. "Cherry is a bit of an optimist. . . obviously."

"Okay nice reunion," I intervened. "But who are those people outside, and are they here to help?"

Cherry twirled around smiling, "Of course, silly! We are the Waters of Peachtree. We've sent a team to help you." She looked at the ground. "I hope you don't mind."

"You've been at the Waters of Peachtree this whole time," Fira's voice cut in. The sentence was stained with hurt and something that sounded almost like anger as she rounded on Cherry.

"I'm sorry Fira, truly," Cherry's eyes searched her face, almost begging her to understand, "I asked everyday to tell you, but they said I couldn't. It was too dangerous."

"You've been so *close* the whole time," Fira's voice cracked and I turned away, feeling like I was witnessing something private.

Arabella cleared her throat. "As lovely as this is, we're kind of in the middle of trying to defeat an ancient evil magic lady, and I daresay Maurelle is going to wait for us to catch up."

As if to prove her point, a small group of soldiers came thundering out of the woods on the opposite end, all wearing the Dark Unicorn on their chests.

"Oh, here they come," Cherry said happily. And without another word, she climbed onto the window and jumped out.

We rushed to the side to see her safe on the ground, sprinting toward the small group of soldiers.

Fira rolled her eyes. "Let's go."

The others barely hesitated to climb up, but I stopped short.

This would be my first time ever actually fighting since my training. Protecting Hattie at all costs was my job but now that it was here, it almost felt impossible.

What if I wasn't ready?

The idea rocked in my chest, unlike anything I'd felt before.

A soft hand on my shoulder brought me away from my thoughts.

Elnora's worried eyes were searching my face and I gulped, shaking my head to clear my thoughts.

The girls stood on the sill, ready to jump.

"Come on, Illis!"

My heart thumped in my chest, and I feared that the others would hear it beating loudly in the room.

Fear of heights had always been the one thing that frightened me out of my senses. My brain whirred into a panic, and my eyes fell upon the ground far below.

I gulped down my fear, and my gaze settled on Hattie's determined face, something in it I had never seen before. It gave me courage.

"On the count of three," she instructed. "Three, two . . ."

Whether she ever said the last word, I never knew, and I stepped off the ledge, my eyes squeezed shut on themselves.

Cries echoed into the air.

My feet thudded on the ground, cushioned by Misty's jet of water from above, and surprisingly my boots stayed dry. I nodded at her, noting that she was still atop, looking scared.

Unsheathing my dagger, I ran forward.

A crowd of Dark Unicorn workers had gathered around the doors at the bottom of the fortress, all looking as terrified as I felt.

"I'm going to find Maurelle!" Hattie shouted.

"Hattie wait!" I yelled, starting to panic, but her face was cut off from my vision as I got swallowed by the crowd.

No one tried to stop me as I pushed through the people, finally making my way to the edge of the mob, and onto the field.

I spotted Hattie following Maurelle, and instantly I began to shake with anger and run after her.

It had only been a minute, and I was already failing to protect her.

The battle twisted around me in a swirl of panic.

I finally reached the center, where Elnora and Arabella were holding their own against Dark Unicorn soldiers.

I quickly took in the gravity of the situation, my eyes tracing hurriedly over the people.

There were fifteen trained Dark Unicorn fighters, and only nine of us– considering Misty was nowhere to be seen– untrained, un-helpful.

We were outnumbered, and all I could do was hope that The Waters of Peachtree knew what they were doing.

I let my senses take over, feeling my brain switch onto autopilot as a Dark Unicorn soldier ran over to me.

Just like in my training, I thought desperately, except that this time it is a do-or-die situation. No big deal.

I threw up my dagger to meet theirs, the clang of metal ringing in my ears.

I clenched my jaw and pushed forward, twisting the dagger and preparing to sink it into their stomach.

My vision narrowed until I could see the exact spot to strike, but I stopped.

This was a person. A real human person, and I was about to kill them.

Apparently they didn't think the same, swiping their blade before I had time to react.

I was frozen, and it seemed to go in slow motion as the dagger neared my side. Abruptly, in the middle of my thoughts, a body crashed into me, sending me and the soldier flying onto the ground.

Sitting up brought me the sight of a panting Hattie. Her hands were glowing. "Hi!" she exhaled.

"Hattie," I breathed. "You're okay."

"Of course I am," she attempted to smile but she looked drained.

I could not help but feel that she was lying, but I stood up next to her anyway, laying a protective hand on her shoulder, "I'm going to protect you Hattie, I promise."

For a second it looked like she might cry, but instead guilt flooded her features. "I'm sorry Illis."

The world was dimming at the edges, and I felt very groggy, my muscles sluggish. "What did you do?" I whispered.

"It'll only last a minute," Hattie said quietly. "But I can't let you get hurt."

She grabbed my arm and practically tossed me to the edge of the battlefield, my limp body hitting the ground with a thud.

I watched as she let a stray tear out of her eye, and ran after Maurelle again.

I shook my head in disbelief. How, after so many years, could she come perfectly back to her power?

But she plunged forward ahead.

I tried to lift my arm, and felt a strange tingling spread over my whole body.

Slowly, it began to move and I let out a small laugh, trying to think of exactly all the ways I could punish Hattie for hurting me.

The rest of my body was paralyzed.

I'd thought I was ready for this, but maybe I wasn't.

Maybe my parents had been right about me.

No.

That was the thought that snapped me out of my head.

No. I'm not what my parents say I am. I'm not a monster. I'm not weak. I'm not useless.

Pull yourself together, I thought, shutting my eyes and pinching the bridge of my nose. You are Illis, you can accomplish anything.

Behind my lids, my hands curled around the hilt of my sword. I reached inside me for my magic, feeling it build up to an explosion of potential energy.

My eyes snapped open, and I let out a sly smile before running forward.

A Dark Unicorn soldier raced toward me, and I death-gripped my hilt.

He swung down, and I threw my dagger up to meet his, my teeth clenching at the effort, a metallic taste filling my mouth. I ducked and swung around, catching the side of his leg.

He staggered but regained his balance, diving forward and swinging his sword sideways.

Time slowed down, and I saw his sword in a perfect position to connect with my neck.

Time sped up again, and I ducked down in the nick of time, feeling a swoosh as the sword passed within mere inches of my head.

My feet slipped, and I fell onto my back. He advanced toward me, and I realized my only option for escape.

I tried to look scared, and took a deep breath as he raised his sword.

On the downswing, I rolled out of the way and delivered a blow to his leg, knocking him down. He hit his head and passed out, and I sprinted away from him, holding my dagger ready for the next challenger.

32

Misty

My breathing was heavy, my heart panicked. My feet were only inches away from falling into the oblivion of the battlefield below.

I shut my eyes, but, even still, the shouting surrounded me, threatening to swallow me whole.

Everyone had already jumped, and I was the only one left on the sill. I tried to muster some courage, but I failed repeatedly.

I heard a banging on the door behind me, and I whipped around, snapping my eyes open.

"Open up!" Guards slapped fists against the cold metal.

"Dark Unicorn!" A furor of voices signalled the arrival of more guards.

"Hello?"

"Anyone in there?"

"We are here to place you under arrest."

I did my best impression of Maurelle's smooth voice, nervously quivering. "All is fine. Report back to your stations, the battle has commenced."

"Does that sound like her?" The guards voiced suspicion.

"No, I don't think so," came a wary response.

As the fear that knotted inside me unraveled, I stepped off the ledge and plunged into the crowd that had gathered below.

My heart pounded in my throat. I stopped myself with a cushion of water, just as I had for the others.

My feet hit the ground, and I looked around, not missing the way that the crowd screamed as I dropped down.

People's faces painted themselves into my memories. They watched helplessly as my friends fought the Dark Unicorn soldiers in the field.

I rushed forward, my eyes squeezed shut.

I ran toward the battle, determined to be brave.

But I quickly redirected myself to the edge of the field, and I crouched behind a tree, hugging my knees in an unbreakable knot.

My eyes flooded with tears that plopped onto my lap.

I was scared.

Purely terrified.

I had never felt so scared in my life.

Not when my brother died.

Not when my parents moved.

Not when I learned about magic.

Not when Hattie left.

No, I was scared now. Because I felt helpless and utterly alone.

I felt a hand on my shoulder, and a pink dress flashed into view.

"Hello, Misty. It's me, Cherry. You don't know me really." Cherry knelt before me, the picture-perfect image Fira had always described her to be.

I began to cry again, and her soft hand brushed my face. "Shh. Don't cry, Misty. It is all going to be okay. Come on now." She twisted her hands, and a flower chain wrapped around mynecke. She stood up and offered me her hand, "Here."

I took her hand. "Why are you helping me?"

"Because any friend of Fira's is a friend of mine," she said with a smile. "Now dry those tears. We have a battle to win."

I felt childish standing there, her hand in mine, her comforting me when she could have been serving our mission. But I accepted her help.

It was a nice gesture and though it didn't stop it, the fear inside me calmed a little.

I put on a brave face and gave her hand another squeeze. "I'm ready."

"I knew you would be."

She ran forward back into the battle, and I barely hesitated to join her.

I looked around and saw four passed out soldiers, but still eleven standing.

"MAURELLE!"

I heard the scream over the din of battle, Hattie's voice like a knife.

All noise ceased to exist, and an eerie silence crept over the field.

A single word had created pure silence among a crowd of hundreds.

"Yes?" Maurelle drawled.

I finally spotted them, both in the very center, circling each other. Hattie's face was hard and determined, while Maurelle simply looked bored.

"What do you want, *Princess* Hattie?"

"I want you to tell your people what you've done!"

She laughed sharply. "What *I've* done. It seems that your blame is clearly in the wrong place."

Hattie's mask broke for a small second, but it was enough to move her to ask. "What do you mean?"

"Oh, you'll see." Maurelle laughed again, the sound sending a shiver up my spine.

I watched alongside everyone else as a new battle unfolded. Hattie leapt toward Maurelle, her hands bright as light blasted out and conflicting with Maurelle's exploding black balls of power.

Hattie's face grew redder in a more concentrated effort, whereas Maurelle's still wore a bored look.

Hattie dove repeatedly, but Maurelle just dodged her moves, laughing as Hattie failed. "Is that the best you can do?"

I covered my mouth with my hand, and an audible gasp escaped me as I realized that Hattie was going to drain herself in the effort to beat Maurelle.

They jumped toward each other again, blasting backward from the collision of their power jets still streaming at a constant rate.

Maurelle let out a quick scream, her face finally showing evidence of fright. As soon as I saw it, it was gone, and she looked at Hattie again with the same coldness, hissing, "You mess with me, there will be consequences." She glanced at her nails with a small smile.

Hattie looked close to boiling over. Her fists clenched and unclenched at her sides. She opened her mouth and closed it again.

Maurelle smiled one last time, and cackling in a mocking tone, she jerked around and began to fly toward the woods.

"GET BACK HERE, MAURELLE," Hattie yelled. Her voice was stained red with anger. "COWARD!"

Illis ran to restrain Hattie. Sure enough, Hattie instantly began to chase Maurelle. Illis's face looked strained as I watched Hattie struggle from afar.

Hattie sunk to the ground.

I ran toward her, noting how the battle appeared to have ceased around me. The remaining eleven soldiers rushed and disappeared into the crowd.

I enveloped Hattie in a hug, and she leaned heavily into my shoulder, saying in frustration, "We have to get her. We have to. We have to. We have to."

"I know," I whispered, trying to inject as much courage into my voice as I could. "We will. I promise we will. We just need a moment to calm down first."

She continued to depend on my shoulder, and I felt something that scared me even more . . . Hattie felt drained.

I continued to hug her lightly, but she felt so weak I was afraid even that might break her.

I looked toward the woods. Maurelle had disappeared into them, leaving no trace.

33

Illis

My eyes stayed trained on Hattie. She was devastated by the loss to Maurelle.

I could still hear Misty's voice comforting her, "There was nothing you could have done. Let's go. We have a lot to talk about."

Misty was certainly right.

The four people– including Cherry– who had helped us were advancing toward the center of the field where we were sitting.

Cherry wandered over to Fira and stood firmly beside her, engaged in deep conversation.

Some part of me was still trying to figure out how the Waters of Peachtree had found us so quickly, but the other part had the sense to stand up and give a curt head nod to the person who looked like the leader.

A woman with mocha skin, of no more than thirty, stepped forward to address the crowd. Her eyes were strong and determined.

"Greetings," her voice boomed across the field. "My name is General Ota, the only commander of the Waters of Peachtree's magical organization present here today."

I saw Hattie straighten up, and Misty did the same. Hattie spoke out, "My name is Princess Hattie Hills of Rolling Hills. I must insist we begin forming a plan soon, or else Maurelle might wander too far into the woods for us to catch."

General Ota smiled. "I admire your authority, sincerely." Hattie blushed. "But I think it may take more than just a plan to stop Maurelle, if you don't mind my saying."

"Of course not," Hattie rushed.

"Well then, if I may suggest, I need a bit of help cleaning up these materials before we send all of us out to get her. We can also call for backup."

Hattie ran over to General Ota and began to help her.

The sun beat down on us with the weight of heavy boulders.

My neck prickled, and I had the strange sense that someone was watching me. I spun quickly around, the speed knocking me off my feet. I scrambled back up, earning a few confused looks from the people around me, but I ignored them.

I looked around, but there was no one there. My ears picked up the sound of laughter coming from the woods, and I turned in time to see a flash at the edge.

Checking to see that nobody was looking, I sprinted over to the woods and hid behind a rock. Unobserved, I let out a sigh of relief.

Everyone was chatting away easily, not a single face showing signs of doubt, or the feeling of being watched, except one, Hattie.

Her body fidgeted as she lifted the materials. General Ota looked at her, and Hattie faked a smile, something only a few would be able to recognize.

As soon as General Ota turned her back, Hattie looked anxiously around.

Her eyes landed on me with an intense look of terror.

I was confused, but a closer look told me that she was staring at something behind me.

The feeling increased, and I spun around. I felt it. It was hotter in this direction. I looked upward.

Maurelle was floating above the trees, wearing a smile of pure evil. Her eyes were locked on Hattie, and I prayed Maurelle had not discovered me yet.

She cackled again before ducking back into the trees.

My heart pounded loudly in my chest, a steady beat.

I sprinted back to the camp, my legs in time with the beating of my heart. The heat was increasing as my face struggled to keep itself composed.

I stopped short at General Ota and Hattie, who were talking about plans.

My panting was beyond my control, and I stayed crouched over my knees, barely squeezing words out in between gasps. "Maurelle. Trees. Change. Plans. She. Heard. Everything."

Sharing a look of shock with Hattie, General Ota said in confidence, "Impossible! We have just had many spells placed around this facility."

Hattie kicked a stone.

I looked at her, raising my eyebrows heavily as a sign to ask her to tell.

Hattie recognized the look and cleared her throat. "She was there, General Ota."

General Ota's look of shock was more prominent this time. "What?"

"She was there. Just above the trees." Hattie pointed to where Maurelle had been floating.

"How–" General Ota stammered. "We must continue as planned," she said firmly.

"What?" Hattie's voice acted in unison to mine. My breath had finally returned, and I straightened up.

"I'm afraid there is no other way, Hattie." The general looked pointedly at her, saying, "You know this to be true, deep down. We will increase protection and forces–"

What did she mean that she *knew deep down*? I was about to interrupt when Hattie quietly said, "That won't be necessary,"

Now it was my turn to look shocked. "Hattie, you can't be serious. You need the extra protection, more than just us."

"No, I don't. The seven of us will be enough." Hattie met my gaze, "She'll just wipe the floor with us if there's too many, Illis."

"Hattie. . ."

"No Illis, it has to." She took a deep breath. "It has to be just me."

General Ota gave me a grave look before turning to the crowd of people, declaring, "We must prepare to venture into the woods. Princess Hattie, Illis, Fira, Misty, Arabella, Elnora, and Cherry will go in. Our job is to create pandemonium toward the other side, forcing the enemy to retreat."

One glance showed me that Dark Unicorn forces were still huddled about the castle edges, waiting for someone to strike.

"Is that understood?" General Ota boomed.

There was a murmur of reply.

"Is that UNDERSTOOD?"

In response, a stronger *yes* echoed across the field.

General Ota smiled thinly.

The seven of us lined up together, and General Ota said, "Good luck. We will be hoping for you."

I noticed that everyone looked a little nervous.

I took in a deep breath, letting my nerves melt away.

We began to walk toward the woods.

34

Fira

General Ota's voice followed us to the edge of the forest. "Be very careful. The woods can be a dangerous place."

I looked back in time to see her open her mouth to say more, but her words were inaudible as we got swallowed by the trees.

Confusion rattled in my brain, making it impossible to think. My heart pounded in my chest.

The woods can be a dangerous place. General Ota's words reverberated back to me as I thought, nothing in these woods was dangerous except for Maurelle, and she was Danger with a capital D.

Without having to look, I felt Cherry appear next to me, for no one carried such an energetic stride. She looked upward at my face.

So the group ahead of us wouldn't hear, she asked me quietly, "Are you all right, Fira?"

My stomach clenched with fear.

"I'm fine," I replied roughly, almost tripping over a root, yelping in the process.

"Well, you don't look fine." Her matter-of-fact tone was annoying, but I enjoyed it. It was the voice I hadn't heard for so long, the one I'd so dearly missed.

I stopped and put a hand on her shoulder, looking her in the eye. "I'm fine, Cherry. I'm just shocked to see you."

Her face dropped a little at my words. "You really thought I was never coming back, didn't you?"

I struggled to answer. Of course I had hoped that she would come back to Rolling Hills, but had I ever really believed that she would return? That things could just go back to normal?

Her smile dropped more when she saw the pained expression on my face.

"I knew you would come back," I answered quickly, but she didn't hear me.

Cherry looked away, tears in her eyes, with no sign of her former optimism. "I tried, you know. To tell you. Where I was, what I was doing. I asked every day, hoping the answer would be different, but it never was. Always the same. 'The answer is the same as yesterday, Cherry. You may not tell Fira where you are and what you are doing.' I tried, Fira!" She looked at me desperately. "But they always said no."

I hugged her fiercely. "I have missed you *so* much." I brushed the hair out of her face. "It's going to be okay." I clapped her lightly on the back. "Also, your magic is awesome."

She laughed in relief, the light back in her eyes. "Thanks."

"I've missed you so much, Cherry," I smiled.

She beamed. "I know."

"So, anyway, what were you doing for the Waters of Peachtree? You were gone for so long, Cherry."

Her grin faltered. "Well, I was, you know, helping people, and doing things. Front lines, training, and all that."

I had the feeling that she wasn't being up front with me. "Training for what?" I asked.

She sighed. "Magic, combat. We were taught normal things too, like language, and math, but they were never as fun. And our trips, oh Fira, you would have loved the places we traveled. And our battles . . ."

"Battles?" But pushing through our conversation was an argument from the front.

Elnora's voice was the loudest. "When are we getting to the other side?" she said, sounding more than a little agitated.

"You know," Arabella said coolly. "Maybe if you stopped asking, the time would go quicker."

"Stop being so straightforward," Elnora complained.

Arabella raised her eyebrows. "Stop being so annoying."

I had to resist the urge to burst out laughing, but Elnora turned toward me.

"Fira," she complained, and I was surprised she even remembered my name. "Please figure out how to get us to wherever we're going. I hate the woods. Besides, I heard you're the smart one."

I narrowed my eyes at Illis, who threw up her hands in surrender, but inside I was dying with laughter. "Fine," I clipped.

I spied a tree near me with several branches sticking out. I leapt and grabbed at them, not realizing how sharp they were, and cut both hands.

"Ow!"

I heard Elnora's laughter below. "You asked for it."

I narrowed my eyes, peering at the length of the forest, and noticed something odd. It was a circle.

But I decided to ignore it and focus on the obvious– that if we kept prodding along as slowly as we were now, it would take us hours to cross the forest.

I called down to them, "At our current pace it will take us forever to get to the center, so we will have to move quicker than this."

Elnora made a strangled noise from the back of her throat. "Why?"

I rolled my eyes in the tree so she couldn't see. How stupid could one person get?

I jumped down from the tree and landed with a thump on the ground. Cherry picked leaves out of my hair as I continued to walk.

Though Elnora had complained before, she now plodded along beside me in begrudging silence.

I couldn't help it as the corners of my mouth twitched, forming a rough smile.

"Stay on guard." Illis's voice from the front brought us all out of our heads and back into the forest. The air felt heavier around me, and the sky darkened. The old trees creaked with age.

Illis whipped around, checking that we were okay.

But my head was beginning to hurt in the way it did just before receiving a message from the Adar.

Cherry barely had time to whisper, "You're glowing."

Before I exploded with pain. It was a good ache, like the kind when I would cry until there wasn't anything left.

Words clouded my vision, and the same voice appeared, reading them to me.

Danger ahead.

35

Misty

I heard a gasp from behind me, and we all spun around to see Fira glowing, her head in her hands.

I rushed over to ask, "Fira, Fira, what did the Adar tell you?"

She looked up, and the glow subsided. Cherry was still panicking about the act of Fira glowing, but I focused on Fira's face. It was an expression that somebody like her didn't wear for fun. She looked sick.

Insistently, I repeated my question, "Fira, what did the Adar tell you?"

She gulped so loudly that everyone could hear. "It said," her voice wavered into a whisper. "Danger ahead."

We all held our breath, and I heard a collective sigh from everyone.

"Um, no duh," Arabella said. "We're literally walking toward the person who's been trying to kill Hattie for the past week."

"She's right, Fira," Illis agreed. "I'm sure the Adar wanted to warn you about Maurelle, that's all."

I saw the nodding of heads, but Fira's violently shook.

She inhaled. "It wasn't talking about Maurelle."

"How do you know?" I asked frantically.

"The Adar knows everything that goes on inside my brain, whether I like it or not. I did that to myself when I picked up the key."

The same prickly feeling crawled through my stomach, but I pushed it down.

"So . . ." Arabella gestured for her to finish.

"*So,* it doesn't need to warn me that we're approaching Maurelle. I already know that. Each time the Adar has told me something, it's because I *unlocked* something new, *new* being the most important word. It wouldn't tell me something I already know. It's not talking about Maurelle. Right now, we have something else to deal with."

"Well, crap," Elnora said. "What do we do?"

"I don't know!" Fira yelled. She recollected herself. "I'm sorry. I don't know. I just think for now we should just keep walking. This whole forest is a circle, and from what I could see in the tree, we're headed toward the center. That's where Maurelle is."

I got to my feet reluctantly, and stuck out a hand to Fira. She squeezed it tightly and threw me a nervous look as she stood.

Cherry instantly crowded Fira. "Are you okay?" she asked, obvious worry creeping into all her features.

Fira hesitated, but she nodded. "It only hurts a bit."

Cherry saw straight through it. "So pain is your price for knowledge? That seems unfair."

"It's not. And I swear it only hurts when I'm receiving the message. And besides, it's not the kind of pain you're thinking of at all."

"Promise?"

"Well, I can't really explain it, I mean, it's all very new."

Cherry rolled her eyes. "Fine."

"Ahem." Arabella cleared her throat. "We need to get moving ASAP. Maurelle won't wait around for too long."

"Great idea!" Hattie exclaimed, taking the lead.

I glanced back at Fira who dipped her chin and followed Hattie.

There was nothing out of the ordinary about the forest. I didn't see what could be so dangerous that the Adar had thought to warn Fira about it.

The seven of us continued forward, and I tried to look for something that might give us a sign that we were on the right track. But the forest appeared untouched by anyone, and since Maurelle had flown over the top, it was completely possible that the center was the only clearing.

The point was we had no path, which suddenly seemed a lot scarier now that we had been warned about *danger ahead*.

I kicked a rock and it rolled around, stopping when it hit a circular stone, surrounded by flowers of all colors.

"Woah," I breathed, crouching down to look at the flowers. "That's really pretty."

"Yeah," Elnora said, but her eyes were focused on Illis's face.

We continued walking for miles, and my feet ached. I adjusted my pacing until I was next to Cherry.

"Hey," I said. "Can I talk to you?"

She smiled. "Of course."

"Um, thank you," I sighed. "For helping me earlier. The truth is I'm scared of all this magic stuff, but thank you. I'm not typically somebody who could ever do that. Bravery is *not* my strong suit."

"Well, you're my friend now, so it's clearly my duty to help you. And let me tell you a little secret." She leaned forward and whispered. "It took me awhile to learn how to be brave too."

"Cherry, why do you think Maurelle is after Hattie's power and *the History of Peachtree Palace*? Does it have to do something with being a legendary power?"

Cherry frowned. "I'm not exactly sure what you know about the legendary powers, but they're strong enough to help Maurelle do whatever she wants. If she got her hands on just one of them, it could be a disaster. That's why we can't let her find out that Fira has the Adar. As for why she wants the book, if I know Maurelle at all . . ."

"Know her at all?"

Cherry cleared her throat, "Strictly research wise, I don't know, world domination? Her fascination with Rolling Hills? As I'm sure you figured out, that's the only copy of the book in the world, and it's basically a free guide to all of the Hills' secrets."

Apparently not all of them.

Without permission, my mind wandered to the Hall of Marble, I'd never seen it in the book before.

Cherry continued, "She has enough power to destroy all of Rolling Hills on her own. But she doesn't like to just strike. No, she likes to think. She wants to watch Rolling Hills be torn apart by its own power. Only then will she be satisfied."

Perplexed, I said, "I can't help but wonder why she was so poorly treated."

"In history, the Hills' princesses have always practiced their magic in secret. However, Azami's mother didn't. She knew the legends, and she hated it. She hated how it made her different, how it had to be discreet. So she wanted it banished from Rolling Hills forever. She hid every book about magic, any object that could teach someone. So when she found out that Maurelle was practicing magic, she wanted her eliminated."

I sucked in a breath.

"Azami's mother wasn't a bad princess or a bad queen. She could even be kind . But she couldn't abide magic. She saw it as something that needed to be disposed of, so that's what she tried to do."

"If she got rid of everything, then how did Azami learn magic in the first place?" I asked.

"She found it. If Azami's mother's goal was to eliminate magic–which, I should point out, is impossible–To be fully rid of magic she would have had to destroy the entire world, everything on it. But if she had truly wanted it gone, she would have burned the books, destroying them. Instead she hid them, and no one knows why. So Azami found them and learned all the magic her mother had rejected. And she found out how beautiful it could be."

Something that looked almost like sadness crossed Cherry's features.

"Umm, guys," Elnora's voice sliced through my conversation.

"What is it?" Hattie asked.

"Well . . ." Elnora faltered. My heart stopped. I could hear the fear in her voice. "The thing is, a while back, Misty and I stopped to admire this rock with some flowers around it. It was almost a perfect circle, so it's not easily replicated."

"Your point is?" Arabella asked.

Elnora grimaced. "I don't want to be the bearer of bad news, but . . . I found the rock again."

Silence settled over our crew.

"So what does this mean?" Hattie asked, but I could tell by her expression she knew the answer.

"We've been going in a circle," Illis said, her voice low and rough.

"But that's impossible," Fira insisted. "We've been going straight."

"We don't have any way to know that," I muttered.

"She's right," Cherry said. "There's no path."

"So we're right back where we started?" Arabella asked, spitting sarcasm. "Fabulous!"

Illis screwed up her face in concentration.

"It's enough to take in without you snapping, Arabella," Fira quipped tightly.

"Oh, because you know everything from the Adar," she said with jazz hands. "Look where that got us!"

I watched curiously as Illis's face scrunched, as though she were listening to something.

"It's not my fault that the Adar didn't tell me!" Fira cried.

"Well, it is your fault that you're not smart enough for it to show you!"

"COULD YOU ALL JUST SHUT UP FOR A MINUTE!" Illis yelled.

Everyone stopped talking and looked at her.

Her face was so tightly wound it looked as if it might twist all the way around.

No one moved a muscle, when all of a sudden she screamed. "DUCK!"

No sooner had she said this than we were all screaming too. I looked up in the sky and saw hundreds of arrows flying toward us.

"Where did *they* come from?" Arabella yelled, snarling like she had much stronger language in mind.

"I don't know!" Illis shouted.

The seven of us ran around, shrieking and dodging arrows. My heart thumped loudly in my chest, as another arrow skimmed by my ear.

I tripped on a root and went sprawling into the grass below. I tasted dirt, and implausibly heard silence. The arrows had stopped.

But the silence was short-lived.

Cherry screamed, and I pushed myself up, rocks digging into my hands, and spun around.

Fira was crouched over her, assessing the arrow flank sticking out of Cherry's arm. Blood poured out of the wound.

"Shhh, shhh, it's okay, Cherry. We're going to fix this."

Cherry tried to smile but grimaced as she attempted to give me a thumbs-up.

Fira got up, leaving Cherry on the ground. We all huddled around her.

"I have *no idea* how to fix this," Fira whispered frantically.

Arabella groaned. "More insightful knowledge, thank you, Fira. I should be shaking your hand."

"Enough," Illis clipped. She turned to Fira. "What should we do?"

"I don't . . ." She had started to glow. She grabbed her head again, but this time it seemed that the pain released more quickly. She stopped glowing and looked at us, saying, "We need one of the flowers by that circular rock to rub on her arm. After we remove the arrow, we'll tie up the wound, and she'll be perfect."

"Well, that's easy," Elnora said. "The rock is just right over there . . . Uh oh."

"What is *uh-oh*?" I panicked.

"Well, hate to once again be the bearer of bad news, but the rock with the flowers is gone."

"What?" we cried in unison.

"When the arrows were raining out of the sky, we all ran, but apparently we ran away from the rock."

She was right. The pretty rock with the flowers we needed was nowhere in sight. I groaned.

"It's okay," Hattie said, a thin facade of calm pulled over her tone of panic. "We can't have run that far. We can probably just retrace our steps."

"Probably," Illis echoed glumly.

"Illis, stay back with Cherry," Hattie ordered, continuing when Illis opened her mouth to object. "The rest of us are going to find the flower."

"Okay, Cherry," Fira becalmed, holding out her hands like she was trying to soothe a stallion. "We're going to get a flower that will heal your arm, and we'll be right back."

Cherry looked about ready to pass out, but she managed to nod.

With Illis at Cherry's side, we set off to retrace our steps.

None of us could find the rock anywhere, and I was sure we were never going to find it. The sun was low in the sky, casting long, eerie shadows in the grass.

"Guys," Fira called. "I found it."

We all scrambled over to find her crouched over the ashen rock.

"But there's a problem." She winced.

"Another one?" Elnora groaned.

"The flowers are gone. All that's left are the stems."

The arrows had destroyed the little garden, along with all the flowers.

Everyone began to argue about what to do, when an idea hit.

"How have I been so stupid?" I asked myself.

"What?" Hattie said hopefully.

I smiled. "Cherry can control plants right? So she can make them grow. We don't need a flower. We just need a stem."

"Misty, you're a genius!" Fira cried. She picked a stem, and we ran back toward Cherry.

She was in the same spot, with Illis standing over her.

Fira handed me the flower. "Cherry, can you make this grow?" I asked.

"Of course I can," she said, but her brows furrowed, and a bead of sweat dropped down as she concentrated on the flower. Slowly, a little bud began to bloom, until the entire flower was open.

"Okay," Fira said. "I'm going to remove the arrow now, Cherry."

She placed her hand firmly on the arrow's shaft and pulled. Cherry screamed, and our whole group winced as her face contorted in pain.

"It's going to be okay," Fira reassured her. She took the flower and rubbed it on the wound. She ripped a piece of fabric from the bottom of Cherry's dress and tied it firmly on her arm.

Cherry was panting, but her labored breathing subsided, and she sighed, closing her eyes. "Better. Definitely better."

We let out a collective sigh, and I turned to Fira. "Nice work," I said, but she was glowing again.

She clutched her head, and Hattie stepped forward. "What is it saying now, Fira?"

Fira coughed, "Maurelle is waiting for you. She is approaching. The next clearing. Stay ready."

My stomach twisted into knots. We were going to confront Maurelle.

"Let's just go," I prompted, and Fira nodded.

Getting to our feet, we walked fast, but with grudging anticipation.

The woods began to thin, and I braced myself. The next clearing, I thought before speaking aloud. "This is it."

The world folded out as we stepped into the clearing.

My gaze fogged because what I was seeing could not be correct. I waved my hand in front of my face. Focus, I thought. This couldn't be right.

Fira's face twisted with recognition. And betrayal.

In the middle of the clearing sat Maurelle garbed in the same black outfit as before. Her smile was heinous. But next to her was someone who couldn't be there. A sheet of silver hair twisted into a rope down her back, slender fingers cupped in front of her face.

Whispering into her ear was Odelina.

36

Hattie

Judging by everyone's faces, I was as confused as they were. Misty and Fira had said Odelina was on our side.

"What are you doing here?" Misty asked, denial lacing her words.

Odelina looked up, recognition in her eyes. "The same as you, I expect."

"Not plotting with Maurelle," Arabella parried. "Not whispering plans into her ear when you are supposed to be in that hall. *You're* coming to destroy her with a slow, painful death. Because that makes perfect sense." Arabella rolled her eyes.

Odelina straightened up, clearly startled that we were here. "I don't have any idea what you're talking about."

"Oh no," Misty whispered.

I wanted to ask Misty what was wrong, for her face evinced a look of horror such as I had never before seen.

A split second later, Fira's face held it too.

Maurelle stepped menacingly forward. "I think that these two have figured it out," she laughed, and before I had time to react, her arm was around my neck.

I choked, her forearm barring my movements. I clawed at her hand, but her fingers didn't loosen.

Maurelle's grip tightened with my struggle. "Care to explain?"

No one spoke.

"Did you ever wonder why it was so easy for you to enter the Hall of Marble? Why it was so easy for you to escape?"

The pieces were sliding together, and I was almost positive that my face now looked as terrified as Fira's and Misty's.

Maurelle had kidnapped me in hopes of using me to attack Rolling Hills. Fira and Misty had easily infiltrated the Hall of Marble. Odelina had helped them find the orb, and transported them to the fortress. Dark Unicorn had let us escape without difficulty. Maurelle had as good as led us to this spot in the woods.

It clicked in one second of pure horror. It wasn't a fight Maurelle wanted, it was my power. And we had brought it right to her on a silver platter.

"You understand now, don't you?" Maurelle purred.

I nodded.

She released me, sending me stumbling to the ground. I coughed and hiccuped. I felt my orb of power burning in my pocket.

Maurelle grabbed the collar of my shirt and pulled me to my feet, hissing, "Give me the power or they die." She gestured to my friends.

This. This was exactly why I should've been here on my own.

"NO!" Misty cried. "Don't do it, Hattie!"

I heard similar echoes from the rest of my friends, and it hurt, more than anything that Dark Unicorn had done to me, hearing their voices.

I wanted to scream. It was my fault that my friends were here, and now they were going to pay the price of *my* mistakes.

But I had an idea. It was a bad idea, definitely, and there were about a million scenarios where it wouldn't work. But it was an idea nonetheless.

I took a deep breath. A *very* deep breath, reached into my pocket, and pulled out the orb, my friends gasping around the clearing.

The orb glowed softly, the silence reverential.

Here, in front of Maurelle, the memory didn't start to replay at all.

I slowly lifted it to Maurelle's outstretched hand.

She began to laugh. I could already see the victory etched on her face. But one moment before it was in her hand, I dropped it.

Such a small movement, but so precise, the effect so startling that no one grabbed it.

It all but fell in slow motion and shattered into a million pieces on the rock below.

I felt the rest of the power flood into me, and the orb was gone forever.

"I wonder," I said to Maurelle's face, a new energy edging into me. "How long did it take you to convince Dark Unicorn that you were the *perfect* leader for them? Because you can't even catch a small orb like this one. No, Maurelle, you can't do anything. So how long was it then?"

Visibly shocked, her face soon turned to anger, more deranged than I had ever seen a person before.

Her fists shook and her eyes raged. She recovered quickly and smiled darkly, frightening me. That smile meant that something was coming, something I couldn't recover from. "How long did it take you to convince yourself that it wasn't your fault your parents are dead?"

Of anything she could have said, this caught me off guard.

Next to me, Fira tensed.

I stopped short, swallowing down a retort, but I was curious.

"What are you implying?" I asked coolly, barely keeping my voice from splintering.

Maurelle choked on laughter and turned to Odelina, who stood uncomfortably next to her. "She has no idea, does she?"

Odelina merely blinked.

"Do you know what happened to your parents?" cooed Maurelle, low and soft.

I tried not to, but, involuntarily, my head shook no.

"Your parents are dead because of *you*," Maurelle said, looking me full in the face. "It is all your fault. That day when you were seven was a big day for Dark Unicorn. We came for the Hills power, but we returned with the orb and more in hand. We had driven your parents into hiding," Maurelle cackled. "They lived in a place we could never find. They stayed hidden."

I knew where. They had hidden in the Waters of Peachtree. I reminded myself that it was not my fault they were dead. This always happened in legends. The evil ones would try to twist your mind. I won't fall for it, I thought.

Maurelle continued her diatribe. "They stayed hidden. Until the day you were eleven. Three years of planning since they had gone into hiding. This was the day we would defeat our enemies once and for all. It was hot out. But it is really not a rarity in the never-ending spring of Rolling Hills. I could tell– for one of our members was a gazer– that you were sitting beneath a tree, content. I linked your brain with another who would be present at the battle. We ushered a faux distress call to an organization who was sure to pass the information on to wherever your parents were. We told them that the Dark Unicorn was planning to attack you and that you needed immediate help."

I could see where the story was going. I shut my eyes tightly.

"We lured them into a cave where we told them we were holding you. They looked around confused," Maurelle began to speak of the exact vision I had seen. "You sat beside a tree, the beautiful pink blossoms rained around you . . .

You gazed at the sunrise, dawn cracking beyond the horizon. Your eleven-year-old body stretched and snuggled into the grass.

Your eyes closed and you fell deep into sleep.

You dreamed.

A dark cave.

Your parents.

'Quickly this way,' your father cried, and you struggled to catch a glimpse of the oncoming conflict.

Fear weaved into your mother's eyes, and she began to run. But your mother was too slow, a blast of light flew toward her, and the room exploded. You awoke with a start.

Your stomach was twisted into knots.

It was a dream, you thought, a dream.

But you felt an emptiness in you that wasn't there before."

"You knew, didn't you?" Maurelle continued. "Somewhere in your small eleven-year-old heart. Your parents are indeed gone, Hattie, they are *dead*. And it was all your fault. We were coming to get *you*. If you had only been able to protect yourself, your parents would still be alive. You would be together. Think of that. Family dinners, goodnight hugs, bedtime stories. All for you. But that doesn't exist, does it? No, because of you. It is all your fault. *Everything* is your fault."

I watched the satisfied look on Maurelle's face from a distance, for my mind was whirring in another direction. "No," I said. "No."

In another world, Fira's hand touched my shoulder. "She is lying, Hattie, it is not your fault." She spoke in desperation. "Hattie, listen! It is NOT your fault. Hattie, please pay attention. Focus, Hattie! Hattie. Hattie. HATTIE, LISTEN TO ME!"

They were all calling to me now, "Hattie. Hattie. Hattie. Hattie. Hattie."

I began to cry even though I tried to stop the tears from coming. I knew the truth now. But was it true?

Yes, I thought, it is all my fault.

It was as though the world had zoomed out.

I couldn't feel the up from the down. I couldn't hear anything, just the thudding of my own heartbeat in my ears.

I couldn't tell what I was doing, but I felt my hands grow hot, and saw them glow, just as they had in Maurelle's room, where I had destroyed everything.

But none of it mattered anymore. Nothing did.

Because I, Hattie Hills, Princess of Rolling Hills, was the reason my parents were dead.

37

Misty

There was no possible way it could be going worse. Odelina had been on Maurelle's side the whole time. It seemed so obvious now. It had been so simple. We should have known.

Fira and I realized that we had been playing into Maurelle's hands while at the Hall of Marble. Would things be different if we had known that by telling Odelina what we knew, we were doing exactly what Maurelle wanted?

A sharp headache was beginning to form as the pieces slid together.

And now Maurelle had brought up Hattie's parents. I had feared that Maurelle would try this card, but Hattie was falling for it easier than I would have expected.

Hattie clutched her head, as if trying to stop the voices reaching there.

From the other side of the clearing, I ran to her. It was unusual to see Hattie so distraught. I wondered how she could really believe it was her fault that her parents are dead.

We all crowded around her now, calling her name. "Hattie. Hattie. Hattie!"

It was impossible to reach her. She was impounded behind an invisible wall.

"Get out of the way!" I yelled.

Hattie had begun to glow again. Without Hattie thinking straight, her executing an attack at this moment could result in disaster.

Hattie unexpectedly charged forward, her hands raised. Hattie's magic hurtled at Maurelle, which she easily dodged before shooting back her own balls of black streaked with a foggy substance.

Illis dove forward, her dagger in hand, aiming to get Hattie out.

Maurelle had no reason to advance toward Rolling Hills. Since Princess Azami had ruled, it had been nothing but a lovely kingdom with barely any prejudice.

Was she simply holding sour feelings from sixty years earlier? But to kill her best friend Azami's descendants because of something that her father did, that was puzzling.

Then I remembered Alvara.

Was the legend true?

Did she really have a grudge toward the whole of the Hills family? But if Maurelle believed it, nothing would stop her, not even our small force of people who knew the legend was real.

A twig snapped behind me, and I spun around to see Odelina, who had simply slipped aside.

Something clicked inside me, an anger I wasn't used to feeling.

Maurelle was trying to murder my princess and friend, taking down my entire kingdom with her.

Inside me a dead flame rose, and I found that the power inside me was stronger than it had ever been before, thumping in rhythm with the pulsing of Hattie's power.

I glanced over at Hattie. Her eyes glowed in a way they never had before. They looked hungry for something that would not sit well in the stomach.

There was life behind her vision, and her gaze fixed on Maurelle.

It scared me immensely, and it took all of my willpower to concentrate on my own self, but then Hattie lunged at Maurelle, her power flying.

I stumbled as one of Hattie's jets came too close.

As it zoomed by, I noticed it was hot and loud. As more jets shot by, I could have sworn I heard voices.

It was becoming harder to dodge her jets, and I noticed the others having the same difficulty.

When I spun back around, Odelina was gone.

I ran over to Illis, who was struggling to get close enough to talk to Hattie.

"Misty." She nodded in acknowledgment. "I need you to find Odelina. She may have disappeared, and we need her here. She can't leave."

"Got it," I said, before starting to look around.

It took me several moments to locate Odelina, but I finally spotted her next to Maurelle.

Odelina was holding something that looked an awful lot like a teleporting device.

I sprinted over and grabbed her wrist. She looked up, terrified.

"You won't be leaving us just yet." I smiled, before quickly adding, "Sorry, this might hurt."

I wheeled my arm backward and punched her square in the nose.

She tottered and stumbled down, startled, but her reflexes recovered quicker than I had expected, and she dove back at me.

I dodged her arm as it came flying toward me, but I landed on my butt as a reward.

Odelina hit me across the face with burning speed, and I scrambled up just in time for her to sweep a leg against mine, knocking me over again.

The world pinwheeled, but I discovered I could stand, and was rapidly on my feet again.

Punch after punch gained me no further ground toward Odelina. We kept dodging each other's blows, getting nowhere.

I finally landed a hit in her gut, knocking her down onto the soggy grass.

I heard what almost sounded like an explosion behind me.

I turned around, shocked. Blinking on the ground was the now normal Hattie, the Hattie I knew, fully aware of her surroundings, looking terrified.

I glanced back. Odelina had disappeared.

I tracked Hattie's gaze to see she was staring at something above.

Closing in on us were hundreds of corvids with wingspans that looked like spread cloaks, and they were diving right at us.

"Call them off Maurelle!" Hattie yelled, her voice still strained with anger.

Maurelle rolled her eyes and swiped a hand. The birds evaporated into thin air.

"If you insist on fighting like an adult, then fight me. Just you. Come on Hattie, you know you can," she drawled.

"No!" I shouted.

No way were we going to let Hattie fight Maurelle on her own.

I rushed over to Hattie's shoulder, and she turned to me, tears in her eyes, "It's all my fault, and now your deaths are going to be my fault too. I can't have that, Misty. I can do this. I can fight her."

"No, you can't Hattie," I took a deep breath. "But if we don't think of something quick, we actually *will* be dead."

She looked like she was about to break down even further when her head abruptly snapped up to look at me.

"Wait, I have an idea." Her eyes brightened. "I'll send you all into a dreamlike state, where you'll be safe. Nothing can hurt you there except your own mind. But it'll affect Maurelle too. It'll give me more time to figure out what to do."

I looked around, "How did you even think of-"

"I don't know," she said in something that almost sounded like annoyance, like she wished she could know too.

I had the gnawing feeling that the mind could be a very dangerous place. But seeing no other option, I replied, "Okay."

Hattie looked at me with aching gratefulness and stood up, her brown curls rising behind her, the glow seeping back to her eyes.

Her hands slowly tilted upward. Through the glow I could see her face etched with concentration and effort.

Everything stopped. Then everything started again, lighting up until looking at anything was blinding. It seared the back of my eyeballs.

I felt as though I was hurtled downward into a haze.

My hands gripped at the edges of nothing.

I slipped.

And then I fell.

38

Illis

My first thought was that I must be dead, for I was falling into an abyss.

Then I hit myself on the temple and felt pain against it.

Maybe I am alive, I thought.

Hattie, it seemed, had used the last bit of her energy to send us all flying into our own minds, from what I had overheard from the conversation between her and Misty.

I took a second to observe my surroundings.

There were stars everywhere, but not normal stars that would inhabit an evening in the sky of Rolling Hills.

They were oddly colored, ranging from red to purple, with what looked like faces. Expressions, at least. That was when I noticed that they were images, floating around me.

Little snapshots of my life, whizzing by.

"Memories," I said, awestruck.

These were my own memories. This was my own mind.

I suddenly felt the urge to throw up. The last place I would ever want to be was in my own head.

I could be anywhere, *anywhere* but here.

I started to panic again. My breath quickened and I tried to round myself, hating how weak I felt.

The concept startled me down to my toes, and in feeling them, I discovered I could move, steer almost.

I noticed an aggravated section of red toward which I was involuntarily floating.

I remembered what Hattie had said. "Nothing can hurt you there except your own mind."

But my mind was a terrifying place. It could do a lot of damage. It already had.

I picked up speed. I was hurtling toward the red.

I blacked out and woke again with a start.

I was on the floor of my old training gym.

Mr. Montair grinned down at me evilly. "A bit too light today, I think." He whacked me across the face, and I knew instantly something was wrong.

The pain burned, then itched, but I didn't scratch it.

Rather I held out my hand, and when he didn't take it, I asked, "Help me up?"

He spat down at me. "Help your own self."

I was startled. Was this seriously my brain's way to torment me?

I sighed. It would take more than this to shake me.

The floorboards creaked beneath me as I stood.

Mr. Montair turned to face me, but he was no longer Mr. Montair. All signs of my teacher were gone, replaced with evil red eyes and a hunched, hairy body. "You shouldn't have done that," the creature said. It laughed wickedly and dove at me.

I grabbed my dagger and began attacking it. Its eyes narrowed before performing a series of attacks that proved impossible to dodge.

My shoulder sliced open from the force of its claws, and I screamed. Unbearable pain branded down my arm.

I dropped to my knees and chanced a look at my injury.

It was bruised, my arm already puddling with blood. Bubbles popped out of the scratch, looking like magma.

I turned to the creature, who had reared and was again preparing to charge. Its claws had the same bubbles that now seared my arm. It had to be poison.

I gritted my teeth and stood, though it hurt like twenty blades stabbing me just to get on my feet.

If Fira were here, she would gasp first, and then recommend a long list of complicated treatments filled with words that I would never understand.

I almost smiled at the thought, but reminded myself to keep a sharp mind, or I would end up sliced in more pieces than this.

I put on a tough face and lunged back at the creature, my dagger flying, and then suddenly so was I.

I was back into the abyss catching a brief vision of myself as if from an aerial view. Then my mind plunged me back into the red zone, into the awful place my mind had twisted for me.

It was the day my parents kicked me out.

The urge to throw up grew stronger.

My brother looked at me scathingly. "I think this housing unit has no need for anyone named Illis anymore."

"Please," I begged. "I'm only ten, I can't leave yet. You can't kick me out yet. I'm your daughter, you can't do this to me."

"Watch us," my mother snarled.

My father moved to slap me hard on the face one last time, but I flinched and he wrinkled his nose, lowering his hand and throwing me out the door.

And him not hitting me almost felt worse.

My tears mixed with dirt as I pushed myself up, desperately wanting to fight back.

But my father walked over slowly and leaned down. "One last thing," he growled before spitting in my face. "*You aren't our daughter.*"

The door slammed closed and I sat panting in the canyon, willing myself to move, to cry, to do anything, but I couldn't.

I was frozen again.

But there was something else that stung more than my father's slaps ever had.

I'd spent all this time convincing myself that I'd forgotten. That everything my parents had done to me didn't hurt anymore.

But here was proof that I'd been wrong. I'd never forgotten, and I never would.

Get up Illis. Get up.

I forced myself to my feet, stepping one in front of the other.

I made my way to Peachtree Palace.

Hattie stood ready, but she was different too, like everything else in this fake, twisted world.

She was an old woman, but she had kept her facial features. Her back was hunched over, her clothing ripped. She looked like a witch, and sounded like one too. "Come in, Illis," Hattie said creepily. "I've been expecting you."

I walked in slowly, my vision blurring at the edges. The hall was scattered with memories, echoes and shadows of events from all periods of my life.

I saw things of the future. Things of the past that I didn't remember. Until now.

Hattie snatched my wrist. "Come with me," she spat.

"LET ME GO!" I yelled, my arm still searing from the creature's slash, "DON'T TOUCH ME!"

She dragged me forcefully with a strength that a body like hers shouldn't possess.

I chanced another look at my arm to see it was bubbling more than it had before.

I cried out in pain. Hattie didn't bat an eye, but the corners of her mouth twitched into a smile.

Hattie dragged me down to a part of Peachtree Palace that I had never seen before. It was nasty, moldy and cold.

A prison.

I was being reared to be thrown into a cell when the world yanked on me somewhere at the edge of my being.

The scene jolted and shook, and it almost looked like an earthquake.

I flew back through the abyss again, but this time I landed with a thump on the ground.

My hands pressed into the dirt, the silence heavy around me, and I knew I was back in the real world.

I inhaled the scent of fresh earth, taking a deep breath.

I'm back I reminded myself, *And I'm not going to let my memories hurt me again.*

39

Fira

With no warning, I was sent hurtling through space. At first glance, it looked like space, but I was too smart to believe that. Judging by the small orbs with images, this was my mind.

I tried shaking my head, and just as I had expected, the world around me shook with it. I tilted my head, and the world tilted with it.

I smiled.

I controlled my own mind, something the others probably didn't understand. I hoped they were okay, but the only way to truly help them would be to escape my head.

It was all one big puzzle, and if I could figure it out, I could get out.

If I moved my limbs back and forth, I could float effortlessly through the space that was my mind.

Suddenly, through some unknown force that I definitely wasn't in charge of, I was hurtled through my own mind in an uncontrollable whirlwind. There was red etching at the edge of my vision.

I was thrown onto a hard floor that was not there before.

I looked up to see Hattie chained next to Cherry, their faces strained in anguish.

This may have been my own mind, but minds are powerful places, and I didn't know exactly what spell I had seen Hattie use and what it did, or even how she'd known to do it at all.

I immediately rushed to the point at which their chains intercepted and moved to unlock them.

Both of their voices growled down at me, "No, Fira. You can only unlock one of us, or you will die a most painful death!"

I knew they were lying, that my brain was just messing with me, but it didn't help the fear infiltrating my heart. "That's not true," I stammered. "Is that really the best you can do? You will die a most painful death?" I mocked, then muttered, "Yeah, not on my watch."

Hattie smirked, then twisted her face in pain. "Would you like to find out?"

"Ugh!" I yelled. "Can anybody give me a break?"

I sharpened my mind, like the feeling of putting on glasses and finally being able to see. What would happen if I tried to free both of them at the same time?

I darted forward and loosened the chain.

Instantly the room turned red, and it was crushing in on me. The space that had been a large hall was now the space of a closet, shrinking down by the second.

I was gasping for breath now, finding very little air to actually take in.

This is my mind, I reminded myself. I pushed my legs outward, willing the room to pop back out again. It obeyed, stretching like a rubber band, constantly moving outward until I thought it would come flying back in.

I placed a hand on the wall.

"Please stay like this," I begged in a panicked voice.

All of a sudden, the space shifted, no longer in the room but sitting on lovely grass in a wide field.

In the distance, I could see Peachtree Palace, but as I looked closer, nothing was the same.

The sky was darker, the town abandoned. The market in the distance was torn into shreds.

Something materialized in front of me. It was a person, but it wasn't. Some sort of hologram.

Its voice was robotic as it spoke to me, "Hello. You are Fira Pele. And I am someone you will never know."

"Um-"

The hologram stared at me.

What is this place?" I asked. Everything I had seen so far bore some connection to my life. But this woman, or hologram, had no familiarity.

"I suppose it is your mind. So you tell me," droned the woman.

"Is this Rolling Hills?" I asked.

"I don't exactly know the answer to that question," the woman replied. "I don't think like you do. I suppose if Rolling Hills is what you think it is, then it is. This is your mind, after all. You get to decide where we are, I think."

"How does it work? I can't do certain things, but some I can." I hoped this question wasn't too difficult for her to answer.

"You cannot change the scenarios, but maybe you can bend them. Bend the things you do, but not what others do."

That made sense. I could manipulate escapes, but I couldn't make others stop attacking. "Thank you," I said, sensing a change in the vision.

"You are most certainly welcome, Fira Pele."

Abruptly I was pulled from the scene and dropped somewhere new. I was standing at the edge of a cliff. I hated cliffs. A nauseous feeling crept into my stomach.

The cliff was at least three hundred feet off the ground.

"A fall from this height would result in death," I thought miserably.

Instinctively, I backed up, only to hit something hard. I whipped around.

Maurelle was standing with her hands on her hips, at almost two times her actual height. Behind her was an army.

They held bows, swords, and knives, and manned several cannons.

"Now," Maurelle said. "You have two choices."

I groaned. Why not three?

"You can jump off this cliff yourself, or–" She smiled sweetly. "We will kill you slowly and painfully. Now, of course, you won't really die, will you? But I can't say that your mind won't choose to inflict pain on you, now, can I? Remember, it is your decision."

In quick time, the army began to close in on me. Everything was moving too fast. Fear gripped my stomach.

My foot felt the edge of the cliff and sent a stone spiraling down to the ground below.

Maurelle smiled. "No pressure, of course, but I am giving you ten seconds, my dear."

"Ten."

My foot once again felt rocks sliding beneath it.

"Nine."

I clutched my stomach for fear of falling over.

"Eight."

Think, Fira!

"Seven."

I control my brain. I am the driver. I can bend my own escape.

"Six."

If I fall at just the right time . . .

"Five."

I readied myself.

"Four."

The soldiers' faces were hungry.

"Three."

Maurelle smiled maliciously.

"Two."

My eyes shut tight.

"One."

I sailed backward off the cliff and into the deep valley below.

40

Misty

I shrieked. A loud sound echoed through the entire space. My mind. I was truly terrified. Warnings could not have prepared me for this feeling.

I was falling through nothing.

Whether up or down, left or right, I couldn't tell, or move for that matter. Yet, I was constantly in motion.

The contradictory feelings were too much for my body to handle. I again tried to grip something that would stop the spinning, but found nothing tangible to make it stop.

I wasn't fully aware of when I actually stopped falling, but all at once I was still.

I panted loudly but must have lost my acute sense of sound, because I couldn't hear anything else around me. It was deathly quiet, which actually made it worse.

I took a deep breath to steady myself, trying to focus on anything but the floating in my mind.

Contrary to what Hattie thought would be a safe haven, I had the discomforting feeling that it was a very bad idea to send us into our own minds.

Why not a giant, conjoined, mind-room thing where we could plan? Or better, a large grassy field where we could take a nap before getting up to fight more evil or whatever it was we were supposed to be doing.

I opened my eyes.

The space around me was actually quite pretty. It was dark, but lights sparkled around me, images of my life scattered about in a beautiful display.

I tried to swim as if I were in the waters of Rolling Hills.

Suddenly, I *was* in water. I surfaced and found myself in a memory from years ago, and not a nice one. My stomach clenched in fear.

It was a sweltering hot day, and Liam and I were swimming in a river just outside the marketplace.

My present self tried to persuade Liam to get out, but it was as though I was in a dream, or peering through a looking glass.

I laughed and splashed around in the coolness of the water, feeling the soft sand beneath my feet.

We splashed each other, the mist spraying us with refreshing coolness. It was fun, but I silently awaited the second when things would go wrong.

All of a sudden, just as I remembered, Liam slipped and fell under the water, the current not hesitating to sweep him away.

I laughed, that is, the image of myself which I was stuck in laughed, but I was panicking. A minute passed, and Liam did not surface. I called for help, but unlike my memory, no one appeared.

I regained control of my movements, took a deep breath, and dived under the water to find him. My open eyes burned as the water flooded in.

The water was somehow much deeper than it had been a second

ago. It had stretched out to look like an ocean, seemingly miles to the bottom. Now tougher to navigate; thicker, darker, heavier.

At last, I spotted him floating lower by the minute, at least ten feet below me. He was unconscious, his head cocked backward. I screamed a strangled cry choked as water flooded my mouth.

I had no time to spare, so I dove even deeper, my lungs filling with cups of liquid. My ears popped as I swam, and I wondered how long it had been. A minute? Ten?

In reality, my father had come to the rescue, diving in and saving Liam's life. But, in this illusion, my father had not arrived.

I plunged deeper into the water, my lungs burning. The world was dimming, but I finally closed my hand around Liam's.

I concocted an idea. My powers were water based. I tried repeatedly to shoot myself upward, but no matter how hard I concentrated, I could conjure no power.

Realizing I was wasting time, I began to swim slowly toward the surface.

My legs and arms ached as I paddled helplessly upward. I longed for a breath of air, but I was still under the clutches of the water around me.

I had lost count of the passing minutes, unaware how I could still be conscious in this slippage of time, but my fading brain concluded the possibility that I could bend reality. I was in my own mind, after all.

After another eternity, my hand broke the surface, followed by my head.

The sand closed again beneath my feet until I was standing, the ground holding me upright.

I gasped before remembering Liam, whose hand I still held.

"No!" I choked, heaving him up and out of the water.

The roughness of the rocks at the water's edge scraped my knees.

Liam was heavy as I dropped him onto the soft sand, so perfect it was almost the same color as his hair.

I shook his shoulders, and tried to blink away the tears pooling in my eyes.

"Come on, Liam!" I cried, only briefly cognizant that this was all an odd and horrid lucid dream. My mind was in panic mode, and trying to save Liam *was* the panic.

As much as I knew that this whole world was fake, I couldn't bear to see my best friend die, no matter what the format. I eventually gave up, resulting in sobbing over him in hopeless despair, my brain in a million different spots at once.

His eyes fluttered open, and he gasped for breath before coughing out, "Misty?"

"Yeah," I said, almost laughing in relief. "Yeah, that's me, I'm here."

He looked around sleepily. "Where are we?"

I decided not to tell the made-up Liam that we were in my brain. "Just outside the marketplace."

He sat up, looking a tad more alert than he had before. "Where is the marketplace?"

"In Rolling Hills," I said, a bit suspicious.

"Where is Rolling Hills?" he asked.

I sat in silence.

He blinked stupidly. "I am just kidding, you know."

I laughed a little too hard for the situation. "Right! Of course. I knew that."

He stood, wobbly on his legs. "I'm sorry, Misty," he said, sounding truly apologetic.

"For what?" I stood as well, putting my guard on alert.

He pulled out a knife.

I screamed and jumped back. "What are you doing?"

"You left me behind," his voice cracked at he cocked his head, "You *always* leave me behind."

"I—"

He laughed wickedly, a sound I would never have expected to come out of his mouth.

He lunged at me and I screamed just as I was yanked to the stars and catapulted to the ground of cold, hard reality.

41

Hattie

What had I done?

Was I really this stupid?

I had just jumped headfirst into a plan that didn't make *any* sense.

Like, any at all.

I didn't know who would wake up first.

What if Maurelle did? Then she would kill us all, and we wouldn't even be able to defend ourselves.

I groaned and opened my eyes, watching the empty space around me.

I refused to let myself think. Rather I just floated. But the tranquility of floating didn't last long. Slammed into the unforeseen ground, I jumped to my feet and looked around.

"Oh no," I said.

I was in a room. Every surface was white, but the thing that most scared me was its manifestation as a maze– of mirrors.

I'd read countless books in which a maze of mirrors was never a good sign. A sign of what, I didn't know, but a sign nonetheless.

Hundreds of pairs of eyes stared out at me from the mirrors, and they were all mine.

I summoned some of my power, and felt it waiting at my fingertips, ready to spring out when necessary.

Was I at the entrance to the maze? To get out I had to reach the other side. But who knew what could be lurking in between.

I knew that I had sent my friends into their minds, but what if the spell had twisted them. What if inside their minds, there was something else?

I heard a scream from inside the maze and jumped.

My power still tingling at my fingertips, I began to creep into the maze. From all angles, my face was projected back out at me. It was terrifying.

I had to hold a hand out in front of me to prevent myself from crashing into the mirrors surrounding me.

I dragged my hand against the wall, keeping to the right. I'd read that in a maze you have to keep to the right, so I took the turns and prayed that I would make it to the end.

But again, I had no idea what I was doing.

The room was steadily growing darker, little by little. I started to pick up my pace.

The mirrors were all the same, all reflecting my face back at me.

Suddenly, my brain fogged up, and I crashed into the mirror in front of me. I screamed and held out my hand, my power close to exploding from my fingers.

I froze and looked at the reflection before me.

I tried not to move a muscle, and noticed something odd. My reflection was still moving.

I gulped, and my reflection smirked back at me. I started to slowly back away, continuing down the way I was headed.

I turned around and had to stifle another scream. The glass was cracking, and my reflection was slowly peeling away from the mirror that held it.

I yelped and began to run.

I heard the footsteps of my reflection behind me, and I glanced sideways to see that another reflection was chasing me through the mirrored hallways.

I kept my hand on the wall and sprinted, taking every turn as fast as I could.

I remembered the power hot on my hands, and I whipped around, blasting my reflection in the face.

My reflection screamed, and I turned and ran.

I could sense that the other reflection was still right alongside me.

I turned and yelled, "What do you want?"

But my reflection wasn't my reflection anymore, it was Misty. I spun around. Fira was standing in the glass behind me.

"Help us, Hattie," Fira whispered.

They both wore looks of pure terror on their faces.

"How do I get you out?" I cried, my hands scraping at the glass.

"Hattie," Misty said, placing a hand on the glass. I put my hand over hers.

"Misty," I whispered, "You need to help me. What do I–"

I didn't have time to scream. Misty's mouth curved into a smirk, "Really, Hattie?"

She yanked me through the glass.

I screamed, "You too?"

It was almost pitch black, and the mirrors surrounding me glowed creepily.

I'd lost sight of Misty.

I heard a low, haunting laugh. It was her.

"Where are you?" Misty sing-songed.

I saw her brief reflection and dove behind a mirror.

Her laugh again echoed through the mirrors. "Come out, come out, wherever you are, Hattie dear."

"It's not you," I whispered.

"What was that?" Misty purred. "I didn't catch it."

Her reflection flashed again, and I dove through a mirror, the glass shattering behind me.

I saw Misty again and shivered, because this time, it wasn't her reflection, it was actually her.

She advanced toward me, and I scrambled backward. I tried to summon some power to my hands, but nothing would come.

"Really? Now?" I asked, exasperated.

Misty grinned, and her eyes glowed.

I shook with fear, and tried to call up the last bit of energy. I could feel my fingers heating up. "Come on," I muttered. "Come on."

I yelled and felt the energy explode from my hand. Misty blasted backward, and the mirrors around me shattered, crashing to the ground.

I shrieked and covered my head as glass rained down on me, scratching my arms.

I looked up and the maze of mirrors was gone. In its place was a vast expanse of land. But it was all on fire. A deep plateau was cut into the middle, and hills surrounded it.

I gasped in fear, realizing with a start that it was Rolling Hills, and I was standing on *the* Rolling Hill.

My hand flew to my mouth, and tears clouded my vision. "It's all on fire," I whispered. "Why?"

I began to run from the Rolling Hill and throughout the kingdom, sprinting across the downtown. I passed the entrance to the market. It was also burning.

I sprinted down the canyon, past Misty's house. I could see through the house windows that all the insides were lit up too.

As the burning leaves fell around me, I wondered what Peachtree Palace was going to look like.

Was this the catastrophe awaiting my kingdom if I didn't stop it?

Abruptly I came to a halt. Before me lay Peachtree Palace. It was in ruins.

Flames were pouring out the windows. Fire engulfed my entire castle.

I wanted to yell. I wanted to cry. And even though I knew that this was only my own mind, I was furious. This was the palace that my ancestor had created, and it was falling before my eyes.

I wanted to kill whoever had done this.

I stopped myself. Why was I thinking this way?

Wasn't I supposed to be kind and thoughtful, a picture perfect princess? But I couldn't help it.

No sooner had I thought this than the woman herself walked out of the burning front door.

Maurelle had dark magic radiating in the air around her.

"Why did you do this?" I screamed.

"I did promise you, Hattie." She grinned.

"What?" I looked at her, horror-stuck. When had she promised me *this*?

"I told you." She narrowed her eyes. "That I was going to watch Rolling Hills burn to the ground, even if it killed me"

42

Hattie

My breath came in short gasps.

I was unaware of where I was.

I sat up slowly, blinded by the light that came from everywhere and nowhere at the same time, giving me an immense headache. Thousands of little orbs were floating around me– my memories.

Now that I had seen what my head could do, I was certain that I had accidentally sent everyone into the worst part of their memories, the worst part of whatever their brain could dream up for them.

Everything was my fault, all of it. My parents were dead because of me, my friends in danger because of me.

I didn't know what to do. There was no way that Maurelle could be defeated, not right now.

I would need to catch her weakness, and I had no means of exploiting it when I was trapped alone with only me and my head.

"Hello, Hattie," said a soft voice, low and calming, a girl's voice.

"Where am I?" I asked. I was aware that I was supposed to be in my mind, but I was confused. The lights were blinding me, and I was still unable to see clearly.

But the voice was familiar in some respects, the kind of familiarity that was very soothing.

Another voice spoke, but this one male. "Hattie, open your eyes."

"What do you mean?" I asked slowly. My eyes were open.

"Think about it. Did you ever actually open them?" The girl asked me.

I thought about it, slowly realizing what she was saying. I hadn't opened my eyes at all, but the illusion of light had induced me to believe that they had been the whole time.

I opened them now, and instantly my headache was gone.

I was in a field with long, green grass, wind sifting through the stalks.

But in front of me was something I willed to be real, my parents, sitting placidly on the ground.

I ignored the voice from my heart that knew that this was all a hallucination.

"Mom? Dad?" I choked up, but didn't cry. "You're dead. And it's my fault, but you're gone." I took a deep breath and tried to will some sense into me, "And I am *not* going to kid myself that this is real. Now, if you don't mind, I am going to get out of here before you say anything that might make me believe that you're still alive or something!"

I stood up on wobbly feet and marched in the other direction. A portal opened in front of me, and I walked through, coming out right where I had been before.

I groaned, turned, and walked away to find another portal that deposited me back where I had been. "Ugh! You have *got* to be joking."

"Listen, Hattie, . . ." my mother started to speak.

"NO!" I cried, "You listen. I've spent years hoping you'd still be alive just to find out that it's been a lie all along. I'm not going to let you lure me into some fake wish just to find out again-"

"Of course we are dead!" My father interrupted.

I stopped short of the portal that reappeared in front of me. "What?"

"We are an image pulled from your mind to tell you the information that you need to know. For years we've been trapped here, somewhere between life and death," my mother said kindly.

"Wait," I protested. "What about the letter you wrote to Fira, the one in which you said you were 'safe in the afterlife.'"

"What letter?" my mother asked, and for a second my heart stopped.

"The one you wrote to Fira," I repeated, so sure that she'd remember that time, but instead she said something even more confusing.

"Who's Fira?"

My stomach twisted into knots, but my mother seemed to recognize my face, "What were you saying, dear?"

"Huh? Oh," I said, taking a deep breath, willing myself to concentrate on the current problems. "So, you're dead, and you know that?" I asked, trying to subdue the now raging part of me that had hoped that maybe this was real.

"Yes," my father said.

My breathing slowly steadied. "So what do you need to tell me?" I asked.

My father cleared his throat., "The full story."

Fear gripped my stomach. They were going to tell me about the day they died. I wasn't ready to hear it again, but I asked anyway, "What story?"

"The story of the day we died," my mother replied gently. She was smiling, but it almost hurt more because of it.

This mother could never compare to the loving, real person I had known for seven years of my life. The one who tucked me in and read me stories at night. No, she was just an image.

One more heartache I could never get rid of.

"I don't want to hear it," I said bluntly.

"The truth is a terrifying thing sometimes. But if you ignore it, run from it, will you ever learn?"

I looked into her eyes and whispered, "No."

"It was hot," my father began. "A rarity in Rolling Hills."

I tightly scrunched my eyes, almost desperate not to hear anything at all.

My father recognized my discomfort, but continued nonetheless. "We had received a warning from a fellow opposer to Dark Unicorn that they had planned an attack on, well, you."

He spoke quietly, "We were scared, Hattie. You knew no defense, had no way to protect yourself. You would have perished. The way you almost did the night we disappeared. Maurelle was always staging attacks on us, in an old longing for revenge. For her old ancestor Alvara, and for her old friend."

"So it is my fault," I said simply.

"No," my mother said, continuing the conversation my father had begun. "It was mine."

"What do you mean?" I asked, awestruck.

"I neglected my duties as a princess. I disregarded the existence of magic, though I saw it in myself every time I performed it. I practiced in secret, but only ever taught you what you needed to know. I was scared because the legend said that the 100th descendant of Charlie Hills would perish by the hand of Maurelle. I thought it would lessen the consequences if I didn't pass down my knowledge of magic to you, until the day we disappeared."

"So you taught me magic?"

"How else do you think you'd be able to use it now? The Hills' magic is a part of you, but you still have to learn if you want to control it. Unfortunately, not teaching you everything resulted in only one thing, Maurelle stealing your power, until today. Hattie, if it wasn't for *me*, we wouldn't be dead."

I was confused. "So I didn't cause your deaths?"

"No, honey," my mother said.

I didn't trust my voice, so I instead went with a safer topic. "So, where are we even? You can hear me, respond to me. I can hear you, respond to you. But you are dead, and you know it."

"I guess," my father replied. "That that is for you to decide. But it's beautiful." He looked around in admiration at the place my mind had created.

And in that moment, watching him admire the field where we stood, I actually believed them.

I stood up, a new fiery determination in my voice. "I have to go save my friends." I smiled, and for once, it didn't feel fake, "And I think I know how."

My mother stood next to me, placing a hand on my face, reassuring me, "My darling, I don't know where we are. But we will watch over you as you face your fears." She cupped my face, "Your destiny isn't set in place, only you have the power to change your future. So if you don't mind my saying so, go get that evil creature and put her back where she belongs."

The tears rushed forth quicker than I could feel them, and I realized something. All these years, I had been holding onto guilt, that it was all my fault. Maurelle had tried to cement that, but in my mind it had always been there.

Here I was standing in my own brain, tears running down my face, and I was letting go.

Letting go of my guilt.

Letting go of my fear.

Letting go of any part of my brain that would ever tell me no.

Finally, letting go felt good.

My parents enveloped me in a hug that seemed to last forever, but it was over too quick.

I felt a tug on my head and knew that I was being returned to the real world. I knew that I would never be able to see my parents' faces again.

All the years of visions, of finding my parents in my dreams, were over. At last, my parents were free to dwell in a place of peace and tranquility where they belonged.

I smiled through my tears, knowing that this was the end. "Don't worry about me," I laughed, feeling an awful sadness inside me. "But wherever you are, just . . ." I took a deep breath. "Look down at me from time to time. Watch over me, okay?"

My parents took a step back, and I saw that they were also crying.

My father looked at me sadly. "Good luck, my little peach. We're so proud of you."

"I love you," I waved at them as I began to disappear, whispering the last words to my parents that I would ever say. "Always and forever."

43

Illis

Fira woke shortly after I did, barely taking a breath before she ran over to Cherry.

Fira shook Cherry by the shoulders. "Wake up, Cherry!" she yelled.

At the same time, Misty woke up, giving a little squeak, "What's happening?" she asked. Her face wore a look of shock and mixed confusion. I wondered what her head had put her through as her eyes darted around, finally landing on me.

"You were in your head too?"

"We all were," Fira said, and I noticed the unfamiliar quiver in her voice.

Slowly the others woke up too, until only Hattie and Maurelle remained asleep.

"What should we do?" Elnora asked.

Arabella rolled her eyes, "Isn't it obvious?"

Elnora shook her head.

Arabella smirked, "We lean down, ready ourselves at her ear, and scream as loud as we can. 'WAKE UP, HATTIE!'" She danced around in a circle, flailing her arms in imitation.

Now it was Elnora's turn to roll her eyes. "That is a horrible idea," she replied.

We gathered around Hattie, poking and prodding at her head to wake her up.

She didn't stir.

Suddenly I remembered Maurelle and whipped around to look at where she had been laying. She was gone.

I jumped to my feet. "Guys. Bad news," I said as calmly as possible, trying not to panic. "Maurelle is gone."

The rest of the group joined me except Misty who simply looked at me, passing a note of agreement before continuing to try and wake Hattie.

"Well, well, well. Hello there." Maurelle's voice came from above, and I raised my eyes to see her floating in the air, awake from whatever visions her mind had provided her with. "I see you have also awakened from that wonderful spell that Princess Hattie kindly gifted us. Oh, but why do you look so depressed down there? Is it the light playing tricks on my eyes? No? I didn't think so. Can't handle a little bit of dark magic?"

A shiver ran through me. *Dark magic.*

"Whatever, Maurelle," Arabella said, seeming to regain some of her snootiness again. "Go step on a thorn or something. You know, why not a whole bush with thorns in it. Maybe even a forest full of thorns. Or a kingdom. I bet one exists somewhere."

"My, that is awfully rude, Arabella."

"Thanks," she replied. "I learned it from you."

Maurelle scoffed, "From me. Now there, Arabella."

Arabella smirked loudly, making something like a retching noise, imitating Maurelle.

She proceeded to raise her voice to a higher pitch, sounding much like an old crone. "Yes, there, Maurelle, from you."

Maurelle cocked her head. "This game is getting tiring," she complained. "So let us switch up the rules."

She raised her hands in preparation to cast magic.

Misty joined me at my side, and I drew my dagger, watching Elnora, Arabella, and Cherry ready their magic from the corner of my eye.

"That won't be necessary," spoke a voice from behind, and Hattie walked gracefully forward, her head raised high.

"She's awake," Maurelle noticed.

"Sharp," Arabella muttered.

"Hello, Maurelle," Hattie said strongly.

"Hello, *Princess* Hattie."

"You know what I realized, in this head of mine?"

"I am afraid I do not," Maurelle said, lowering to the ground, "Enlighten me."

Hattie kicked a stone on the ground playfully. "I've learned that you–" she pointed her finger squarely at Maurelle. "–are wrong."

"I am afraid I am not," Maurelle said, but something had flickered behind her eyes.

Hattie ignored her, "*And* I'm happy to say that I have let go. Let go of all the guilt that you purposely replaced my magic with, the guilt you put in my head eight years ago. It is all gone, because I know the truth now. I realized it as quick as one snap of a finger. The truth is that you are afraid. You want power, and you are scared that I will get in your way on the road to victory."

"That is not true," Maurelle forced. "I am Maurelle. I am afraid of no one."

"A ruse. The person you are most afraid of is yourself."

Maurelle laughed eerily in an attempt to cover up the fear that was slowly creeping into her face.

"Yes," I whispered. "Keep going, Hattie, you almost have her."

And Hattie did. "Do you want to fulfill the legend so that you will be the most powerful being on the planet?"

"Yes," said Maurelle. "I'm most deserving, and a silly gang of teenagers is not going to stop me."

"I *happen*," Hattie said sternly. "To be the princess of Rolling Hills."

"The best princess," I whispered fiercely, willing her to use my words.

"The best princess," Hattie smiled over at me, and for once I felt good tears pricking at the edge of my vision. "That Rolling Hills can get. *Your* princess, if I am not mistaken."

"I abandoned your slimy little kingdom decades ago," Maurelle yelled. "It is nothing but a pile of garbage. But with me ruling–"

"The results would be nothing but disastrous," Arabella finished.

"Bingo," Cherry chirped.

Maurelle screamed in rage. "You know nothing of power! This is power. I am power. Not you."

"See, you're wrong again," Hattie said. We lowered our defenses, and she walked over to stand by us. "We have power together, and that is something you will never have. I'm not *alone* like you are. I have something worth fighting for."

A soaring feeling entered my chest in a way I had never felt before. I felt as though I could fly to the clouds and never return.

And all at once we turned to face Maurelle, some newfound energy in the air.

I could feel it changing. I could feel *us* changing. And we were still scared, but there was hope now too.

44

Fira

Now I stood firmly next to all my friends with a look of pure determination on my face. Maurelle had no right to ever harm them, and I swore she would never get to try again.

"Maurelle," Hattie started. "Think sensibly about what you are doing. Going around destroying kingdoms and reeking havoc on the Hills family. This is no way to live."

"No," Maurelle retorted, "*You* think sensibly. It is the best way to live. Look at me, Princess Hattie. I am power. I am confidence. I am beauty."

Arabella grimaced before muttering, "I wouldn't be so quick on that last one if I were you."

Maurelle, enraged, growled, "You know nothing!"

"Maurelle, listen to me. You can change. Join us, please. Forget about the silly old legend and live a normal life."

Part of me wanted to smack Hattie for even *thinking* that this was a good idea, but I stopped when I saw the hesitation on Maurelle's face.

She was quick to regain her sneer, "This is the life I want. I would never stoop to a life as low and dirty as your life in that stupid kingdom of Rolling Hills."

I angrily stepped forward. "Stop. Just stop. Stop everything you're doing. You don't understand."

"Oh, hello, Fira Pele. Have I mentioned my observation over you? You are quite the young genius. Studying in that small room of yours. Is that really all Princess Hattie gave you to do?"

"She's given me more than you would ever have the capacity to give anyone." I glared at her, my fists clenched by my side. "Stop talking to my friends like that. You wouldn't understand because it seems that you had *no one* who cared about you like this. No one who you would risk everything for, even if it meant leaving the job you were supposed to be doing and putting your life on the line, if it had any chance of saving them! I wonder, did you *ever* have someone that special to you?"

"Oh yes, you did, Azami," Arabella said. The blow was low, even for her, but I saw something change behind Maurelle's eyes, some sort of burning that had lived inside her for a long time finally resurface.

"Do not dare to speak of my past," she said, her voice thick and low.

I knew that the others had seen it too, for Elnora clapped obnoxiously. "You hit a nerve, congratulations." Elnora bowed before Arabella. "I am honored to be in your presence."

I frowned. "Not now."

"Why not?" Arabella responded. "Who knows," she paused in dramatic silence before continuing darkly, "We may not ever get the chance again."

"True." Elnora nodded before clapping Arabella on the back "Well said."

"Hey guys? Hate to break this up," Hattie paused and assessed the situation quickly. "But we're in the middle of something."

"Righto," Elnora said.

With a ghost of a smile dancing across her face, Hattie turned back to face Maurelle. "I am going to try again. But you have to listen to me. You can be good, like us."

"Like you?" Maurelle cackled, but a serious expression overtook her face. "Your kingdom took *everything* from me."

"Look at us," Illis said. "For three generations we've tried to get to you, to convince you that we don't hate you anymore." She yelled. "WHY ARE YOU SO THICK?"

"I am not the thick one in this situation," Maurelle said quietly. "You seem pretty dim-witted."

Illis groaned.

"Don't say that!" Cherry blurted. "You have no right, absolutely none. And they've tried. Everyone has. To change you and make you good. But you won't give anyone a chance."

"You're right."

All of us froze, because there was something different in Maurelle's voice this time. Something quiet, afraid.

"Maurelle?" Hattie approached her.

But she couldn't have heard Hattie, for her eyes looked miles away, just like Hattie's had only an hour before.

Maurelle continued, "I won't try because I know what will happen. It is always the same, ever since Azami. I try to be good, but something inside me stops and remembers her father, hurting me when I did nothing wrong. The shock on Azami's face, the horror. Even that cannot bring me to my senses. No. So I will not try, because I don't think there is one person in this world who is actually good, and I can't love anyone like I loved Azami again."

Loved.

That was the reason Maurelle hated Rolling Hills. It was because she loved Azami, and her father hurt her anyway.

I focused on the second half of her confession.

"Are you saying. . . that you can't control it?" I asked

Maurelle sank to her knees and shook her head *yes.* "Therefore," she said. "I am a danger to everything and everyone."

I knew what would happen before Maurelle even raised her hands to perform magic.

She cast a shield around herself, sending Hattie flying away from her.

"No!" Hattie yelled. "Maurelle, listen, this is not the answer."

"Yes, it is," Maurelle whispered.

I realized what was about to unfold. She was going to kill herself. She was giving up.

There was nothing to do but watch and wait.

Maurelle began to twist her hands and cast magic on her own body. She let out a yelp of pain and clutched at her leg.

When she took her hand away, her skin was melting. It looked like hot bubbles as it boiled and dripped.

I clutched my stomach and resisted the urge to throw up, but I couldn't look away. It was too horrifying, "What are you *doing to yourself?*"

"Making sure I never have to live another day."

She let out another cry, "But before I go, remember something," she raised her voice, and I recoiled in disgust as her arm actually exploded with a loud splatter. "NEVER TRUST ALVARA. I MADE THE MISTAKE TOO LONG AGO."

Hattie's face twisted. "Never trust . . ."

"ALVARA!" She screamed, "NEVER, EVEN IF IT KILLS YOU. YOU WILL DIE EITHER WAY."

Maurelle's other arm exploded, and though she opened her

mouth to say more, she could do nothing but scream louder than she had ever before. It was painful to listen to her.

She cried and yelled and screamed. We could do nothing but watch in painful silence as she melted in front of us.

And she was gone.

All signs of her lost except for the tiny specs of dust littering the ground where she had knelt.

45

Misty

"Oh my god," I whispered. "Oh my god."

The days I had spent thinking of the ending to this horrible nightmare, I hadn't ever thought about what I would do if we managed to defeat her. And here she was in front of me.

Well not in front of me. She was just . . . gone.

"She's dead."

"Yeah," Arabella said coldly, not a hint of regret touched her voice. "She is."

Hattie sat down. "All this time, and it ended like that. It feels too easy."

"I agree," Fira muttered. "There has to be something we're missing here."

"There is," I hesitated. "Odelina got away during battle."

Illis groaned. "And I didn't even realize it."

"Let's go back," Cherry said gently. "I think we've all had enough action for the day.

But even as we set off through the woods, something was tapping at the back of my mind. A question.

What had Odelina been plotting with Maurelle?

I rubbed my class badge with my finger. Sunflower. The word was comforting, as if it had always been there, and I just hadn't noticed it.

I began daydreaming of attending Peachtree Academy. I wondered if after this all was over, I could take a trip there, maybe live for just one day as a normal girl who was allowed to attend.

I wondered what the food would be like. I pictured a big great hall full of all the things I could eat.

Suddenly my stomach gave a loud grumble that warned me to stay away from thinking about food.

"Misty? Misty? Misty? MISTY!"

I snapped out of my daydreams when I heard Illis next to me.

"What?" I asked, agitated.

"We're here," she replied, in an odd voice that made me think that she may have had her head stuck in the clouds on the walk as well.

"Oh," I murmured. The field was different than it had been before. General Ota was helping Dark Unicorn soldiers off the battlefield, and tending to their wounds, as well as those of the soldiers from the Waters of Peachtree.

Hattie marched up to General Ota, apparently not yet registering that these were Dark Unicorn soldiers.

"Maurelle is dead," she said stiffly.

"What?" General Ota dropped the bandage she was holding.

"She killed herself after a battle."

General Ota, rather than jumping for joy, looked confused. "That seems—"

"Too easy, I know." Hattie scratched her head, but something told me that's not what General Ota was going to say. "And someone else was there, a girl named Odelina. She was plotting with Maurelle, but she escaped."

At the look of shock on General Ota's face, Hattie responded with a nod. "Yes, the one from the legends."

General Ota found her voice. "You say she escaped?"

"Unfortunately," Hattie said grimly.

"Well, while you've been away, we have made our own discoveries." General Ota gestured around her at the Dark Unicorn soldiers. "It appears that they were brainwashed to some level. They say she did it yesterday at a meeting with you, Hattie. Some sort of dark magic."

"Wait, I remember her doing something to all of them yesterday!" Elnora exclaimed.

"So what you are saying is that these people are not guilty as we thought?" Cherry asked cautiously.

"That is exactly what I am saying," General Ota replied with a grin. "You always were the brightest."

I had a feeling that this wasn't the full story, but I smiled, tucking the information in the back of my mind. I was going to need it.

Cherry beamed, and Hattie cleared her throat.

"Right," General Ota said. "Well, we had best be headed back to the Waters of Peachtree. These soldiers need a home. Arabella, would you like to come with us?"

Arabella had since thrown off her Dark Unicorn lanyard, but her outfit still resembled something of an attendee. "No," she said, glancing around at my friends and me. "I think I found where I belong."

"All right," General Ota dipped her chin. "How about you, Elnora?"

Elnora gazed at the ground, and then looked up at Illis and Arabella, "I have too."

Arabella smiled warmly, and Illis began to furiously blush.

Suddenly Fira clutched at her head, and her body glowed blue as she received a message from the Adar.

Fira looked up with wide eyes, and I rushed over to her. "What's wrong?"

Fira gulped. "Something is attacking Rolling Hills, and we aren't there to protect it as we should have been."

I swallowed hard, my throat dry. "So they're–"

"All alone," she finished.

"We have to go!" I called. "All of us."

"What?" General Ota asked.

"Something is attacking Rolling Hills," I said rushed. "And there is no one there to protect it, or the people."

One of the magical girls looked sideways. "That's not really–"

"Oh, come on," Cherry fumed. "It is completely our business. All these years we have fought for one thing: PROTECTING ROLLING HILLS. Do *not* chicken out now."

"All right, everyone," General Ota yelled across the field. "We have to go."

In a series of minutes, everyone was on their feet, and we were marching back down the path. It wasn't long until we reached the cavern described by Illis, the one used to imprison everyone.

Children and adults wandered the cavern looking lost. I wondered if after Maurelle had died, they had been set free. Even her sidekick Pompy looked shocked at the scene unfolding before him.

I saw Elnora turn away from the people, looking slightly sick.

Lily rushed up to Hattie and gave her a hug. "You know what, Princess Hattie?"

"What?" Hattie smiled.

"When you were being carried away, I heard you. You thought in your head that you would save us." Hattie grinned, and Lily said, "Well, guess what? You did!"

Hattie returned the hug before stepping onto a rock in the center of the cave, her shoulders drawn behind her.

She cleared her throat. "Okay, everyone. Hi. We have a job to do. Rolling Hills is under attack, and we are the only ones who can help because *they* don't know about magic. Only we do. You may stay here if you'd like. But you cannot turn back once we get there. So head to that side of the cavern if you are staying behind." She pointed with her finger, but not a single body moved, not even Lily.

Hattie took a deep breath. "Okay then. When we go out there, fight with everything you have. This is for my parents." We all cheered. "This is for all the people we can save." The cheers grew louder. "But most of all, this is for the kingdom of Rolling Hills so that we can wake up tomorrow and say that we survived!"

I glanced at Fira, to see her eyes set on Hattie, and a look of such pride was in her eyes that for a moment I could tell it would all be okay. Hattie would be okay.

And we could do it.

We could save everyone.

46

Illis

I cheered loudly along with the others in the cavern, feeling a chaotic, joyful, wonderful energy seep into me.

The woman beside me turned to face me. "I have been locked in this place for eight years, from the first time people started disappearing. I was only a kid when they took me, thirteen. Time flies, I guess."

As I examined her closer, beneath the tiredness and fright, I could see a young woman wanting to be a kid again, for she had lost her childhood.

"Don't worry," I said with a sad smile. "You can enjoy your life once we get back to Rolling Hills."

"Thank you," she replied, tears in her eyes.

I opened my mouth to inform her that I didn't actually do anything, but she looked so truly happy that I sighed, "You're welcome." Deciding that it would be the best response.

We began to hike up to Rolling Hills, and Elnora joined me at my side. She was walking with quite a pep in her step.

"Hello, Illis," she said, slinging an arm around my shoulder.

It took most of my concentration not to flinch away.

"Hi, Elnora." Even I was aware that my voice sounded more tired than usual, as if I hadn't slept in a day.

When I thought about it, I realized that was true. I hadn't gone to sleep since being in Tulip's hideout, and I was positive more than a day had passed since then.

"Um, Illis?" Elnora asked quietly, fiddling slightly with her hands.

"Yes?"

"I just wanted to thank you." She looked almost sheepish.

"For what, Elnora?" I asked.

"For letting me come with you. For letting me take the step outside the cavern. For not leaving me in there with all the other people. For allowing me to help and actually make a difference. For helping me learn about magic. For helping me become stronger."

I nodded. "All I did was let you come. You did the rest yourself. You cooked up the courage to ask and step out of the cavern. You were helpful. You were strong. I didn't do any of that. Besides, I think it is time you start having a *lot* more faith in yourself."

"Oh, and for one more thing." Elnora nudged my arm. "For being my friend."

If I could have leapt into the air in absolute giddiness, I probably would've, but I *also* would have hit my head on the ceiling. And it probably wouldn't have made me seem very professional.

I cleared my throat awkwardly. "Thank you for being mine."

And as I saw the smile that captured Elnora's face, I was positive that I could have gone back and fought the whole battle again.

"Come on."

She took my hand in hers and raced up to the front of the line. I could have listened to her laughing the whole way, but both of us stopped when we saw the expression on Hattie's face.

She looked more depressed than I'd ever seen her before, and I felt the need to ask, "What did you see?"

"Huh?"

"In your head."

"Oh. My parents," Hattie replied, blowing out a long breath. "I've been carrying them around since they disappeared. I guess they have been living *somewhere* between life and death all the years they've been dead, because I was too stubborn to let them go."

"Oh, Hattie." My heart ached for her. I couldn't imagine living my life carrying around the guilt of my parents' deaths, even though I hated mine.

"Never mind that right now," she said with a shake of her head. "We are here after all. We've made it this far."

And she was right. The Rolling Hill's secret passageway door opened, and the sunlight streamed in. I turned around to see the people's reactions.

They clutched their eyes because the light was too bright, but soon they smiled and cried at the beautiful sight of nature. They had lived in the dark for so long that the sight of the sun almost blinded them. The saddest thing was that it wasn't even all that bright outside at that moment.

People began to adjust to the light, and soon they straightened up, attentive and ready to listen to Hattie.

"Okay, everyone, we are looking for signs of something attacking Rolling Hills. Everything looks peaceful at the moment, so we just have to wait for something to happen, I guess."

No sooner had she said the words had a dark shadow appeared over our heads.

It was massive and hot, the temperature increasing miserably.

It was hard to tell exactly what it was, but it swirled in a sparkling kind of beauty, mesmerizing to look at, a giant metal machine. But then it began to shoot a deluge of lasers at the kingdom.

It reminded me of the lasers and jets I had seen in only one place before.

"Hattie," I whispered. "That's not just a machine. That's magic."

"You're right," Elnora whispered.

"Okay," Hattie called out loudly. "Umm, change of plans. So that object in the sky above us, *that* is what we are fighting. Just go and–" She struggled to find her words, so I simply took over.

"Attack!" I yelled.

The crowd paused.

"Yeah, um . . ." Hattie said, glancing at me for reassurance and half-smiled, half-grimaced. "Do that."

We ran forward quickly.

It was truly an awesome scene. The people attacked viciously with magic, shooting all kinds of objects conjured from hands at the thing that still hovered above us.

The market was burning. I could see that in the distance. But the people began to form a shield over the kingdom. The machine's jets now mostly bounced harmlessly off it.

I was snapped out of my observation by the sound of one of the lasers flying straight toward me.

"Illis!" Hattie yelled, and threw her hands up.

Hattie's magic barely made it in time to deflect the laser, and I still had to jump out of the way to avoid it.

I brushed myself off and tuned to Hattie and sternly said, "You know that's supposed to be my job right?"

"What was that?"

I grabbed her shoulders. "THAT'S SUPPOSED TO BE MY JOB."

She just shrugged. "You're going to have to be quicker next time."

I turned to Hattie with a sly smile on my face.

We were going to do things the way we always tended to, together. Hattie, my best friend whom I'd always protected and who

I would always protect, stood ready, knowing what I was going to ask.

I smiled again at her. "Are you ready?"

"Apparently I was built for this, so I was ready the day I was born," she smiled back at me, and in one swoop, we charged forward to join the fight.

47

Hattie

I felt myself entering my glowing state.

Instantly, my head cleared, my thoughts less jumbled. But I was quickly getting tired. My muscles slowed, and I felt more drained than I ever had before.

No one had stopped moving, but from what I could see, the magic of the hundreds of people we had brought with us were not making a single cut in the metal machine that floated in the sky.

I let out a cry of exasperated anger as I continued to fight.

A young girl wearing the Dark Unicorn symbol, her eyes frantic, ran up to me yelling, "Princess Hattie!"

"This really isn't a good time–"

"Please," she begged. "This is important. It's about Dark Unicorn. They aren't who you think they are. Neither were your parents. You need to trust them. It's essential."

"What?" I spluttered.

"Please listen to me," the girl began to cry. "If you don't, you'll perish too. They–"

Suddenly, something hit the ground in front of us and blew up. The girl was thrown backward against the canyon wall with a sickening crack.

"Oh no," I bolted over and knelt down. There was no doubt in my mind, she was dead.

I saw the tears falling on the dusty ground before I felt them. But before I could contemplate what she had just told me, I saw Illis rushing to someone's side a couple meters down the canyon. Laying on the ground was Misty.

I ran over to Misty and squatted down beside her.

Her breathing was labored, a deep cut ran down the side of her leg.

"Oh my god," I whispered. I had never been good with blood, as it nauseated me to a point that was almost unfathomable, but here was one of my best friends lying wounded on the ground gasping for breath.

Oh, suck it up, Hattie. I took a deep breath, "Okay, Misty, what happened?"

She gasped in breaths. "The thing, it's attacking with jets of magic, but I think that they're poisonous." She sucked in sharply.

I took a closer look at her leg to see what she meant by *poisonous*, and almost vomited. Decay was setting in. It was possible that it would heal in time, but it was burning off, like the end of a match.

I turned to Illis, my back to Misty. "What do we do?"

Illis grimaced. "I don't know. She definitely can't fight like this."

"Maybe we should move her to the edge of the canyon."

"I can hear you," Misty said. "And you know I don't even know how to fight normally right?"

Illis opened her mouth to argue, but looked around. "Fine," she said. "On the count of three."

Illis and I both grabbed one of Misty's arms and hoisted her to the edge of the canyon.

"Stay safe."

"I'll try." Misty smiled apologetically.

Illis ran away in the other direction.

I surveyed the battle with an idea tapping at me that there was something else we could be doing to defeat this thing, whatever it was.

It came to me in one sudden start. The idea that could save Rolling Hills. The questionable idea that had been nagging at me since the six of us had combined our magic the first time.

One question.

One idea that could steer the course of the battle. I spoke the question aloud, as if hoping that someone would answer it:

"What would happen if the whole kingdom banded their magic together?"

It was as though verbalizing the question sent a magical spirit into me. The wind swirled around me, and I felt on top of the world.

This was the answer that I had been looking for.

I remembered what Misty had told me, Tulip's words: Everyone has some inkling of magic inside, even if it is small.

"ILLIS!" I yelled across the battle.

Further down in the canyon, her head whipped around to look up at me. She took off at a run, reaching me in less than a minute.

"Yes, Hattie?" Illis panted.

"I have an idea that could save Rolling Hills."

Illis raised her eyebrows, "So what is it?"

"We need to band the entire kingdom's magic together. All the people, the soldiers, the Waters of Peachtree. Everyone."

"But the people don't know how to use magic. I don't know how to."

I shook my head frantically; "Do you remember at the compound, when I first touched the orb? The guardian of the place that's not real or fake told us that the Hills's magic is like an amplifier.

That's how you were able to use your powers. And if we could do it with six people, why not everyone?"

"That might work," Illis chewed her nails. "Hey, that might work!"

"Okay, you go get everyone in line. I'll help. Then we can use our magic to defeat this thing. Let's go."

"Okay, OKAY!" Illis turned and ran back down the canyon, calling, "Come on, follow me!"

I scrambled to collect people. From across the canyon, I saw Fira, and hollered, "Fira, come here."

In haste, I explained my plan.

"Okay, Hattie," she paused and looked at me with great pride in her eyes. "You really are something special."

I smiled at her as she bolted away.

Just past the canyon I could see the group forming.

If we could get everyone together fast enough, then we could defeat the machine before it drifted straight above the kingdom.

I ran as fast as I could, running around the mob to stand in the front.

I reached inside myself and found the same pulsing energy as I had before, letting it beat faster and faster until it raced in time with my heartbeat.

Everything stopped. The machine froze in air, not a sound was uttered.

I stepped forward, and cleared my throat loud enough that it hurt.

"We do not know what or who you are, but you are attacking our kingdom. And I may not be the strongest princess. I may not be the bravest or the smartest. But I'm still the ruler of Rolling Hills. And if you won't leave, we're going to make you."

I slowly began to lift my arm, feeling the energy from everyone in the kingdom pulse faster and faster until I was positive it was going a million a second.

I stepped backward into the line, feeling an aura among us that was so powerful, I knew that my plan would work.

In one moment of pure clearness, I remembered the prophecy, knowing that it was coming true.

Magic inside, do not hide.

The magic inside of us was not hiding now. It burst forth and tackled the world. A ball of all the colors I could imagine started to form in front of me, pure light.

Show your class, through the glass.

The light began to expand until it formed a sheer layer of raw power in front of us– all the classes that had always been there. And here I was, looking through a sheet of magical glass.

Broken,

I saw my kingdom in front of me.

Building.

I saw the people.

World unfolding.

A new world was evolving, and I could be there, helping it.

Magic reveal what you feel.

My heart soared as I whispered the last line of the prophecy, "Magic is real."

And all the real magic in the country was unleashed in a roar of power that rushed past me and into the air.

48

Misty

Light burst forward, and the machine in the air reared up, looking like a sinister monster. The world was filled with a terrible roar as the monstrosity simply dispersed from the sky.

Slowly, it began to float away in particles, little segments that turned to dirt.

I felt a soft breeze tickle my nose, and some of the particles landed in my outstretched hand.

The monster was gone, and I realized that all of our magic combined had temporarily dampened the pain in my leg, for I suddenly began to feel it again. Burning like a smoldering fire, shooting pain all through me.

I felt Hattie at my shoulder. "Misty, are you okay? You look like you're in pain."

I laughed, but it winced through me sharply, causing me to gasp. "Yes," I said. "Yes, I suppose you could say that."

"Here, let me help you." Hattie held out her hand to help me up. I accepted it, hurting myself in the process as I tried to put weight on my leg. I cried out, and Hattie squeezed me tightly on the shoulder. "Come on, Misty."

We staggered through the canyon, my leg searing the whole way, although slightly less with Hattie supporting my weight.

I yelped again as I stumbled over a stray rock in the canyon.

Among the crowd of people who littered the canyon, I spotted a mess of sandy blonde hair down at the other end.

"Liam," I whispered, then yelled, "LIAM!"

He turned around, caught one look at my injured leg, cursed loudly, and sprinted over to me at a pace I had never seen from him.

He arrived quickly. "Oh my god, Misty, what, what happened?"

Hattie loosened her grip on me, and Liam lowered me to the ground, his soft touch reminding me of safety and comfort.

"I took a hit from one of the monster's lasers." I winced again.

"Are you okay?" he asked, but behind his eyes I knew the real question he was about to ask. He looked so sincere, the way he always did, so caring.

"Not really," I gasped again as I shifted my weight to catch a better look at my leg.

Liam hugged me.

It lasted a long time, and he whispered something in my ear that I could barely hear, but I made out the words "thought you were dead."

When he finally pulled away, his eyes were serious and filled with questions. "Where were you?"

"What do you mean?" I said, trying to sidestep the question.

"Where have you been these last few days? Don't think I haven't noticed when you just disappear."

"Didn't you get my note?"

"What note? Where were you, Misty?"

"I was on an adventure," was my answer, suddenly feeling a bit woozy, my head spinning.

My vision clouded, and I finally gave into the exhaustion and blacked out, falling into Liam's arms.

Everything was dark.

I was in a sleep state, cocooned into my own body. But I could hear everything.

Liam called out for me and began to panic when I wouldn't wake up.

"It is okay, Liam, she just blacked out," I heard Hattie tell him.

"Yeah, as if you would even care if she hadn't just blacked out," Liam responded.

"What's that supposed to mean?"

"Don't think I don't know it's your fault she was gone all this time. If it weren't for you she probably wouldn't be hurt."

"If it weren't for me *everyone* would be dead!"

There was a beat of silence.

"Listen," Hattie said, her voice still stained with hurt. "We could stand here and fight all day, but she won't get any better. Let's take her to the infirmary in the palace."

I felt my body being moved, and heard Liam shout, "Do *not* touch her, I'll carry her."

I was lifted off the ground and shuttled to the infirmary.

The gentle rocking of Liam running through the canyon was enough to exhaust me even further and in one swift move, I fully blacked out.

* * *

The first thing I noticed was the ticking of a clock. Then the soft warm sheets beneath my tired body. And finally the pain that still lingered in my leg.

I slowly opened my eyes and was greeted with a bright light that temporarily blinded.

But eventually, I was able to fully open my eyes and was now greeted with the sight of Liam sitting beside me, looking down with a nervous expression, biting his nails.

"Liam?" I croaked, my voice tired from lack of use.

He looked up, startled, but immediately looked relieved to see me awake, "Oh, Misty, I've been so worried, you have no idea."

I looked around the infirmary, noting the white blankets and the lovely nurses with smiles on their faces. At the bottom of my bed sat a low brown table packed with sweets and peaches.

Liam traced my gaze, "It was the least we could do after you helped save the kingdom from certain destruction."

I smiled, but then remembered the fight between him and Hattie. "Liam," I said. "Why did you say those awful things to Hattie?"

He scooted closer to me so that I could properly see his face. He took a deep breath.

"Honestly?"

I nodded my head.

"I was jealous to be stuck here while she was spending time with you saving the kingdom," he confessed. "I was worried that someone was replacing me."

"Liam," I sighed. "I don't think anyone could ever replace you."

"You mean it?" he asked, a giddy look upon his face.

"Of course I do. You're my best friend in the world."

His expression dropped, but he passed it off by running a hand through his hair. "Really?"

"Yes," I replied. "But Hattie means a lot to me too, and nothing you try to do will change that. I have a lot of friends, and if it weren't for Hattie, I would be dead, literally."

He exhaled loudly and slowly. "Okay," Liam said. "Okay, all right."

"So you two are good."

"I said some horrible things to her," he admitted with a guilty look.

"I heard," I replied.

"You know, she was waiting here too," Liam laughed. "In total silence. The others dropped in as well, but she stayed the longest. Fira had to pull her away, though, to do *princess stuff.*" He made air quotes around the words.

"Ooh," I said dreamily. "The Cherry Blossom Festival is coming up."

"Yep," Liam said. "in two days."

I smiled. Maybe my perfect kingdom would go back to normal after all.

"Nothing will be the same, though," I pinched the bridge of my nose. "Not with the new magic. I don't even know where to start."

"Magic, yes," he said, leaning closer to me, and an unfamiliar whoosh filled my stomach.

He lingered a moment before moving even closer. My breath caught, and I . . .

Someone cleared her throat, and Liam yanked his head back, sheepishly pulling his hair in front of his eyes.

Elise stood at the opposite end of the infirmary. Her head tilted at me in a gaze that seemed to say, *WHAT-WAS-JUST-ABOUT-TO-HAPPEN?*

When I noticed Liam looking in the other direction, I shrugged.

"Hi, Misty," Elise crept.

"Hi, Elise," I mumbled.

"Not here for another visit about her brother are you?" Liam joked, but I could see the hard set of his jaw as he looked at her.

"If only."

She took her hands from behind her back, and in her hands was a small bag.

"Here you go." She sidled over and plopped the bag in my lap. I stared at it until she said, "Well? Aren't you going to open it?"

I carefully pulled the pink paper out of the bag to reveal a small bottle in the shape of a heart. The elixir inside was blue, and a sticker on the front read *Misty's Masterful Concoction.*

"Ummm . . ." I glanced at her apologetically. "What is it?"

"It's for whenever you need me," she smiled. "I hope you'll never need to use it, but if you do, simply grab hold of your friends and drink the elixir. You'll know when the time arises."

I wanted to point out that I had absolutely no idea what she was talking about, but she had taken the time to make it for me, so I nodded stiffly and gave her my best smile.

She looked uncomfortably at the floor.

"So," I said, attempting to make conversation. "Dark Unicorn is gone, huh?"

That seemed to make her even more uncomfortable. She opened her mouth to say something that I had a feeling was going to be different from the words that came out. "Yeah, maybe."

"Maybe? Do you think they could still be out there?"

"No of course not!" Elise said. Her hands fidgeted until she glanced at the clock on the wall. "Crap, time! Sorry, Misty, I have to go!"

She bolted out of the door.

Liam cleared his throat, and my face instantly flamed again as he said, "That was weird."

I became very interested in my hands, wondering to which moment he was referring.

A puzzled look still on his face, he said, "What were we talking about?"

"Magic," I mumbled and sighed.

"You know what I have come to learn in these days you have been asleep, Misty?" He grabbed my hand firmly.

"What?" I asked.

"No amount of magic could ever change what's already been here in Rolling Hills the whole time."

I smiled, not sure if is was the firmness in his eyes or the small feeling of hope that caused me to say, "You know what Liam? I'm starting to think you might be right."

49

Fira

I nearly exploded with joy when Misty walked flawlessly into the main hall of Peachtree Palace the morning after Liam had talked to her.

He seemed to accompany her everywhere, and, sweet as it was, I wondered if maybe Misty needed some time alone to contemplate the things we had been through.

"Misty?" I beamed.

"Fira!"

She hobbled over to me, and I squeezed her as tight as I could.

"I am so happy to see that you are okay," I said with a little chuckle. "I've been so worried."

She laughed, and I assumed she might have already been told that by everyone in the kingdom she'd seen so far.

"Okay, Misty, we actually have some things to discuss with you if you feel up to it."

Liam started, "I'm going with her."

"Liam," I said gently. "This is private."

He opened his mouth to speak, but Misty cut him off. "It's okay, Liam. I'll be fine. Besides, they'll protect me if anything bad happens."

Liam turned to me. "You promise?"

I crossed my heart. "I promise."

I led Misty up the stairs to Hattie's bedroom.

She lay face down on the bed in the dark, so I flipped the light on.

She sat up quickly, brushing the hair out of her eyes. "Hey Fira," Hattie said, then noticed Misty standing beside me. "Oh my god, you're ok."

She ran over and hugged Misty tighter and longer than usual. Hattie pulled away and looked at her with a small laugh, "You're okay!" she said again.

"Yeah," Misty said. "I am, aren't I?"

Hattie laughed again, and I cleared my throat. "But that is not why we're here. We need to discuss what happened."

"I know," Hattie mumbled.

She sat back down on her bed, with Misty now by her side.

I sat in the desk chair, feeling like a teacher about to lecture her students. "I know what the magic was," I stated simply.

Hattie, who was in the process of drinking water, choked. "What? What was it?"

"I read about it the other day," I said. "It was the magic of the ancients. Mechanical machines that shoot out poisonous jets. The book said that it was used by . . ." I took a deep breath. "The book said it was used by Alvara."

Misty gasped. "The one that Odelina serves."

Hattie continued, "And we think Odelina was working with Maurelle."

"And Maurelle told us to stay away from Alvara," I added. "The pieces sort of fit together. Alvara was using Maurelle for something, and Odelina was just the messenger. But whatever Alvara was using Maurelle for resulted in something awful, so Maurelle's good ol' 'change of heart' told us that we needed to stay away from her."

"But," Hattie interrupted. "Alvara's dead, right?"

"She has to be," Misty confirmed. "Every legend says so."

I wanted to point out that the key word in the legend had been *disappeared* but instead I just said. "All right. I have to go. The festival won't plan itself. And the bridge won't open on its own."

I stood up and walked out of the room, heading down the stairs.

Liam stood ready at the door, a nervous look engraved on his face.

"Where's Misty?" He asked quickly.

"She's fine," I assured him. "We just had some things to discuss."

"Like what?" He asked stonily.

"None of your business," I wrinkled my nose and inclined my head.

He groaned, and I tipped an imaginary hat to him. "Good day, sir," I said, and walked out the palace doors.

Outside, the kingdom was bustling with business. The Cherry Blossom Festival was the next day, for Hattie had forbidden postponing it.

So now the kingdom was struggling to clean up and prepare for a festival in the space of a few days.

I walked over to Aubrey who was busying herself with a sheet of paper, ticking boxes in a checklist.

"Hello, Aubrey," I said.

"Hello, darling," she replied, pushing her glasses down to get a better look at me. "Are you ready to open the gates to the Waters of Peachtree?"

"Yes," I said confidently. "It's just odd to picture letting a whole new society into our normally isolated Rolling Hills."

She chuckled. "Honestly, I feel that way too."

I blew out a long breath. "Glad I'm not the only one."

I strode toward the spot where we were going to conjure the bridge.

It was to the right of the palace, where there was just enough room to make the passage.

I was waved over by a couple of workers from the Waters of Peachtree who specialized in building.

"Ready?" they asked me.

"Yeah," I said, pushing up imaginary sleeves and reaching inside myself to gather some magic.

I let the Adar take over, and we pushed our magic outward, and slowly, a bridge began to form. It cut into the ground, creating a tunnel that burrowed beneath Peachtree Palace.

A few of the more decorative casters put little details on the bridge to spruce it up. Cherry wrapped the archway in flowers.

In the end, a wide tunnel with a beautiful arch at the front stood completed next to the palace.

I clapped my hands together lightly, and Cherry ran over to hug me.

When she pulled away, I found the courage to speak. "You don't know how much I have missed you."

She smiled and whispered, "Yes, I do."

I gripped her hand, and we ran forward to see the people, those who had dreamed their whole lives about this kingdom, come flooding through its gates.

I was distracted by a group of soldiers standing with smug smiles on their faces, but the thought left my mind as I spotted Rosie coming through with a look of pure wonder on her face.

It made me smile so wide I thought my face would fall off.

She spotted me in the crowd and raced toward me with surprising speed, knocking Cherry out of the way to hug me. "Thank you," she sobbed. "Thank you so much."

"You're welcome, so welcome, Rosie."

She stepped back and wiped her eyes, "It is all thanks to you and Misty, you know, like the legends say, the ones who will save everyone."

I was about to object when I realized I deserved a moment of bragging.

"Yeah," I grinned. "I suppose it is."

50

Illis

I watched from the window at the front of Peachtree Palace as the residents of the Waters of Peachtree seeped under the archway and into the kingdom, looks of joy etched upon their faces.

I saw a young girl approach Fira and hug her. I assumed that this must have been Rosie.

I imagined being seventeen, dreaming my whole life of coming to Rolling Hills, and finally arriving. I let out a long breath, my heart aching for her.

Fira and Rosie began to walk toward the palace, and I readied myself at the bottom of the stairs, waiting for them to walk in.

When they did, I smiled at Fira and gave a sharp nod. "Who's this?" I already knew, of course, but I thought it the most polite thing to ask.

Fira gestured with a hand. "This is Rosie Hills, Queen Mariana's younger sister."

Rosie smiled widely, speaking very fast. "Only one year older than you, actually. You have no idea how long I have wanted to be here, in this kingdom. I have dreamed about it my whole life, and now I am here. In Rolling Hills!"

Squealing with delight, she continued. "And now the Cherry Blossom Festival is tomorrow, something I've wanted to go to my *entire* existence in this world. Do you still have the market? I have always wanted to see it. I have a picture of it that I ripped out from a book. Also your housing units are amazing, and I'll probably buy one, that is, if I can get a job back at the Waters of Peachtree. Then I can save up enough to move here, live out my days with you, and," she gasped, "Hattie. I GET TO MEET HER! Oh my goodness. Where to even begin. Should I spruce up? I probably should. How about a bow in my hair? Maybe that is overkill. I don't know! Oh gosh, I am a hot mess, and I haven't even talked to her yet. But I will be almost a cousin's age to her, so there would be no point in calling me aunt. I will absolutely forbid it." Rosie took a deep breath and looked at me. "You must be Illis."

I could not suppress a grin and a laugh at her bubbly energy, which reminded me slightly of Cherry. "That would be me."

"Well, hello then, I guess. I have got to get going. Apparently I am going to be meeting Hattie for lunch. I am so excited, I can't even put it into words, can I? Nope, I am going to answer that myself. I *cannot* put it into words. I am beyond words. Actually, I should go now." She jumped around in excitement. "Okay, bye." She waved a hand and sprinted out of the palace.

"Um. . ."

Fira laughed. "Don't worry, she'll get used to it here soon enough." She regained her solemn tone. "There is something I need to talk to you about though."

"What?" I asked.

Fira took a deep breath, "The machine, the one that hurt Misty. It was ancient magic used by Alvara."

"No," I whispered.

"Yes," she confirmed.

I sunk into the floor with a plop, my brain whirring. "I still have a feeling that Tulip has more to do with all of this than just her working for Maurelle. And that the Dark Unicorn is still out there. Is that crazy?"

"Not at all," Fira answered. "And actually, I agree. I believe that Tulip might have been there to observe Maurelle, making sure she didn't step out of line."

I dipped my chin. "That is a valid point."

"I have to go prepare for the festival," Fira said as if the thought had been a million miles away, worry in her eyes.

"Fira."

She turned towards me, hope puckering her lips, as if she was waiting for someone to tell her it would be alright.

"We're going to figure this out."

"I know," Fira replied, but she didn't really look like she believed it.

I walked slowly to my bedroom to find Elnora sitting in front of the door.

She was wearing a beautiful white dress with small yellow flowers, her makeup perfectly done, her caramel hair lightly curled. I found my breath caught in my throat. She looked absolutely gorgeous.

She noticed me standing there and smiled, her teeth glistening like diamonds. She looked self-consciously down at her outfit. "Do you like it?" she asked timidly.

"It's beautiful," I replied breathlessly.

"Thanks! I don't usually wear dresses. To keep, you know, the edgy vibe," she laughed. "But it's for the festival tomorrow, and I, um," she drew out the word, nice and long. "I wanted to show you first."

I fiddled with my bracelet, finding it hard to speak. "Did you want to come in?" I gestured to my room.

She shrugged, and I opened the door, letting her inside.

We sat on my bed in silence.

"Hey, Illis," Elnora said softly. "I was thinking. Do you want to maybe go somewhere sometime?"

"What?" I asked, my stomach exploding with butterflies.

She exhaled slowly, running her hands down her thighs. "Well, I mean as friends, we could do a little friend date. You, me."

I found no words. Right. A *friend* date. "Oh," I choked.

She laughed again, the low sound vibrating through the walls.

It was then that I noticed how very close to mine Elnora's face was, her breath hot on my cheek.

My heart thundered in a way I had never felt before. I was staring into her brown eyes.

She shot to a stand.

"So," she said awkwardly, smoothing her dress. "Sometime. Place. You. Me. Cool?"

I was shocked, but I tried to compose myself with a small nod. "I'd like that."

She twirled out of the room, gifting me with a small wink.

I sat breathless on my bed, pinching the bridge of my nose.

"Oh, Illis," I groaned, "What has gotten into you?"

The day tracked on, and I found myself in Hattie's bedroom, the sun setting slowly behind us.

"So, how did your lunch with Rosie go?" I asked her.

Hattie hugged a pillow. "Well, I think that she was very overwhelmed when I offered to let her live in the palace, but she accepted. From tomorrow on, she will have a permanent room here in Peachtree Palace, though I assume she will mostly want to live back in the Waters of Peachtree."

"It's really awful what happened to her there, being locked up, even in a place as lovely as the Waters of Peachtree."

"You are right," Hattie said. "It is." She stood up on her bed, speaking with conviction. "As long as I'm in charge, I'll never do something as awful."

She stomped her foot so hard that she fell backwards, collapsing back onto her bed.

I smiled, noticing she looked wary at my expression.

"What?" she asked.

"How did we end up with a princess as wonderful as you?" I asked.

Instead of pleased, she looked sad, and I instantly wanted to take the words back.

We ended up with her as the princess because her parents were dead.

Hattie quickly fixed her expression to impassive stone. "I think I'm going to go to bed now."

"Okay, Hattie. Sleep well. Sweet dreams."

There I went again, saying the wrong thing.

As if she wasn't going to dream of every horrible thing that had happened.

As if I wasn't.

I shut the door tightly and pinched the bridge of my nose as if the act could keep away the thoughts threatening to swallow me up.

Just one more nightmare I couldn't escape.

51

Hattie

I woke up with a start. Shaking the images of Maurelle, Odelina, and every mystery we hadn't solved out of my head.

My curtains were open, and I instantly sat up with anticipation. Today was the festival, and I was wired with excitement.

I could use today to forget. Everything.

The Cherry Blossom Festival was my favorite time of year, a time when we could just ignore unpleasantries and have fun. A time when no one was busy caring about power or position.

I threw my sheets aside and kissed Teddy on the head, vowing never to leave him behind again. I got up, ready to begin my day.

I hummed a soft tune as I put on some makeup and dressed myself in a white pleated skirt and an oversized pink sweater, just in case there was a breeze. The outfit complimented my brown curls that were tied in a high ponytail, while a plain white bandana was finished in a knot around my head.

I smiled at myself in the mirror. My goal was to try to simulate the beautiful cherry blossoms that grew outside in the long beautiful spring.

I had given Lovedaya the day off to celebrate the festival with their family. Besides, at some point, I knew I would have to learn how to do things on my own without relying on the help of others. Especially getting ready in the morning without Lovedaya, no matter how much I loved them.

Today would be the first time in eight years that I could celebrate the festival without carrying around the hidden guilt inside me. I took a deep breath and then a step outside my bedroom door.

I flowed like a flower in the breeze as I exited Peachtree Palace. Instantly, I entered a world of pure pink.

The skies were pink, as was the ground.

The dirt was barely visible underneath all the petals that had fallen from the trees. The kingdom had long ago decided to hold the festival in celebration of the beauty that we took for granted every day in spring, in hopes that we might remember to always look at the beauty in life.

And I had always tried to do that, from the first festival I attended.

I strode briskly down the narrow canyon, the same as I had done just weeks before the entire dilemma began.

It all seemed so far away now.

I was grateful to be back in the kingdom with something other than a prison bed to sleep in.

Though it may have been a mere five days, in my brain I had been stuck in a cell for weeks. It was true that we had defeated Maurelle, but there was more to the puzzle, something big we were missing.

I remembered the dead girl in the canyon, mulling over what she had told me.

But everything seemed to fit perfectly. Dark Unicorn was gone, and the Waters of Peachtree had finally been welcomed back home to where they belonged.

It would be easier to forget, for now.

But as much as I wished it were, I knew it wasn't over yet. I knew that from a glance to my side.

Even though some of the kingdom had cleaned up, most everything still held signs of the attack. Some windows were smashed,doors hung ajar.

There was still debris that littered the canyon.

I considered telling my friends what I'd heard. I wanted to, but some secrets had to be kept. It was safer this way.

Next time, I wouldn't let them risk their lives for me. I could do it on my own.

I took a deep breath in and pulled my mind away from these disquieting thoughts.

I had finally reached the end of the canyon, and was greeted with a different sign than the one that usually hung above the market.

It was pink with the signature blossoms on it, reading *Cherry Blossom Festival.*

I smiled at the sight. Though I never liked to brag, I did feel that I was doing my best to help my kingdom, and I was doing a pretty fair job at it. Ignoring the mess behind me, that was.

People everywhere were dressed in pink and white, so that the whole festival looked like a giant cherry blossom tree.

I knew that my friends would be arriving soon, so I took to munching on the many delicious treats that lay waiting to be devoured.

Soft and sweet tastes lingered in my mouth as I traveled around the Cherry Blossom Festival, admiring my council's work in pulling it all together.

After another hour of wandering, I spotted my friends at the edge of the market and rushed over to them.

Illis, Misty, Fira, Arabella, Elnora, and Cherry stood waiting for me.

"Hey, Hattie," Illis said with a bow of her head.

"Hello, Illis," I said, and then greeted everyone in turn.

"Hey," Elnora said. "Come with us, we have a surprise."

She grabbed my hand and pulled me up, laughing the whole way. We walked out of the market and into Peachtree Grove, traveling for a brief while to a spot that was unfamiliar to me.

As we approached, Cherry looked at me and squealed. "Close your eyes, silly."

I did as I was told, and we continued to hike upward.

At last, we halted, and Elnora dropped my hand.

"Do not open your eyes yet," she instructed.

Anticipation gripped my stomach as I wondered what the surprise could be.

"Okay," Fira whispered. "You can open them now."

I did, and my breath caught in my throat. We were at the edge of a hill, the tallest one in the kingdom. A cherry blossom tree soared above us, creating a tent of petals. I could view the entire kingdom from my perch.

Just beneath the tree, my friends sat on a picnic blanket, smiles on their faces.

"It is beautiful," I said, awestruck. "I've never even seen this part of the kingdom before."

Misty smiled. "I knew you would like it. We can go back to the festival after, but I thought it might be nice to get away for a minute."

"You were right."

I sat down, and they pulled desserts and sandwiches out of a picnic basket.

At once, we began to eat and talk, and my heart soared along with my soul as I paused to enjoy this moment.

I turned to Misty. "Oh don't worry, I haven't forgotten about your appointment with Lovedaya."

She giggled and turned to take in the view of the kingdom.

"You can almost see Peachtree Academy from here." She joked.

She then sighed, cradling her chin in her hands. "I've always wanted to go."

Cherry choked on a sandwich. "Haven't I told you?"

We all shook our heads, with not a single prospect of what she was going to say.

She beamed. "Peachtree Academy is a school for Mythics. Your class badges, they're the ones we use there. I went. We spread the rumor that only rich families can attend, because we know what happened the last time everyone learned about mythic. People got hurt. That's why the villagers aren't allowed to go. But I suppose anyone could attend now, if they showed enough potential."

Misty wheezed. "I could go?"

Cherry chuckled. "In theory."

I grinned. Everyone was having such a good time, and that's why my suspicions had to be kept quiet. My friends would know someday, but for now, I gushed, "Thank you for this."

Misty's face glowed. "Of course, Hattie."

The night continued on until the sky was touched by the sun's pink beams.

I had always thought that I would never have a family again, once my parents were gone.

How grateful am I that I had been really and truly proved wrong.

As my heart sank into the open night, I looked around at my friends, friends who had followed me everywhere. My friends who had become my family.

And it was better than any magic I'd seen.

But while surrounded by them, even within this serene moment, a trace of suspicion lurked in my mind. I was absolutely positive they'd want to know what I'd heard, but there was no imminent need to worry them.

After all, what harm could a few secrets do?

Epilogue: Odelina

From my ship in the sky, I stared in distaste out of the window.

Inside one of the mechanical monsters, what people around here liked to call them.

The Cherry Blossom Festival was still in full swing below, the people living in their perfect fairy tale.

It disgusted me– pretending they were the saviors of the day. It would be soon enough to tell the girls, but we still had to wait. A little longer.

As in the days previous, I was itching to launch more jets of magic down, but my master was furious at my failure, and I had to meet her in ten minutes.

I sat in the command center, people bustling around me. The world of metal was my world. My home.

Ever since the time before time, I had served the one great master, she who should have been ruling Rolling Hills. But instead she had stepped down from power.

I, as her second in command, had protested, but she insisted on the decision.

But ever since Maurelle had come around, my position had become less important to my master, my value diminished. But it had finally come to the master's attention that Maurelle, in addition to ignoring every policy in place, had been trying to harm everyone we needed to keep safe. The Dark Unicorn fort had been destroyed, and its people pleaded brainwashing. But they were just trying to spare themselves from having to explain to Hattie, which we could certainly not do under any conditions.

I checked my watch again, noticing the time. My stomach lurched. I was going to be late.

My boots thumped on the ground, and several heads turned in my direction as I rushed around the ship. Eventually, I skid to a stop in front of her door.

Two guards stood next to it, and I showed them my identification.

They let me in, somewhat reluctantly.

The room was dark, and I could barely see a thing.

"You're late," a booming voice spoke from the back of the room.

I spotted it now, a chair turned to face the wall opposite me, preventing me from seeing my master's face. I looked down at my watch. I was one minute behind.

I kicked myself internally. "I'm sorry, Master."

"I have a matter to discuss with you, Odelina," she said.

"What would that be, Master?" I already knew the answer.

"You know you messed up," she said. "Horribly. You almost killed the entire kingdom before anyone was ready to know the truth about us."

She paused to regain herself. "I appreciate your getting rid of Maurelle, but interacting directly with Hattie's friends was a risk. We'll have to be more careful next time."

I breathed a sigh of relief, but my master continued. "That being said, I have a new mission for you."

I nodded, wondering if she could see me.

"I need you to keep those girls away from Peachtree Academy, never to let them find what is hidden there. Until they know, we cannot risk them learning anything that will harm us."

I scowled.

"I won't mess up again," I protested.

"Oh," my master laughed, a low sound that tingled unpleasantly under my skin, warning me to follow my instructions. "You don't have a choice."

Acknowledgments

So. . . that's it. Sorry, but I guess I just have a lot of fun writing horrible cliff hangers :) But don't worry, I'm already hard at work on book two. You won't have to be away from Rolling Hills for long. That being said, there are many people I need to thank that made this entire adventure possible.

First and foremost to my parents, who helped me so much with publishing all while being my biggest supporters. You were the first to read it, and I'm so grateful for everything you did to help me make my world a better place. And thank you for making *me* a better person, I love you more than words can describe.

To my editor, Susan Arnold. Rolling Hills wouldn't be anywhere near what it is now without you. You helped me take it from an idea to an actual book that I can show people and say I wrote. I'm beyond grateful for the amazing things you helped me accomplish.

To Sydney Hamilton, my friend, beta reader, and fellow author. You helped me with my book when I was unsure if I even wanted to continue. You helped me have faith in the characters I created, and learn to love them again. LOVE YOU FOREVER!

To my sister, who gives me character names based on her favorite celebrities, and always listens when I read her an out of context scene that I love. You mean the world to me.

To Bev Johnson. The cover of this book was just a weak image in my head until you brought it to life. I'm so happy to have gotten the chance to work with you.

To my friends who supported me and believed in me beyond even I could myself. Thank you for screaming with me every time there was an update.

To all the teachers over the years that encouraged me to follow my dreams of becoming a published author. I hope I made you proud.

And finally to you, the readers and my followers. Thank you for believing in me before the book even came out. I will *never* forget all the messages and comments of support I got, they mean everything to me.

Until next time,
-Michaela

Classes of Mythic Guide

Marigold
Mythics that belong to Marigold are creative, and love to show their works to others. They are almost constantly thinking of new ideas, and may struggle to focus on one particular thing. They are very passionate about the things they love.

Sunflower
Mythics that belong to Sunflower are very kind and caring to others. They would w]put down most anything to help someone, even if it means putting themselves second. They always bring a happy aura with them wherever they go.

Protea
Mythics who belong to Protea are extremely courageous and will rarely back down from a challenge. They are always up for adventure and have a good knack of recognizing the good qualities in people and befriending them.

Aster
Mythics who belong in Aster are hardworking and devoted. They tend to be fast learners, and are clever enough to solve even the hardest of puzzles. They enjoy working and finding new material.